A MATTER OF WIFE & WEALTH

The Siblings - Book One

RAFFAELLA ROWELL

Published by Blushing Books
An Imprint of
ABCD Graphics and Design, Inc.
A Virginia Corporation
977 Seminole Trail #233
Charlottesville, VA 22901

Raffaella Rowell
A Matter of Wife & Wealth

eBook ISBN: 978-1-63954-004-4
Print ISBN: 978-1-63954-005-1
v2

Chapter 1

Mollie Sorensen and Kathryn Ellis had called in to see the old man.

"My husband wouldn't leave the room until I pushed the 'delete' button on my laptop, my lord. We had no choice. Your son was not in agreement with this. Without his approval, we had to wipe out all his information from our dating app. I am sorry, sir, Fergus made quite a fuss. He got us into trouble," Mollie said with a serious expression.

Gustave Waltham, the tenth Earl of Buckley, was ill. Everyone knew this. His days were numbered. He had been ill for some time. The doctors thought he was declining rapidly and would not recover. So, in his illness, the earl wished to see his son, and heir, settled with a good woman.

They were in his sitting room, in his grand home in the outskirts of Oxford. The man was propped up in a comfy armchair with cushions, wrapped up in blankets, with a hot-water bottle on his lap.

The earl's face was wrinkled by age but still fascinating, while wispy white hair covered his round, elegant head. Though his body was frail, his eyes, under bushy grey eyebrows, were as alert as they had ever been, as if in those of a curious, spirited child. His mind, as sharp as a knife, had not lost its acuteness or its brilliance, as if he were still in his prime. His intellect was sublime.

Time had not completely misshapen his frame, but he looked frailer and weaker than ever. Mollie could not remember seeing him this feeble before. He had lost a lot of weight and seemed fatigued. It was a blow for the girls to look at him so poorly. It shocked them, but they put on a brave face for him. He was in good spirits that day, entertaining them with his wit and stories. A gifted raconteur, the old fog was amusing. The girls liked him. They had always got on well with him and had struck up a friendship.

"We had no option, my lord. Fergus hadn't given us his permission, not to mention he was livid about it," Kathryn emphasized.

"Yes, I understand, ladies. Not to worry, I know Fergus was not happy. He told me in no uncertain terms, I can assure you," he said with a little naughty laugh. "But out of curiosity, did my son match up to anybody on your dating app?"

"Yes, he did," Kathryn replied with a satisfied grin.

"Really?"

"Oh, yes. A 'top pick' too, a ninety-five percent score! A top match!" Mollie pointed out. "You can't get much higher than that."

"My fiancé and I, you know Finley Harman, don't you, sir?" Kathryn went on with a smile.

"Sure."

"Well, Finley and I scored ninety percent match on our dating app, and look, we are engaged to be married now. See my ring!" She proudly showed her engagement ring, a modern and refined round twist solitaire diamond with a clean edge platinum band.

"Oh, it's beautiful, Kat, congratulations. You deserve it,"

he said, while the girl lifted her hand to the light to make her engagement ring sparkle, smiling with satisfaction, showing it off.

"What a rock on her finger, hey? Finley spent a packet on it." Mollie snorted. "And they adore each other. Fergus and his match scored even more, imagine that. Unbelievable! Ninety-five percent score, my lord. It would have been an incredible match for your son. What a pity we had to delete everything," Mollie said, rubbing her ear with a soft shake of the head.

"I can't believe that ill-tempered son of mine matched to somebody. Ninety-five percent, you say, eh? Who the hell will want him?" he said, but a sudden twinkle flashed through his eyes.

"Yes, sir, he did. I can assure you, and our dating app hasn't been wrong so far," Mollie stated primly.

"He is a good-looking chap all right," the earl said. "Women find him handsome, irresistible; it's a family trait. All of my children are attractive if I may say so myself. Their mother, God rest her soul, was a beautiful lady, but Fergus has a waspish, short-tempered attitude. After a while, women run. They fear him. He is not like his brothers. My younger sons can charm the pants out of a stone, but Fergus and my daughter, Belinda, she is my youngest, you know her, don't you?"

"Yes, of course." The girls nodded vigorously.

"God, I despair of those two; they are my burden to bear. Still, Fergus is my heir and some woman will have to put up with him," the old man sighed with a resigned expression.

He had pushed his son to marry for a long time, but to no avail. He wouldn't budge. He found something wrong with every girl his father tried to push on him. The young lord was against marriage.

His father was convinced his son was incapable of love. Only brief affairs were his style, nothing serious.

The earl was a sick man and he realised he didn't have

long in this world. Thus, he wished to go to his grave knowing that the irascible, crotchety son of his had a woman to look after him and ready to produce the next heir, too.

So, Lord Buckley had taken it upon himself to solve the issue. Failing everything else, he grabbed his chance with Mollie and Kathryn's dating app without his son's knowledge, though it had backfired on them when the young man had discovered what they were doing. He'd complained to Zac and Finley to put a stop to it, immediately!

Fergus was furious about the girls meddling in his life and using his data without permission. Hence, the girls were forced to delete every scrap of information on him from the dating app.

"He matched! We had paired him, but it's all academic now. We have deleted everything," Mollie said with a long sigh.

"I wonder! Who is she? She must be an interesting creature if she paired up to my son with that high percentage rate," he claimed, lifting his eyebrows. He shook his head with a brittle laugh, as if not believing any woman could.

"She is the gentlest girl ever, but she has a determined personality. She can be tough when she needs to be."

"Do you know her?" the earl asked, surprised, his eyes lighting up with that clever sparkle of his, tipping his head to one side while a slow grin curled up on his face. *Well, she must be strong if she is to cope with my son.*

"Yes, we do."

"What's her name?" he urged, as curiosity flashed across his eyes. He leaned forward in his armchair, ready to discover all about her.

It wasn't to be.

"My lord, you do realise we cannot tell you that. You'll get us in trouble," Kathryn said with a serious tone, and the mild rebuke was not amiss, "Fergus wants nothing to do with our dating app. He warned us already, please... He said our app was nonsense!" She went on with a wounded look and thin lips.

"Typical! He would, wouldn't he? Only the first name then."

"What? Oh, no, my lord, it isn't a good idea," Kathryn replied with a concerned expression.

"What am I going to do with a name?"

"Well, I suppose so..." The girls glanced at each other.

"Come on, just the first name. You'll give an old fool who is a step away from his grave a thrill. I can still dream, can't I?" he uttered with a crack in his voice and the most sullen and grave of faces.

He slumped back into his armchair, heaved a long sigh and hunched his shoulders. He took a handkerchief out of his pocket and stroked his forehead with the most pitiful expression on his face. In his current state of health, it was not too difficult to achieve the overdramatic impression he intended to portray.

Tenderness flooded the girls' hearts for him. They had a pang of remorse at not wanting to tell him.

"Oh, my lord, you mustn't say things like that, please, you'll soon be well again," Kathryn replied with a tear in her eye, slowly releasing a deep breath.

"Ladies, I am afraid I'm worthless now. Good for nothing but the grave. Look at me! The doctor said so, my time has come."

"What do doctors know, hey? You have a wonderful spirit, my lord," Mollie spoke. She wrapped an arm around her midriff, and the other went to her heart with a heavy sigh. She was fond of the man and it hurt her to hear him talk like that, defeated, ready to die.

"Sweet girls, just the first name, and you'll make an elderly fool dream a little in his last hours."

"Marguerite!" Mollie blasted out.

"Ah, Marguerite. What a sweet name."

"You would have liked her. She is lovely, pretty, determined, firm. The most efficient administrator in the Senior Post-graduate office," Mollie blabbered in a rush, wanting to brighten the day for him, hoping her news would make his imagination flow. Aware he was ill, if this gave him a little joy, then why not? It was only the first name, anyway. *What was he going to do with that?*

Kathryn elbowed her in the ribs and scowled.

"What? I didn't say a thing!" Mollie massaged her ribcage, despondent.

"Perhaps it's all for the best that we deleted everything." Her companion glared at her.

"French, hey?" His question was rhetorical, but Mollie nodded eagerly, earning another scowl from Kathryn.

He laughed.

"He likes French women. We spent many summers in the South of France. Fergus enjoyed it there over the years. I remember one particular summer, it was the happiest I had ever seen him. We suspected then, it was to do with a girl. Never known him that cheerful in all my life. Mind you, it didn't last long. Soon, he returned to his usual, grumpy self, if not worse. He must have scared the poor wench off. Marguerite, you say... Ah, such a pretty name."

"My lord, I said enough. I'll be in trouble. Your son will kill me! And if he doesn't, my husband will, if he knew I have told you her name!" But there was a little mischievous glint in her eyes, too, Mollie wasn't a fool. On one side, she wanted to please the old man, and on the other, she realised full well what she was doing.

"Yes, sir, please. After today, you must forget it," Kathryn echoed, concerned at Mollie's lack of restraint after the trouble they'd had.

"Sure!" The old man nodded. "Don't worry. It's all hush-hush!" He zipped his mouth shut with his fingers and winked. "What am I going to do, bound as I am to this armchair, anyway?" He flapped his hand over his frail body, dismissing the notion he could do anything at all these days, confined as he was to a chair.

"Well, w-we—" the young women stuttered in discomfort.

"Your secret is safe with me, ladies." He tapped his nose with his index finger. "But you've made an old fool happy today. Bless you!"

They stayed a while longer, laughed and joked at his stories, then they said their goodbyes and left him.

The old fellow was not a clever man for nothing. He'd gotten what he wanted.

When they were gone, the earl called his secretary. "Perkins, find me a French girl named Marguerite who works in the Senior Post Graduate office. Bring her to me."

"Which office, my lord? Which studies?"

"Studies?" the earl pitched, wide-eyed, then he scowled.

"Yes, what discipline? There must be dozens of such offices. This is Oxford. What's her last name if I may ask?" the super-resourceful Perkins replied, unabashed, and used to combat with the old man and his extravagant requests.

"Hell, what do I know! No idea, on either. Get me the girl; hurry! I want to talk to her on Saturday."

"But today is Thursday, sir. With no full name and not knowing which office—"

"The lady is French! How many French 'Marguerites' are you going to spot in a Post-Graduate Office in Oxford? I tell you, you'd better hurry! I might kick the bucket by the end of the week, so off with you," he urged. His wrinkled hand clutched his hot-water bottle and brought it to his heart. "Are you still standing there? Go find her!"

"Yes, my lord!" the man replied, knowing full well he wasn't going to win that particular battle. He was about to dash out.

"Oh, and, Perkins, call my lawyer. I want to see him right away. We have work to do. Make haste, as there is not a second to lose. Time is of the essence. I have a new will to write, my last testament."

―――――

A week later, Marguerite Morel was behind her desk in her office in the Senior Post-graduate department of Physics at Oxford University. She had finished an interview with a graduate for admission. The chap left behind his newspaper on her desk.

She didn't like a messy desk, *an uncluttered desk means an uncluttered mind,* her usual thought on the subject. She took the paper and was about to put it in a drawer, out of sight to read it later, when one news headline on the front page of the Oxford Mail caught her eyes. It was the name that attracted her attention.

Though she was not expecting it so soon, she felt it in her bones. Old Lord Buckley had died, the news headline read. Marguerite went perfectly still, while a pang of sadness surged through her frame, and she shivered. When she recovered, she scanned the half-page article on the Oxford tycoon and member of the House of Lords. As she read it, she bit her bottom lip, torturing the poor flesh, while she rubbed her forehead with her hand.

His son, Fergus Waltham, had become the new eleventh Earl of Buckley.

Suddenly, her head twirled, she felt her body swaying and she gripped her desk with both hands to steady herself.

Breathe, Marguerite, breathe, she told herself. She couldn't believe what she read, but it was true!

It sounded a good idea at the time, but now she was not so sure. In her mind, this was not supposed to happen for a long time. Had the old man lied to her? Marguerite should have gotten used to the idea, but she hadn't yet. Barely two days had passed since she had accepted and signed the old earl's proposal. She closed the paper and sat motionless in her chair when it dawned on her what would happen next.

Oh, dear God, what have I done? She blanched, still dizzy. Her limbs went numb as a violent shock ran through her body.

Chapter 2

A rising dawn scattered the sky with yellow, orange, and reds, and it weaved on the horizon in a splendid feast of colours and light.

Marguerite closed her eyes to commit this beautiful morning to memory. It was a significant day for her, perhaps the most important of her life. It would be a memorable one, for better or for worse, no doubt.

Her name would change. Another one!

How many names have I changed over the years? She exhaled a heavy sigh with a pained expression. She let her hands fall at the sides, clutching her nightdress for a moment.

Never mind, now! You must focus on the day ahead. Today, my wedding day, will bring a new name for me. This one was real. There was no pretense about it.

She took a deep breath, trying to calm herself before she got too agitated. She bit her bottom lip and darted her eyes to the clock. *Still early.* She hadn't been able to sleep much since she read the news two weeks ago.

She was fond of her name as it was. Marguerite Morel.

For the first time in years, she would not mind the change,

though. In a few hours, she would become the new Countess of Buckley.

In the past, she had assumed false names for herself to conceal her identity, sometimes a different persona too; but countess was new! This one was true, nothing invented or pretense about it.

Marguerite came from a modest background, and she was about to become a countess. The aristocracy had never crossed her mind. Not in her wildest dreams, it was so remote from her life. She had known hardship growing up, but poverty had not troubled her much.

What shattered her spirit were the pain, the fear and the hurt she felt with Alain Basset, her ex-boyfriend. A terrible period of her existence which had seen her run from the man, hide, and change names to keep herself safe from her abusive ex-boyfriend. This was now in her distant past, and with Alain in prison for years to come, he would never bother her again or ruin her future.

A cold perspiration burst on her upper lip at the awful memories, and she struggled to put them out of her mind. *Focus on a pleasant memory instead, you silly woman!* she told herself, and she did.

Her mind cast back to her only loving memory when, six years ago, for three brief weeks with another man, she had experienced a deep passion. It was true love. When this man's pale blue eyes had landed on her that first time, long ago, it felt as if the dazzling, warm sun had caressed her skin after a long, dark, cold winter.

She had fallen in love. Alas, it was short-lived. After only three weeks, she had to run away and hide again, leaving behind the love of her life.

She had wished to escape her fate for so long, the terrible memories, start a new life. But it had not been possible until two years ago, when her sick mother died and she could move to England, to Oxford. She found a job, working at the university in the Senior Post-graduate office. She loved her new country; her own held too many terrible memories. A new life, and with Alain out of her world, in prison, she could move on to have some kind of normal life.

That day, though, her past seemed as if it belonged to someone else and it was not hers any longer. It was a long time ago.

But would Fergus remember her? She wasn't sure. She told the old man everything when he came looking for her with his proposition.

She opened the large window and glanced out at the sky. The air was crisp in April, and a cool puff stung her face.

But in spring, she always felt lighthearted, her mood and spirit high. She would have to make it work. She was determined to bring it off, to accomplish it. She had promised the old man. It had been his father's doing, not hers. She had only accepted the terms.

"I'll do this, with or without you, Marguerite. If it's not you, it'll be some other girl. Trust me, I'll do it! I am not going into the ground without marrying off my son," the old earl told her when she hesitated.

She thought it was a crazy idea. But she wouldn't be able to bear it if it was some other woman. *If his father was working to impose a wife on Fergus, it had better be me!*

Now that she had a second chance, she would take it, she told herself. She would not waste it. She shook her head and came back from the whirlwind of thoughts.

The day will soon warm up. I have a long day ahead of me, so focus, Marguerite, she said to herself.

A new life awaited her. She took short, deep breaths. Yes, the most fantastic of dawns on this most particular day gave her joy.

A good omen? How the devil should I know! But she believed in omens, in signals of prophetic significance. If she had to hazard a guess, from what she had learned of him lately, the answer would be a resounding "No!"

No, I don't think so! Even more so if Fergus were to remember their affair. She had transformed her appearance. *Perhaps he won't recognise me! Umm...* She was taking a monumental risk since she'd left him without as much as a goodbye six years ago.

Later that day, she would become a married woman, Fergus' wife. The problem, he had no idea whom he was marrying. Would he recognise her? They had not met yet since she had accepted his father's proposal. His father wished to keep her identity a secret from Fergus until the wedding day.

After a lifetime of insecurity, of uncertainty, of running away, of fear, she'd marry the man she had fallen in love with six years ago. Not a stranger like he would think of her right now.

Yes, she met Fergus six years ago; they had a fleeting fling. Given the time they had spent in bed, at least they knew each other's bodies intimately. She could still recall the tiny strawberry birthmark on his right buttock. A smile formed on her lips at the thought of Fergus's shapely bottom. Though she left him three weeks later. She didn't want to, but she made a speedy departure and unexpectedly disappeared out of his life. She had to.

There is the distinct possibility he won't recognise me. Perhaps...

Men like Fergus Waltham didn't remember silly flings when they only lasted a few weeks. *Was it meaningless for him?* She couldn't say.

When she moved from France to Oxford, she had seen him a few times, always from afar, secretly. She doubted he would even recollect their affair.

How could he? The most exquisite and sophisticated women

in society escorted him. When he tired of high-ranking ladies, it was the turn of models and actresses. These women were his playground, but no one seemed to last long enough. Perhaps if she had not left him, it would have fizzled out, anyway.

If she had to rely solely on his looks, she should be as pleased as Punch! Though she was aware of his personality, too, through gossip. Not during their love affair; he was caring and tender then, but to all accounts, in recent years he had turned into an ill-tempered, grumpy autocrat. His wish was his command, people said.

She would have a hard job on her hands. Now, here she was, about to become his wife. No doubt the man was still in shock.

Fergus had no choice. His father's will and last testament had dictated the terms upon which he would inherit. Old Lord Buckley had seen to that.

It was a marriage to her, or the new earl would have nothing. Fergus would give up his fortune and inheritance if he didn't marry her. Even the aristocratic title would bypass him if he didn't. And he had no clue whom he was about to marry. It was a damn crazy idea, but he couldn't refuse it.

How long will it last? she wondered.

The contract said she had to wed Fergus and live with him for a minimum of eighteen months to get her money. His father had been generous—two million pounds to stay married to his son for that time. The old earl had dictated the terms to them.

Everyone would think she would marry him for the money, including Fergus. Though it wasn't the money that attracted her to the proposition. It had always been him. She would have done it for nothing. Six years ago, she would have stayed with him if she'd had the choice, but she hadn't. So now she had another chance, and this time, she wouldn't waste it.

Marguerite had to admit, he had the looks of an

Olympian god, handsome, powerful and manly with the grace of an athlete, mingled with a hellish personality.

Fergus' hair looked dark at first sight, flowing long as he walked always with purpose, but at a closer inspection, the rich russet hues in it made his hair a remarkable, glorious tone. She loved it, and with his chiseled good looks sculpted to perfection, he spellbound her. The fellow was tall and imposing, and his pale blue eyes had an unmistakable hard glint in them.

One wouldn't overlook Fergus for his beauty or temper, that was a fact, accustomed, as he was, to boss people around to get what he wanted.

"His great lordship" Kathryn said some guys in his office called him, while others hailed him as "The Dark Lord!"

For her sins, she was about to become his wife! He would know the name of his bride only today, on his wedding day, at the ceremony. Not that it would say much to him, anyway.

Six years ago, she had used a false name. Fergus had known her as Lisette! So, her actual name, Marguerite Morel, would mean nothing to him, anyway.

Good Heavens! Her breathing quickened. *He'll be furious once he finds out! Who am I kidding? Of course, he'll eventually recognise me, and he'll kill me! Dear God! Please tell me I am doing the right thing.*

For a minute, she closed her eyes. She kneeled and prayed for God's help. Her hands united in devotion, all of her childhood's prayers in her mother tongue, fast French, dashed out of her mouth. Then she halted, grasping the side of her nightdress with both hands. She clung to the material hard to steady herself again, inhaled, and as she rose, she flattened some wrinkles in her nightgown.

Breathe, Marguerite, breathe!

She glanced up to the heavens. If she believed all she heard lately, his character was another thing altogether. That was not good. Bloody dire if she had to be honest.

She thought of the fellow she had known six years ago, and the Fergus she was going to marry today was a different man, from what she heard of him, but he wasn't. They were one and the same. Perhaps, she had not spent enough time with him then to find out about the real Fergus, his actual personality, more than likely. Her forthcoming marriage would be like a game of hazard. No one could guess how it would turn out.

She was so ill prepared for this wedding, apprehensive. *Oh, sweet merciful heaven... what the hell am I doing? Too late to change my mind now. Breathe, Marguerite, breathe! Calm down, get on with it.*

Though worried and nervous, she didn't regret her decision, not really, if she had to be honest.

The old Earl of Buckley wanted her to marry his son and heir. 'To safeguard my title,' he had stated, 'to prevent my son from being alone when I am gone.'

She had been tempted to say yes straight away. How could she not? Fergus was so handsome. She'd had him for three weeks, so she knew how wonderful he could be, despite what people said. One look at him and her legs turned to jelly. Yes, according to everyone, her husband-to-be was an ill-tempered man, a beast, but the handsomest of all. He had the face of an Adonis, with sculpted high cheekbones and dark hair, with russet hues, flowing long. The pale blue eyes made her dream when they were on her. *I'll swoon when his eyes will land on me again today.*

He knew how to look at a woman, really see her. She knew that better than anyone. The way he had looked at her all those years ago still made her shiver now, and he was about to become her husband. *Dear God!*

The Earl of Buckley was one of the wealthiest landowners in England, with a grand country estate in Gloucestershire. His financial investments corporation was listed on the London Stock Exchange as well as other exchanges world-wide. The huge office building, as well as his home, was in Oxford, with other houses scattered over the country and around the world. Not to mention, a prestigious aristocratic title, almost as old as that of the Queen of England herself, came with him, too. But that was not what interested her.

Marguerite was comfortable, independent, her own woman now. She had finally risen out of the dark. She considered herself as lucky now. So why marry him… risk everything again for a man? She was her own mistress now. She really didn't know why. If she had to hazard a guess, it was because she still loved Fergus; she couldn't help that.

She had regretted having to leave him six years ago. She could not have done otherwise, though she still adored the man.

Once she became Fergus' wife today, she would be at his mercy and will. She would give up being the mistress of her own life to be married to him. But she couldn't refuse it. Her body and soul wanted it, demanded it of her, despite her logic to the contrary. There was a struggle between Marguerite's soul and her mind, but her heart had won the battle by miles. So, she had agreed to the old earl's proposal to marry his son.

And Fergus had no choice. He would have to marry her whether he liked it or not. So, he was doing it because he must, not because he wanted to. She wondered what the hell went through his mind. *What's he thinking right now? Nothing good, I am sure. He'll despise me.*

Today, Marguerite would give up her freedom to be married to Fergus Waltham, the Earl of Buckley, in return for money, with a minimum of eighteen months of marriage. And with luck, she would produce an offspring too. Those were the terms of the contract she had signed up to. And here she was, ready for him.

One thought was keeping her sane. The dating app had done the matching, too. It had surprised her when Mollie told her but elated her, even if they had deleted everything from the app. She had only agreed to take part in the dating app test because, one day, while Kathryn was working on her laptop while waiting in her office for a meeting with Marguerite's boss, she had seen a picture of Fergus on her companion's laptop.

"Are you busy?" Marguerite asked, trying to keep her voice steady.

"Yes," Kathryn replied, bashing at her computer.

"Is it a special project for Uni?" She was curious. *What the hell was Kathryn doing with a photo of Fergus?*

"Yes, it is, but not for University," the girl countered.

"What is it?"

"I'm working on a dating app. Mollie and I are almost finished with the work, and I am inputting people's profiles for matching."

Is he using a dating app? Marguerite wondered, astonished.

"Interesting," she said nonchalantly, darting her eyes from the girl to his photo on her laptop. She asked more questions about it.

Marguerite decided there and then, she would take part, too, on the off chance she would match to him. It was a long shot, but who knew. So when Mollie had told her she had matched up to Fergus, she almost fell off her chair. Marguerite and Fergus had matched to a high score. He was her 'top pick.' *Unbelievable! Surely, the damn thing was wrong!*

Nonetheless, when her apprehension got her down, she felt invigorated by this. *Even the app said we are a suitable match.* She was skeptical about it, but it was an additional reason to do it, to agree to his father's plan. Any reason, however flimsy to her, was worth holding on to.

Now, she must convince Fergus, too—they were a great

pairing. She would have to show him. The likelihood was he'd think she was marrying him for the money.

Breathe, Marguerite, breathe, she told herself time and time again. There was a whirlwind in her mind that morning. Her thoughts flashed fast and furious, between past, present, and future, and back again.

It was her wedding day, and she had the right to be nervous. She was yanked out of her reverie as the door opened.

"Good morning, darling," said Kathryn, followed by Mollie holding a breakfast tray. The girls were excited. A wedding was a big thing, one somehow they had instigated through their dating app, and they couldn't contain themselves.

"Hey, girl, you need to get moving. There is a groom waiting for you, but breakfast first. You must keep your strength up for tonight." Mollie winked at her.

"Then we need to get you into your beautiful wedding dress. You must look divine for your new husband. He'll adore you," Kathryn added with a warm smile, and her companion echoed her sentiment.

Zac and Finley had told the girls about Fergus' impeding wedding to a complete stranger, forced on by his father. The news shocked them, but nobody knew the identity of the bride. Even if the girls had their suspicions, but they could not be certain.

That was until a week ago when Marguerite had come to them for help. The bride-to-be was having a panic attack. She had not known how to approach this marriage with days to go, too nervous to think straight.

She asked the girls for guidance to prepare for it and

explained how the old earl had reached out to her with the proposal. But she had begged Mollie and Kathryn for confidentiality until the ceremony had taken place and not to disclose her identity as the bride, to abide by the earl's wishes.

For once, the girls had kept the secret. Though, as expected, when pushed, they had caved in at the last minute and revealed to their partners the name of the bride on the morning of the wedding.

Chapter 3

"What do you know about this woman? Who the hell is she? On whose recommendation has my father inflicted her upon me?" Fergus Waltham, the eleventh Earl of Buckley, huffed disconsolately.

"Finley and I have only known her identity this morning. The funny thing, she was in my house since last night. But we must abide by your father's wishes until the ceremony. We cannot reveal who she is. But she is a lovely girl, I tell you," Zac reassured him and patted him on the shoulder.

"Bloody Hell, not you too! I suppose the hefty reward tag in the damn contract attracted the woman. This is ludicrous! I just hope this eighteen months fly by. She gets her money and gets the fuck out of my life." He was seething.

"Calm down! She is a clever girl. Her beauty, her mind and simplicity recommend her, and that's all you need to know. The app matched you perfectly to her, whether or not you think it nonsense," Finley added with a grin. The whole thing rather amused him.

"Jesus, not the bloody app again! Anyway, where the hell is she?" The bridegroom rolled his eyes.

"She spent the night at my house. She'll be here with the girls soon," Zac informed him.

"How could my father do this to me? Forcing me to wed a stranger, otherwise I'll give up my lands, my money, my company, my title, everything! God, Dad was mad. Totally bonkers!" he huffed and shook his head as perspiration burst onto his upper lip. "I tried to contest my father's will, to stop the wedding, you know, through the courts. But the judge said he was of a sound mind. Does this seem to you the work of a rational man? A person in his right mind?" He swiped the back of his hand over his upper lip and curses as black as the night came out of his mouth. Fergus had even sought to bribe Perkins, his father's secretary, to know who the woman was. He had appealed to him repeatedly for the two weeks leading to the wedding. Though Perkins had been his father's secretary, he had also been his devoted friend for over fifteen years. He had given the old man his word as to his silence about the identity of the bride. The young lord had even threatened to fire him, but Perkins stuck to his guns and kept his silence. He complied with the old man's wishes. So, considering Perkins' integrity and loyalty, the new earl made him his own secretary thereafter.

So, it was Fergus would not know who his bride was until his wedding day.

"Cheer up, Gus, you might enjoy being married. Look at Zac; he adores his wife," Finley said with a crooked grin. "And I am engaged. Kat and I will set a date for our wedding soon. I can't wait!" he concluded, slapping his friend's back vigourously.

Zac was the groom's best man and winked at him to echo Finley's words with eagerness.

"Forgive me if I don't share your enthusiasm, boys, with a woman like this. She must be a gold-digger. And remind me to strangle Mollie and Kathryn when the day is over," the earl scoffed.

Zac snorted.

"Enough talking! Are you ready? Your bride awaits. The priest has another wedding this afternoon. Hurry, let's get this over with," Finley urged him.

————————

The earl's white Georgian house had been prepared for the occasion. It was a massive mansion on the outskirts of Oxford, where they would live, gleaming opulently and polished to a high standard for the wedding. His loyal domestic staff, considered as part of his extended family in his large household, had seen Fergus and his siblings grow up since childhood. They were ready for the newcomer, too, and invited to the ceremony.

If he were to reflect about it, Fergus couldn't accept that the house, his country estate in Gloucestershire with all his lush farmlands and rich in income, even his investment business in town with high yielding had been placed in peril by his father's will unless he wed the damn woman.

How could he do this to me? To his own son! Another deluge of silent curses scattered in his brain. Would he survive this? Would he get through these eighteen months with her? Whoever she was, who knew.

Perhaps his dad was right on one thing. Fergus required an heir now, a successor like he'd succeeded to his father and at thirty-three years old, it was prime time he did.

He ran a hand over his face in surrender. He cursed aloud. "Bloody Hell!"

————————

They had set the grand ballroom up for the ceremony, with a makeshift altar where the priest was standing. Rows of elegantly draped chairs filled the room for those attending the wedding. Later, the earl would host the wedding lunch, too. The groom was in the anteroom, ready to make his way to the altar. Marguerite was now in an adjacent room, waiting for the appointed time for the ceremony.

'You'll do as I tell you, my boy, or you'll not see a penny from me, and my title, my estate, my business and my money will bypass you. I promise you. I've had enough of your antics. You had better shape up. I'm doing this for your own good. You'll thank me when you understand,' his father had stated in a recording that accompanied the will, and at that instant, his voice haunted him. He couldn't believe his ears when he heard his father's voice utter those words from beyond the grave. The reading of the will had left him flabbergasted. The old earl had had the last laugh!

How Fergus wished he were one of his younger brothers right now. They were to leave for the continent soon after the wedding. His lucky siblings were to go on government errands, Sebastian to Italy and Fredrick to Switzerland, no doubt assignments full of fun with the Italian and Swiss ladies, while he was about to commit to a foolish marriage to a complete stranger.

His brothers had roared with laughter at the reading of the will when they understood the proviso for Fergus' inheritance. They laughed so hard, they almost choked. Fortunately, the lads would soon leave on their errands, happy that their big brother had been put out to pasture.

The youngest of the brood, his sister, had giggled too, but Belinda snorted because she was upset with him. His sister was not thrilled with him, since he was sending her to Dr. Stewart's clinic, to ensure she could control her temper and do no more mischief. He'd had enough of his sister's escapades and was glad she would be out of his way for now. Though it overjoyed the girl that there would be another lady in the household to counterbalance all those male hormones.

"Bloody lucky for them they won't have to see the disaster that will ensue; this will end in tears. You mind my words. The girl will run a mile when she knows she is marrying the Dark Lord, and then a scandal will hit us." He peered through a crack of the door at the priest waiting at the altar and at the few guests waiting for the ceremony to start.

"Nonsense," said Zac, "the young woman is as sweet as pie. If I weren't married, she's a girl I would go for." He was trying to appease his friend.

Fergus launched a dubious look at him and snorted.

On her side, there were only a few friends he didn't recognize. Apparently, she didn't have any family. His faithful staff, his valet, his butler, the housekeeper, the maid and the old cook were welcomed to attend the ceremony. They were sitting amongst the guests now waiting for the service to start.

Fergus was perspiring. He gave himself a cursory look in the mirror, passing a hand on his dark-reddish hair. It was shoulder length. He wondered whether he should tie it up.

Oh, what the hell, who cares? He tugged at his tie, which suddenly seemed too tight, and adjusted his charcoal grey tailored suit, which fit him to perfection. His pale blue eyes sparkled with vivacity despite his atrocious mood.

He looked elegant and sophisticated, and at thirty-three, he was handsome and one of the wealthiest aristocrats in England. The suit enhanced his wide shoulders and trim waist. His beauty and amorous escapades were the talk of many drawing rooms in town. Soon young women would mourn another golden bachelor biting the dust.

"Have you told Lucy yet? Does she know you are getting married? Have you told your long list of women? One or two may be troublesome, you mind my words," Zac said, raising an eyebrow with a grin on his face, looking at the groom intently.

"Leave Lucy out of this. Everyone has been warned not to say a word about her. This woman must have nothing to do with her. And my women are none of her business, either. The bloody chit!"

"Honestly, Gus, I can't believe your attitude. Your bride should know before someone tells her."

"I won't, though."

"I can't believe you won't tell Marguerite, man," his companion said with a shake of his head.

"Marguerite? Is that her name?" Fergus repeated, with a questioning expression.

"Sorry, I shouldn't have said the name. I understand your dad's wishes, and I am legally in breach. But hey, you'll be married in half an hour, anyway. So, I reckon it doesn't matter now. Unbelievable, he told you nothing at all about your bride. God, really!"

"I tell you, not a word. This is the first I've even heard of her name. I am completely in the dark. And not for want of trying." Fergus shot a resigned expression at his friends that said, *a hell of a disaster!* Shaking his head, he wished he could become invisible and escape his destiny.

"Incredible!" Zac puzzled with a grin and echoed his disbelief.

"I am just blindly doing what my father has forced me to do. Is she at least passable, this bride of mine? Why couldn't I meet her beforehand, why all this secrecy, is she ugly? What's wrong with her?" Fergus asked, and he fidgeted with his tie and cufflinks, suddenly feeling hot.

"How should I know? I bet your father figured that if she recognised you for who you are, she might take a fright, change her mind, and not marry you," Finley said and laughed, "And yes, you'll thank him, she is so pretty. Now enough talking, you go and wait by the priest with Zac. I'll bring your lovely bride along shortly."

Chapter 4

They made the brief journey to the earl's house and came in through the back door as agreed with Perkins, so as not to be seen.

"I can't see anything. He is not there." Mollie peeked through the intercommunicating door, now ajar, once they settled in. They were waiting for Finley to collect the bride in the adjacent room to where the ceremony was to take place. He had agreed to give the bride away.

"Soon you won't be just merely Marguerite. You'll be the Countess of Buckley." Kathryn wriggled her eyebrows.

"Yes, for my sins," the bride said with a low sigh. The girls curtsied ungainly to her in jest, as if they were a pair of clumsy ducks.

"Oops." And they all chuckled.

"You don't curtsey to an earl or his wife!" Marguerite said with soft eyes for her friends, a tender smile on her lips, but Mollie shrugged her shoulders with a laugh.

"Let's see," said Kathryn, "if he looks handsome in his groom's outfit." She went to the door to peek, but he wasn't there yet, so she returned to her friend. The girls were giddy with joy, which made Marguerite even more nervous.

"Please, girls, no more nonsense. Focus on the wedding now," the bride chastised them.

"We must call you *my lady* after the ceremony, you know that." Mollie couldn't help a crack of emotion in her voice. She was happy for her friend.

"God. Stop that, I am nervous enough as it is," Marguerite urged them, fidgeting with her earrings and her necklace. She smoothed her gown. She was restless.

She wore an elegant white wedding dress; it had an illusion lace appliqué fitted bodice over a tulle wide, full-length skirt. It suited her to perfection. She looked heavenly, and it enhanced her figure. Normally, a somewhat lackluster dresser by choice, Marguerite was not a fashionable lady. Since her past life, the plainer her clothes, the better. In the past, she had avoided dressing in any way that could attract attention to herself. So, all her outfits were black or brown.

Marguerite was a pretty girl, striving to look plain. Her pale grey eyes and harmonious features made her graceful. She had a tallish figure that embraced a full, sensuous bosom and round, womanly hips that rendered her sexy and feminine. She needed very little to turn herself into a stunning woman.

Kathryn had adamantly opposed her wearing a drab outfit for her wedding day. They had chosen it together. Marguerite was now glad she complied. She had to admit, even if she said so herself, she looked splendid and feminine in her dress.

Mollie urged her to scrap the black and brown going forward; she needed to have more trendy clothes now that she would have a husband who must find her cute and sexy.

Marguerite wasn't quite sure about this. Since her arrival in Oxford she had not dated. Not for lack of invitations from men, but she had felt no inclination to it. Even in France, she hardly dated. Alain had put her off men. That had been true but for one man, Fergus! And she was about to marry him!

She hardly ever used her best black or brown dresses. She thought it would be a waste of money to ditch her outfits, or as Mollie called them, Marguerite's uniforms. In the end, she had gone along with her companions. That day, she was so glad she had listened to her friends and updated her wardrobe.

She was sure Fergus wouldn't pay much attention to her, in particular if he recognised her, but at least it made her feel more appealing and more confident about herself.

Her wedding dress was graceful. She loved it. She felt like a movie star at the Oscars and looked stunning. So, she decided she would wear it for the luncheon as well. Elegant bridal shoes made her feet seem small and dainty, and a veil covered her face, falling long at the back. This completed the ensemble.

It had been a long time since she had felt this good about herself. Her ex-boyfriend, Alain, had messed up her self-esteem and confidence big time, taking them away from her. Fortunately, these personality attributes were now slowly making a comeback in her, and she was feeling more at ease in her new life in England.

One thing she refused to compromise on—she insisted to have her hair in her conventional way. Her long, dark, ebony hair was up, tied in her everyday tight and severe chignon, only embellished with two tiny fresh flowers. Somehow it gave her strength…

Her hairstyle had been so different when she had met Fergus, she'd had to change it to disguise herself.

Will he know me, looking like this? She smoothed her hair with her hand, apprehension creeping up on her again. *Honestly, Marguerite,* her inner voice said, lashing out, *grow up, girl! How on earth do you think he won't recognise you?*

For a moment, she contemplated the door. Was it too late to run away?

"Hey, what's wrong! Cheer up; it won't be that bad! Any man would be honoured to have a wife as beautiful as you," Kathryn declared with a gentle smile, caressing her friend's arm.

Marguerite took a deep breath. *Breathe, girl, breathe.*

"Oh, you are gorgeous. He will love you the minute he sets eyes on you," Mollie said, squeezing her hand.

The bride launched her a skeptical look, and clearing her throat, she shuffled on her feet.

"I hear footsteps," Kathryn said. The girls were her maid and matron-of-honour and overexcited. They both looked beautiful in figure-hugging, pale pink, long dresses.

"At last! I am nervous as it is. The quicker we go through this, the better," Marguerite replied.

Kathryn rushed to the door to peep inside the ballroom where the wedding was to take place. "Ah!" The young girl made a squealing sound. "Oh, he looks splendid! I must admit, he may be an ogre, but he sure is handsome." Kathryn bit her tongue, realising what she had just said. The word 'ogre' had slipped through her lips unaware. She had put her foot in it, with Marguerite already worried. Too late! She turned to the bride and gave her an apologetic smile. She dismissed her remark with a wave of her hand and a shrug of her shoulders.

The girls peeped at him through the crack in the door, with "ooh" and "ah."

"Oh, wow, he is so tall, so elegant. Fergus just tugged at his tie. He looks nervous. He is wearing a charcoal grey morning suit, and he is dreamy," Mollie said. "He has the most astonishing pale blue eyes; they twinkle. If he had a beard, he would look like Jesus."

"Twinkle? Are you sure? It is probably fury, I should expect. You can count on that," mumbled Marguerite.

The ladies laughed.

"Shush, he will hear you. Come away from the door, this instant. Girls, stop snooping, he is going to see you." Her uneasiness was growing by the minute as the moment was coming closer.

"The man is gorgeous. Wide shoulders and trim waist," Mollie said with a sigh. "Good thing I am already married!"

"You can see your face in his black, high-polished shoes. He is looking serious, though," Kathryn stated as she turned from the door and reached the bride.

"Serious? Well, I suppose if someone forces you to wed a stranger, you wouldn't be too thrilled, either," Marguerite replied.

The girls recognised her emotions.

"Hey, what is it? You won't cry now, will you, my lady?"

"Oh, stop it!"

"You will be in an hour, my lovely countess." Kathryn hugged her close and took away a small tear from her eyes with her hand.

"Oh, Marguerite, don't fret. You'll be okay; you'll see. Besides, you don't want to ruin your makeup. He looks delightful to me," Mollie said. "I am sure it will be fine. You still wish to go ahead with this, don't you?" The girl went on, suddenly feeling apprehensive for her friend, thinking she may have changed her mind at the last minute.

"Yes, of course, I do. I am crying happy tears, in a way… I am a bride, am I not? I am allowed to cry on my wedding day."

Happy tears, Marguerite, you liar, her inner voice lashed out again, *more like tears of terror.*

Fergus and Zac were at the head of the small congregation invited to the wedding.

"It's time. Settle your nerves for a minute or two before your bride comes in."

"This won't work. I know nothing about her," Fergus whispered through clenched teeth.

"You'll find out soon enough. In an hour, you'll have a beautiful wife and your entire life to discover everything about her and all the pleasures to be had," he said with a wink.

"This is lunacy," the groom spat.

"There is nothing you can do about it now. Just get on with it, stay calm, don't scare the poor girl before the day is out," Zac reiterated with a warning look.

"Madness, pure madness!" Fergus mumbled, shaking his head with his eyes closed and taking a deep breath.

"Stop fussing, Gus. A man at thirty-three should have a wife, a family. Finley'll be next. Yours is long overdue." Zac chuckled. "Only the future counts now. You must try to work at it," he went on with a grave face, while Fergus granted a hollow, guttural sound.

"Don't blame me when things won't work and everyone will be miserable," he mumbled, looking at the congregation.

He caught the eye of one of his brothers. Sebastian launched him a wicked smile and a wink. A curse erupted from Fergus' mouth, which could only produce a stare full of rebuke from the priest. Then he darted his eyes around to her side of the guests.

"Where the hell is she?" Where was the minx? He just wanted the whole thing to be over!

"Patience, Buck," Zac said, using his friend's old Etonian nickname, "she'll be the only lady you need to worry about from now on, soon your wife, and a pretty girl she is too. You won't be disappointed."

Fergus wondered what Lucy would make of this. But this was his secret until he could decide what to do.

Perhaps...

"Are you listening, Gus? You must give it a try, apply yourself, strive to get along with your bride," Zac resumed, interrupting his musing with a crease between his brows.

"It'll be a bloody disaster! You'll see," the groom mumbled to himself.

Chapter 5

The door opened and Finley came in. Marguerite inhaled deeply. *Good Heavens, here we are.* Her time had come. Was she ready to marry him?

They all stood up. Kathryn ran to her fiancé and kissed him adoringly.

"Soon, I'll be the one waiting for you," Finley whispered to her.

"Oh, darling!" And she kissed him again.

"Hey, you two, it's not your day. It's Marguerite's, so stop smooching and attend to your wedding duties." Mollie snorted with a mischievous grin.

They chuckled, and he turned his attention to the bride. "You look so beautiful, quite a treat for him, I dare say. Delightful," he said, scanning the bride with a pleased expression and turning his thumbs up.

"Thank you," Marguerite mumbled, blushing to the root of her hair.

"Ready then?" he asked with a tender smile.

She opened her mouth to say something, but no sound came. She cleared her throat several times, but words wouldn't come. Emotion was getting hold of her. So she just nodded firmly. Her nervousness caused her to pat her necklace twice, and she fidgeted with her earrings.

Finley winked at her and gave her a crisp nod. "Ladies, could you please get ready for the ceremony? Come on, you two, off you go," he added, and for a few moments, the girls busied themselves, smoothing their dresses with a great rustle of fabric.

"Come on, girls, move on." Finley gently marched the two attendants out of the room, while the bride waited and gave the last twiddle to her wedding dress.

"Come, Marguerite, you aren't scared now, are you? Nothing to be frightened of," he said gently, seeing the girl had turned as pale as a ghost. But he went on, "Everyone thinks he is a blackguard, and he is! Most of the time…" He laughed chirpily. "There will be times, he'll look wild, ferocious, but deep down he has a good heart. I have known him most of my life. Believe me, he has. It's still there, somewhere. Bring his kindness out again. He'll love you; you'll see. I have a funny feeling he'll fall head over heels in love with you, girl! You are his salvation. Besides, the girls will be close to you, so they'll help you. You can count on me, too, anytime, if you need me. But once he gets to know you, he won't let you go." He patted her arm softly.

His tender speech took her by surprise. She gulped at his words, trying to contain her tears. Her mouth went dry. Her heart thundered in her chest. She looked up at him. Then she turned away for a moment and fretted with the flowers in her hair at the mirror.

His heartfelt speech was heartwarming. A small, soft smile appeared on her face despite her anxiety.

"Ready?" he repeated, and she gave him a nod with pursed lips. "Good, let's roll, girl!" He offered his arm to her.

After years of suffering, she was going to marry the man

she loved. She dared to dream she might finally be all right. *An illusion? Stupid optimism? Perhaps! Only time would tell.*

She pulled her veil over her face and took his arm with a heavy sigh and a trembling hand.

He heard the door open and light footsteps advance into the room, but Fergus didn't turn. He'd resolved he wouldn't turn to her, he would not give the woman the satisfaction of looking at her. But he could not help a sly glance over his shoulder as a procession of women entered the room.

The girls came in, one by one, Mollie first, then Kathryn. He caught the young maid scurrying to her seat at the back, too. He realised his bride would be in next, so he pivoted back to the priest.

When the footsteps behind him become louder, heavier, he knew they were Finley's sizeable boots. He often wore boots, even at weddings, an ex-soldier habit.

She must be with him. Don't turn, man, don't, Fergus thought.

A groom who wouldn't turn to look at his bride? Well... he didn't. His tenacity stood firm. He waited. He looked right ahead in front of him, tall, rigid and straight as a pillar until Finley deposited her by his side.

He gave his friend a curt nod and mumbled a "Thank you."

He shifted then, unsmiling, toward her, with a severe expression on his face that would have sent his worst enemy scurrying. A veil covered three quarters of the woman's face down to her chin.

Damn, still can't see her! Bloody woman.

She turned to him too, and curtsied.

What the hell!

She dropped a low curtsy in perfect dignity, elegance and

grace. For a moment, it disturbed him. Fergus was an earl of the realm, but he wasn't a prince or a royal himself, so people did not have to curtsey to him. Yet, on occasion, people mistakenly did, but no one had done it in years.

He didn't understand why it should disturb him, or what he was expecting, but not dignity and grace from her. Even with her etiquette mistake, for a tiny moment, his eyes turned soft and danced with mirth.

He noticed the fine line of her jaw, just about visible under her veil. Fergus assessed a profile that seemed harmonious. He looked at her graceful hands, displaying long fingers, with fiery red fingernails atop, and shapely, slender arms. The attractive long neck and the round, full bosom heaving had not escaped him, either, under his watchful eye.

While the priest started reciting his lengthy sermon to marry them, he became incandescent with the lady, frustrated at the peril she had exposed herself to.

What woman would wed a total stranger? He could have been a bad person, a mean and violent man, and she wouldn't have known what hit her. *I bet this lady has no common sense. What if I were a vicious, wicked man?* he thought, aghast. As it was, yes, she would just get a bad-tempered husband, but not a violent one, the lucky chit.

What type of woman in her right mind, having a career and free to be happy, as his friends had told him she had, would marry a cantankerous, blackguard like himself? Didn't she know what he was?

The silly girl.

Didn't his notorious reputation precede him everywhere he went? Didn't she realise the pitfalls? And there were many.

How could she do something like that, put herself in danger by marrying a total stranger just because I have a title, he thought.

It was apparent to him, only his riches were in her mind, the two million pounds at the end of the eighteen months' marriage, shouting louder and clear, despite the danger she was running by marrying a stranger. She married him for who he was, what he had, for his money!

The minx! How shameful! I should spank her, the dangerous, venal, sleepyhead! Thank God, I am not a cruel or a violent man! Jesus, what his bride had risked! *The foolish woman.*

He doubted she was clever, as his father mentioned in his recording, if she had not thought of all the worst qualities a man could have. Even if the money was considerable, she was taking a substantial risk for it. She placed herself at the mercy of a husband who, for all she knew, could be a vicious pervert. She had gone into this matrimony without meeting him, not thinking of the pitfalls. Without getting to know him, an ill-tempered man like him!

She'll soon wish she hadn't, that's for sure.

He would have wanted nothing better than to put her over his knees and thrash her backside, to teach her a lesson. *The dangerous gold-digger, impudent, selfish, wretched minx. The woman was reckless!*

He was tall and imposing, looming over her, his spine straight as a rod in his full height, with a tight jaw, and a harsh squint in his pale blue eyes. He shot an incandescent glance at her, stocked with fire. He could have scared an army away with that expression.

Her heart thundered in her chest. It puzzled her how the entire congregation didn't hear it and roar with laughter at her. It sounded so loud to her, ready to explode.

She had a peek at him as she curtsied. *Damn curtsey.* Why would she do such a foolish thing? *He'll chuckle at me now.*

Marguerite's eyes darted to him every so often while the priest presided over the wedding mass. He was as handsome as ever, no doubt. Better than she remembered. There was a new maturity to his appearance. He looked grown up, which only gave him a more seductive quality. He resembled Adonis, the mortal lover of Aphrodite in Greek mythology, a man resplendent of beauty and desire with whom the goddess had fallen in love. Beauty called upon beauty. A vision! And like the deity herself, Marguerite worshipped Fergus.

But contrary to the myth, it is a fact I am no goddess, nor a beauty, she reflected. *He'll take one glimpse at me and loathe me. Assuming he doesn't recognise me, but if he does, he'll despise me even more. He won't talk to me for eighteen months, until it's time to send me away.*

That day, he seemed so aloof and remote from her, like an unreachable dream.

She sensed his sight on her. When she spun to him, the expression in his eyes took her breath away. There was a look on his face that terrified her. She knew now why they called him the Dark Lord. He could kill a person with that one look.

Dear Good! He is furious with me.

If her neighbour's cat could see Fergus' face at that moment, the poor creature would have arched its back and hissed, running away in fear, exactly like she might do at any moment if he kept staring at her like that. She inhaled, hinted at a smile, but he turned his head to the priest without reciprocating.

Marguerite gulped. *Blasted man! He hates me already!*

She'd heard from everyone how he was against this marriage, how he fought tooth and nail, in the courts of law, trying to upturn his father's will, to avoid this wedding at all costs, but to no avail. His father had won from beyond the grave. She saw what this meant to him. His face said it all; he hated her! He wasn't even disguising it for her. Fergus told her loud and clear without a word. He was protesting at this matrimony even now, at the altar. His expression confirmed it for her; he had not wanted her.

She was certain now; Marguerite had underestimated the entire affair. She had misconstrued him! This was not the man she had met six years ago; he couldn't be. So harsh. So unpleasant. So irritating!

She swallowed a lump in her throat, and for a moment, a sudden and overwhelming surge of panic took hold of her. She tried to take small, shallow breaths. The room twirled around her. A sob escaped her. She was dazed, and her body swayed. She was about to pass out. She clutched the pew in front of her to steady herself.

Fergus realised what was about to happen, when he saw her swaying through the corner of his eye. He gripped her upper arm hard, almost painfully, and leaned into her. "Don't you dare to pass out! Pull yourself together," he whispered into her ear, but the harsh command was clear.

The sound of his cultured, velvety, and masculine voice in her ear, with his almost inaudible harsh command in it, gave her a shock to the system. With the obnoxious remark still ringing in her ears, blood rushed through her. She could virtually feel it gushing in her veins through her body and limbs, and it pumped to her head. This served its purpose. It was the vicious tonic she needed. The words were nasty in the circumstances, though it made her recover quickly.

She would not give the bastard the satisfaction of fainting. *Oh, no, sir!* So, she collected all her internal strength and pulled herself together. *Breathe, Marguerite, breathe, be dignified! Don't show your emotions again.*

The priest finally pronounced them man and wife.

He could kiss his bride.

He turned, giving a quick glance over her person. His eyes swiped all over her frame, from the heel of her dainty shoes on her pretty feet, up through her body, landing on her heaving bosom. A small, appreciative, amused smile curled up on one side of his mouth. It made her tremble, and he wasn't sure if it was fear or lust.

He held her veil in his hands and raised it over her head, disclosing her face to him. It happened in a flash, an instant was all it took for him to figure it out.

With a tiny step backward, his head drew back too, and then it dipped swiftly forward a tad, while his pale blue eyes became as big as moons. Next, he blinked, struggling to process what he had just seen. For a nanosecond, he squeezed them shut, feeling he was mistaken. When he opened them again, she was still there, watching him.

You!

The shock subsided with the same speed it came on. He was used to it, squashing his emotions, keeping a tight lid on them.

Praise God, was the blunt, irritating, and sudden notion that shot through his brain, though. By then, he had regained his composure. He was a master at controlling his feelings.

He cursed silently. His mind surrendered to all the blasphemes and obscenities he had ever learned. *The damn minx!*

He recovered quickly enough for all his sudden emotions to go unnoticed, giving nothing away, noticing her agitation instead.

Was the chit nervous? Or did she like him? Well, no wonder there. Women always liked him, at least physically. Why would it surprise him if this one did too?

She'd pleased him abundantly back then, though it didn't last long, did it? She had soon moved onto pastures new with not a care in the world, without even saying goodbye to him.

The tease, the flirt, the damn woman!

The priest intruded in his reverie, "Go on; kiss the bride!"

Her bow-shaped lips tightened. He glimpsed at her for a

moment, scrutinising her now. He lowered himself, offered her a small peck on the lips, and one on her cheek. *Why, the second kiss was unnecessary,* he told himself.

The touch of her plump, sweet lips and the silky skin on her rosy cheeks sparked something inside him. It kindled a rush of pleasure in his gut, awakening his senses, and his cock stirred. He forced them down, prepared to crush them without mercy.

While he pecked her cheek, though, a devilish pang overtook him. "Congratulations, my lady," he said. "In eighteen months, you'll walk out of here a wealthy woman with all that cash. But I'll make you work for it. By the time I'm finished with you, you'll have earned every penny, I can guarantee you," he then murmured, leaning into her ear in a vicious flash of spite to punish her.

Then he straightened, to search into her eyes now gleaming with tears. Those beautiful pale grey eyes of hers, misty. He saw the hurt his remarks had intended to cause, and they had hit her hard. A sudden qualm of remorse at having humiliated her replaced the moment of triumph at his wicked, hateful words.

He inhaled and turned to the congregation with a smile instead; he was used to hiding his genuine feelings. Fergus composed his features into an emotionless expression for the guests when he offered his elbow to her without looking at her. He didn't want to look at the pain in her eyes. He felt awful at having hurt her, and this irritated him even more.

What the hell!

He should be satisfied at having mortified her instead. So, the bridegroom grew irked with himself for feeling sorry for her.

She looked anxious when he lifted her veil. He was struck motionless for a second, and she didn't know if he had recognised her or whether he found her ugly.

He scrutinized her, while her grey eyes skimmed swiftly over his face, seeking to read his emotions, but she couldn't. She noticed the small lift of his brow, but then his hateful words had devastated her.

Marguerite turned slowly and, with a shaking hand, took his elbow. Despite the hurt his words had caused her, touching him, even through his jacket, made her heart thunder. Butterflies crushed at her core, as if an electric current had shocked her frame. Her body trembled. She didn't know if it was fear or anticipation. At a guess, she would have said a mix of both.

They exchanged kisses and congratulations with their guests for a few minutes. He had wanted to keep the invitations to a bare minimum; she was glad of it now.

The deed was finally done. She was a married woman, his new wife. The Countess of Buckley wed to the hellish Dark Lord! Champagne followed, to celebrate the newlyweds.

There would be no honeymoon, she knew. Fergus had put his foot down on that score. He wanted nothing to do with her. The excuse, they were in mourning, still bereaved by the old earl's death.

No Honeymoon! Thank God for that now!

Next, she had to go through the humiliation of wedding photographs with not as much as a peep or a smile out of him. Then, it was time to adjourn to lunch with the guests.

She was told Fergus could have easily dispensed with this, too, and he tried, but his brothers and Perkins had insisted they must at least have a wedding banquet after the ceremony. So they did.

A sequence of deep breaths got Marguerite through the next few hours, and they passed in a whirlwind of emotions, as if in a blur.

He didn't look at her once through the sitting of the lunch, not even a pleasant word for appearances' sake headed her way. He seemed out of sorts, annoyed, gloomy and wretched; she was sure he couldn't bear to be near her.

Barely two hours into the wedding festivities, her new husband took his leave.

"Until later, my lady," he said casually, without meeting her eyes. "Bancroft will help you settle in your new home. Don't wait up," he went on, kissed her hand, his lips not touching her skin. His manner was so icy and harsh, he could have frozen her hand just by handling it. He was so bleak to her.

His younger brothers were full of praise for their new sister-in-law and they looked rather apologetic, but they had no choice and followed him.

"We have matters to discuss before we leave this afternoon," Sebastian told her before they left, with a sorrowful expression, "unavoidable, I am afraid. I am sure he'll make it up to you later. Fergus will adore you; you'll see."

What Sebastian hadn't mentioned was it would be best for him and Frederick to be with their big brother while he licked his wounds. Not great for the bride, but it would be prudent to keep an eye on Fergus in case he did something foolish. Thus, he made his way out with his brothers. He was gone!

It worried Marguerite. The wedding lunch wasn't even over yet.

Zac tried to persuade Fergus to stay until the end of lunch at least, but the earl was in a vortex of fury, and his friend thought, perhaps, it was best for him to leave after all.

So, Zac came to the rescue and sat next to her. "Don't concern yourself, Marguerite. This is his little victory parade. Let him have it. He will come back to you and your new home later."

"Where do you think he's gone?" she asked in a whisper, her voice barely audible, her eyes misty.

"Oh, well, if we are lucky, to his club. If not, to one of his more sordid hangouts. Who knows? His brothers are with him, so don't worry; they'll look after him. That's why they have gone with him. They were adamant I should tell you that, no slight on their part intended. Just protecting their big brother from himself. You must be patient with Fergus. Rome was not built in a day."

"The trouble is, Zac, patience is n-not one of my v-virtues," she replied desolately, with a slight tremor in her voice. She was dizzy and humiliated, but of course, all the guests knew the circumstances of their marriage. So, it came as no surprise to them.

Still, it was shocking to her to see Fergus leave. Her wedding day, and her groom had fled. *Disgraceful! Shame on him.* She wanted to burst into tears, but she would not give anyone the satisfaction, least of all him.

Zac noticed her pained expression and rubbed her arm in consolation. "Come, my dear, let's talk to Mollie. She will cheer you up."

Chapter 6

At the start of the wedding lunch, Marguerite talked to Fergus' twenty-year-old sister.

"Are you hungry? I am starving. It was a long ceremony, but you look so beautiful. I am sure he is pleased with you. For an instant, I saw it in his eyes. Whatever else he says, he is, you know," Belinda scoffed, looking at her for a moment. Then the tall, strawberry blonde young woman next to her pointed at the mouth-watering delicacies for lunch.

"If you say so…" was all Marguerite said, giving her a dubious look.

"I suppose you have seen something in the newspapers or the glossies about me?" the girl replied with a sigh.

Belinda was notorious. Some would say scandalous, and renowned for it. Marguerite had read about her in the papers often, but she couldn't remember what was her latest escapade. The rich socialite, Lady Belinda Waltham, had more money than sense, some would say, a foul temper like her big brother, which had plunged her in trouble with the law several times.

"Well, I can't say exactly..." the bride replied with a pink blush as they savoured their food.

"Oh, my last boyfriend didn't want to drop the charges. I battered his car with a baseball bat! I tell you, it was unrecognisable as a Ferrari when I finished with it," she uttered with a nervous laugh. "The bastard had cheated on me and had the temerity to deny it to my face!" She moved a lock of hair from her eyes in an elegant movement of her hand.

Marguerite thought how uncanny the physical resemblance between sister and brother, both in appearance and in personality. "Oh, I remember reading something like that," the bride said, flabbergasted at the account.

"My dear father was still alive then. He had to promise to refurbish two children's homes to see me out of prison. It wasn't my first offence. So, the judge deliberated a prison sentence. Daddy moved Heaven and Earth to get me out of there, until the Lord Justice could not justify refusing complete refurbishment of two children's home, with hefty donations, when the budgets for these wretched places are so tight. I am a patron for them now. I enjoy raising money, writing to friends and acquaintances, asking for donations. I am quite good at it," she said with a proud smile on her face. "Anyway, the detective who arrested me, you know, the man has arrested me twice! He said I should do something about my temper. When Dad died, the police officer insisted with Fergus as, apparently, I am not fit for society yet... the mean bastard! So they ordered me to a clinic for therapy. Can you believe it? That's where I am headed this afternoon, to the clinic. Sebastian had to plead with the Home Office to let me attend the wedding. He used all his contacts so I could be here today," Belinda said, opening her arms wide, showing how outlandish it was, and thundering a few curses, but she went on. "The judge said I must learn to moderate my temper. He made it a court order! I have no choice but to go to the clinic. If not, he will send me back to prison. But with bureaucracy and all that, I spent three months in jail before I could get out, witnessed a murder while in there! So, now the damn police officer keeps interviewing me about it. I'll never get rid of the man. Great, ha? Anyway, the judge doesn't want to see me in court again, or he swore, next time, I won't escape a heavy sentence which he'll make me serve until the very last day." She shrugged her shoulders and rolled her eyes.

Marguerite was astonished at the exploits of the young woman. Belinda seemed so delicate, even angelic! She was gorgeous, curvaceous and delightful. Bewitching, despite her atrocious behaviour, and almost as tall as Fergus. It was like looking at a beautiful painting from which you couldn't take your eyes. Marguerite couldn't imagine the things she did, the curses that came out of that delicate mouth.

The girl was a little devil in an angel's body. *By comparison, her big brother is a saint!* Marguerite thought.

"So, this afternoon, I am going to the clinic when the boys come back. Fergus is Dr. Stewart's friend. I'll be in his clinic. I think the judge said six months. Six, what the heck! Though this is a great opportunity for you, Marguerite. You can get to appreciate Fergus without me trampling all over the place. He is okay, you know, not that bad when you get close to him. When he is not ordering people about, that is. He has a good side. You'll love him, won't you? Even though we argue like cats and dogs, I love my big brother. I want him to be happy with you." Belinda gave her the most angelic of smiles, with a blush and an unexpected bear hug.

It overjoyed her as the day finally came to an end. Marguerite was so tired and stressed, she was glad when everyone had gone. The girls and their partners had stayed for some time following the wedding lunch to keep her company, but eventually they left too. Then, she changed into comfortable clothes and helped Belinda pack for the clinic to have something to do.

Frederick and Sebastian returned late that afternoon, a little under the weather. Marguerite guessed they'd had a few cups… of celebration? *Not in my honour, if Fergus had anything to do with it, that's for sure!*

They picked up their things, as they were about to leave and travel to the continent. The lucky brothers were bound on government errands, one to Italy and the other to Switzerland as attachés to British embassies.

She wished she could go somewhere, too, and far away from their big brother.

"Where is Fergus?" she asked them as a flush marred her face, but the boys just shrugged their shoulders and smiled apologetically.

"He'll be back later," Sebastian said with no further explanation, but he avoided her gaze.

"I see," she responded, lowering her eyes. She could only imagine the scene between the brothers; Fergus' siblings trying to get him home again, but he refused categorically.

"Hey." Frederick put his arm around her shoulder, giving her a cuddle, pressing her to him. "Give him time, he'll come around to it, I am certain. Be strong and patient. He hates people who whimper." He ruffled her tight chignon, which didn't even move an inch.

The siblings soon said their goodbyes, offering her a lot of advice on the "dos and don'ts" about their elder brother.

They had been driven off to their destinations, Fergus' brothers to Heathrow airport to catch their flights, and Belinda to the clinic in the Cotswolds. The boys would be away for months, and who could guess about her sister-in-law…

They left Marguerite alone in the house with only the domestic staff for company. She wasn't sure if it was a good or a bad thing.

Bancroft, the family's longstanding butler, Fergus' valet, Crispin, the housekeeper, Mrs. Briggs, the housemaid, Cora, and the old cook, Ethel, had made her welcome when everybody had gone.

The mansion was enormous and draughty; she had the feeling she was in a hotel and not a home. It was too big to appear homely to her at that moment. *I will have to get used to it.*

Bancroft and Mrs. Briggs showed her the way around the house, every single room. It was four, large floors. One room on the fourth-floor had small drips of water coming through the roof. The domestic staff quarters seemed a bit shabby to her, compared to the high opulence of other floors.

The glorious, several reception rooms were all exquisitely done and in pristine conditions, but some of the primary bedrooms on the second floor were not in any better condition than those of the staff quarters. It seemed to her she was in an old mausoleum. It needed a feminine touch and some urgent repairs.

Luckily, her rooms were perfect, gorgeous, in fact. Her bedroom, her sitting room, and her study looked as if they were out of a house magazine, so stylish, elegant and large. Apparently, the old earl had given directions and strict orders for the preparations of her chambers until his dying day. This brought tears to her eyes. At least the old earl had cared for her.

Bancroft had told the old man about the parts of the house that needed attention. Though, with his lordship's illness, his preoccupation with his son's marriage, and the problems with Belinda, these things had taken a back seat until he died. When Fergus took over, time had been scarce, not to mention his mind was elsewhere after the reading of the will and his own impending doom.

"His lordship is busy, my lady, but he'll get 'round to the repairs," Bancroft said.

"Busy? Doing what? He should ensure his home is well cared for," she replied. "The scoundrel is right now getting drunk somewhere, cursing me, and spending more money than the costs of the repairs in his own house," she said and turned red at her own outburst.

It'd been a stressful day; she'd been glad she had done nothing to offend anybody until then.

Bancroft and Mrs. Briggs smiled in understanding, indulgently, and there was a look of compassion in their eyes.

Oh, dear God!

"Madam will soon turn things around. The earl is a good man. Perhaps you could remind him to take action with the repairs, my lady."

"Please, call me Marguerite."

"Oh, no, we mustn't. It wouldn't be appropriate," they refused categorically, in unison.

Marguerite sighed. She missed her little apartment in town. It was tiny compared to this, hell, even compared to one room, but it was all hers, a pristine home and in perfect working order. The earl's enormous mansion, was a house of contrasts. Some parts elegant and refined, while others left a lot to be desired.

***

She had dinner in the huge, luxurious dining room, sitting all alone at the massive cherrywood table, while the antique clock on the mantelpiece was ticking loudly in the silent room.

Marguerite felt sorry for herself, sitting at the head of an empty table.

Her bottom lip quivered at one point, and a visible shudder went through her body, but she would not give Fergus the satisfaction of crying, even if he wasn't there. In particular when Bancroft was standing by in the room, so she soldiered on. When she finished her meal, she rose from the table and glanced out of the window.

"The weather has turned, madam," the butler said. Clouds had been gathering during the afternoon, and now persistent rain was coming down.

"Yes, what a pity." She couldn't help exhale, a deep, audible breath with a groan, and it plunged her into abject misery.

She took a long bath. She wished she could stay in the water forever; and in the absence of the coveted groom, she went to bed with a book.

After a while, she glanced at the clock, it was 2:00 am. She had read until then. Despite her tiredness and the long day, she was too overwhelmed to sleep. She was restless, and she wanted a hot chocolate to soothe herself. It always worked well on her nerves.

Her dark, inky hair was down, long to her waist, natural in her loose, curly ringlets. She put a dressing gown over her skimpy night shorts and camisole and made her way downstairs.

The butler gave her a fright when he appeared out of nowhere in the kitchen. "Can I help you, my lady?"

"Sweet Jesus! Bancroft, what are you doing up at this time of night?" she asked, perplexed. "He doesn't ask you to wait up for him, surely?"

"Oh, no, my lady, I couldn't sleep. I am a little worried about his lordship."

"Worried?"

"Well, he is out of sorts."

"Oh, I think marrying me has put him out of sorts, all right," she replied with a snort.

"He's often out of sorts, madam, if I may be so bold as to say so myself. I have known his lordship since he was a tiny, weeny boy of two."

"Oh, jeez, that's a relief," she said ironically with a nervous giggle, raising her eyebrows.

"On the contrary, marrying you is the best thing that has happened to him if you ask me. You know, when he pulled your veil up at the altar, I moved from my chair to catch a glimpse of his face. I tell you, he liked you. I saw it in his eyes. He had the same expression as when his father brought him his first train set for Christmas. He was three years old then. He loved that little train. He still keeps it in the nursery at Penningbrooke Hall, his country estate. That's how he looked at you today, my lady, no matter how much he complains about his father's orders, remember this. I saw the furtive glances he darted at you later, too, whatever he says." The butler smiled, satisfied. He was a dignified, tallish, rotund man in his late fifties, with a pleasing look and a full head of pearly white hair.

Marguerite cleared her throat several times, trying to think of something to say.

"I just want some hot chocolate. I can make it myself," she mumbled instead, hugely embarrassed, shifting on her feet with a flush on her face. She didn't know what else to reply. She couldn't deny Bancroft's remarks had flickered a little ray of hope in her soul.

"No need, my lady, I made it already. I was having some with Crispin. It seems tonight, sleep is eluding the household. But you go to the blue sitting room, and I'll bring you some. A warm fire is still burning there."

"Which one is the blue sitting room?"

"On the ground floor, two doors down from the entrance hallway." He nodded encouragingly, and she moved onward to find it.

She stood now by the fireplace in the sitting room. She added to the fire, logs blazing in the hearth as she poked at it. A small red flame sparkled up the chimney. She watched the logs flare up, and the blaze mesmerised. It was cozy, and she felt better already. She moved to the window and peered out into the garden. The weather had turned outright nasty. It was a dark, thunderous night and the April rain was lashing down heavily.

She sighed. It seemed the elements outside were mirroring the darkness in her soul. Marguerite glanced at the clock again. It was 2:30 am. She pressed her lips tightly. *Good Lord,* her wedding night, and there was no sign of her groom. Fine for her, though, given the horrid words he'd uttered. The only words he had expressed to her the entire day. *The brute!*

Should she believe what Bancroft said? *No, it would be best not to!* Otherwise, she would crash and burn harder. *Fergus hates me. I'd better get used to it.* Perhaps, it would be wise if they stayed apart, at least until he accepted the idea of marriage, let alone to her. The entire issue seemed so distasteful to him, she could tell.

He believed she was in this marriage for the money, that she would stay married to him those required eighteen months stipulated in his father's will, to get her cash as by contract arrangements, then go her way. That's what he thought! That she was a venal, money-grabbing woman, and who could blame him?

If he only knew how she had craved him! For six long years, she'd never stopped thinking of him, loving him.

The butler was wrong… She was sure of it. *Fergus abhors me.* He hadn't even recognised her. Well, why should he? He had given no sign of it. He had looked a little disjointed because he believed her ugly. *That's it. He thinks of me as ugly!*

Bancroft came in with a tray, taking her out of her reverie. He poured from the pot and offered her a cup. She took it and inhaled the rich, chocolaty drink. Her nostrils dilated, soothing her.

"Thank you," she said. She sipped at her cup. "It's delicious."

"Anything else I can do for you, my lady?"

"Is Fergus not back yet?" she ventured timidly, even though she knew the answer.

"No, not yet."

"I see. Well, good night. I won't keep you," she said.

As the butler moved toward the door, they heard a commotion.

"What is it?" she asked, getting up from her armchair.

"It seems his lordship has returned. I suspect he could not get a taxi on a thunderous night such as this, and he is probably soaked to the bone, having walked from his club in this rain. I am sure he is none too pleased. He doesn't like to disturb his driver so late, in particular when the man has driven his siblings all over the place today. He is not all bad, you see."

"Dear Lord, this racket will wake up the entire household," she scoffed. The butler settled a slight smile on her as if to say *get used to it!* She deposited her cup on the small table and followed Bancroft out of the room toward the hall.

Something told her she should stay out of it. Let the butler deal with him, while her new husband was ranting and imprecating like a trooper at his bad luck that day, in more ways than one. But she couldn't help it. Marguerite wished to have another glimpse of him. Besides, she wasn't a coward. She would not hide.

Bancroft went to the hall to him. She followed behind, her

dainty form obscured by the man. There, she saw Crispin, her husband's valet, trying to give Fergus a hand at getting him out of his wet clothes. He was still wearing his wedding suit, now dripping with water.

His valet helped him take his drenched coat and suit jacket off. Fergus pulled his tie off with a jerky movement, almost tearing it. His shirt was soaked and sticking to his body, that's how wet he was, though a glimpse at his rippling, hard chest underneath his soaked shirt produced a warmth through Marguerite's body, giving her a shiver.

"Bancroft, good evening, man, what the hell are you doing up!" Fergus said, his words rather fastidious.

"Good evening, sir," the butler replied, moving aside, exposing her to Fergus at the precise moment she licked her lips, looking at his powerful chest, through the wet shirt.

Fergus, slightly inebriated after an evening of drinking frolics, stared at her. He had barely recognised Marguerite with her rich, alluring dark hair flowing about her, untamed and free.

In her haste to follow Bancroft, her dressing gown had come undone at the front, displaying her long legs in her shorts, while he could plainly see her pert nipples showing underneath the flimsy camisole. It was a glorious sight, and with her jet-black hair down, long to her waist, natural and luscious in her soft loose ringlets, it stirred something within him.

She looked like a goddess in a dream of his youth, and when the tip of her small pink tongue licked her bottom lip, blood flowed to his manhood.

He was agape but soon recovered.

"And pray, what the hell are you doing up?" he uttered garrulously instead, clearing his throat to take the attention off the awakening of his cock. "I told you not to wait up," he said sharply, sobering somewhat and hissing a loud breath.

He fidgeted with his cufflinks in irritation, trying to take them off, launched a furtive glance at her, and muttered an oath under his breath when he could not undo them until Crispin came to his aid. He took hold of his shirt, pulled it off over his head and gave it to his valet, leaving his sculpted, naked chest on view.

She would have gladly stared at his chest muscles to her heart's content, but his belligerent tone irritated her, and his presumptuous assumption flooded her body with exasperation.

She rolled her eyes and placed her hands on her hips, a deep frown on her face, staring at him. "Oh, don't flatter yourself, Fergus! I was not waiting for you, I was having a hot chocolate. There is a fire in the blue sitting room. I suggest you come in and warm yourself up, and have a cup of the hot drink before you catch your death."

"So convenient for you if I were to die, wouldn't it?" he mumbled under his breath, disgruntled.

"Bancroft, tell his lordship not to behave like a child," she said in frustration. When Marguerite was irked, her lilting, sexy French accent was even more inviting to Fergus. Her words, as if they were sweet notes of music, harmonised in a titillating symphony out of her pouty little mouth. He remembered that sexy velvety sound well, and it still gave him goosebumps. That night, it did something to his insides.

"What?" he groaned instead, trying to crush all witless, foolish emotions toward her.

"I am going back to my hot chocolate, that is unless The Dark Lord is nervous about being in the same room with me." She turned on her heels and she was gone.

"Nervous! Come back here, this minute! I have not dismissed you yet. Do you hear me?" He stomped with wet, sloshing shoes after her with his valet and butler following on his heels. He got rid of his shoes and socks on the way in a tantrum of temper. So when he showed up in front of her again in the sitting room, he was barefoot and bare chested.

He was Adonis himself, reborn and reincarnated! She had no doubt. No man could be this beautiful. The gods had sent him to Earth to make her suffer. She must keep her wits about her with this man partly naked, even in his hostile mood.

The rain had soaked him and upset him, but it was not the only source of his dismal humour. He was troubled, incensed at being married to her, and cross at his father for pulling this stunt on him. Mad with the entire world, and most particularly, he was so annoyed with her, with a humongous bone to pick with her.

He moved to the fire.

"Dark Lord? Didn't you hear me? Are you deaf?"

"I heard you," she said calmly, but not really feeling it, sipping her chocolate.

"Let me make something clear to you!"

"Oh, shut up, Fergus, stop arguing! Take your trousers off. They are dripping," she replied. He looked at her agape, then at his trousers.

No one dared to speak to him like that, but she wasn't finished.

"Crispin, can you please get his lordship's dressing gown?" she said with a huff. The valet nodded and went on his errand. "And, Bancroft, would you be so kind as to pour a cup of hot chocolate for my husband?"

The word 'husband' visibly shook the furious lord.

"Yes, my lady," the faithful man executed with a glint of humour in his eyes. Fergus took the drink in silence, still stunned at her ordering him and everyone around her about.

"Thank you, Bancroft. I'll see to his lordship. You go to bed," she said.

"Thank you, madam." The butler retired with an amused expression.

When Bancroft left, she took off her own dressing gown and placed it around his shoulders.

"What the hell are you doing?" Fergus asked, but she tidied it along his broad shoulders as best she could, to keep him warm, leaving herself in her tiny shorts and camisole.

It was his turn to lick his lips, and with the touch of her soft, delicate hands on his shoulders, a spark ignited within him and rushed straight to his cock, standing on alert for the occasion. She looked divine in her sexy and skimpy nightclothes.

"I don't want people to say your new wife caused your death. And take your trousers off; they are dripping, I said, move! Chop, chop," she repeated imperiously.

His eyes grew big.

"Oh, don't look so shocked, Fergus. There is nothing you have that I haven't seen before."

He raised an eyebrow and scowled at her. He knew what she meant, but he ignored her statement, not giving her the satisfaction of recognition, not even then.

An abhorrent thought appeared in his mind, though. *I'll bet she has experienced a lot of them too.* His wife and other men... was not something he wished to consider. He gave her an impatient wave of the hand.

His valet arrived with his dressing gown.

Fergus quickly placed himself in front of her, to prevent Crispin looking at his wife in her tiny shorts and transparent camisole.

Marguerite had forgotten that. She was only thinking of keeping him warm, not used to having domestic staff in her home, and she flushed.

Fergus yanked the dressing gown off his shoulders, swung her around roughly, with her back to him, and slid her arms into the garment, putting it back on her instead. He turned her around to face him, covering her well with the robe and with his body from Crispin's eyes. He tightened her robe at the front with the belt in a hard tug that made her shriek, and she raised her eyes to him.

Their eyes locked, and they gazed at each other searchingly for a moment.

The affection rose in her heart, and something between her legs stirred. A divine warmth spread across her body, while more blood flowed to his manhood despite himself, and this time it throbbed.

He cleared his voice, gesturing to his valet for an instant. "Thank you, Crispin, I'll take it from here. You go to bed," he said.

The young man nodded, placed his robe on a chair and bidding goodnight, he left them.

Fergus spun to her with fire in his eyes. He was still holding the belt of her dressing gown tight in his fists, so close. He stared at her. "Don't act like a floozie in my house," he said at length, with venom, alarmed at his undeniable attraction to her, a desire that had not diminished six years on, to punish her. "You'll behave properly while you are my wife. At all times! Understood? After that, you can take your money and fuck out of my life. What you do after that, I don't care," he sentenced harshly.

Her mouth dropped. His remark hurt. His words were uncalled for. He was out of order!

"F-Fergus..." she stammered, but words failed her. She tried to move her lips, and nothing came out.

"You damn teaser!" he cried out with fervour. His eyes flashed at her like lightning, and if they had been able to shoot the proverbial arrows, she would have been dead at his feet there and then.

Suddenly, she felt so provoked at his dreadful words. "Damn you!" she spat. With her indignation still flaring at the way he had treated her throughout her wedding day, she became incensed. A fit of temper rushed through her frame. Her hand struck his cheek. *Crack, slap!* The sound of the flesh of her palm meeting his face in full, reverberated in the room.

He took it hard, but it didn't stir him. He stood his place, with a scintillating stare, unmovable and unreadable. A small grin appeared on his face at having hit home with his words, even though his inner voice told him, *that's low even for you!*

He laughed at her to hide his momentary qualm of remorse at his words.

She was about to slap him again, when he caught her wrist in his hand, dragged it behind her back, immobilising her, and crashed her against his chest with a thud.

"You thought you had fooled me? Didn't you? I know who you are... shall I call you Lisette! What do you say? Wasn't Lisette a shorthaired blonde? Or is it Marguerite? A long haired-brunette? Umm... I wonder... What's your real name, hey? None of these, I'll bet. You hustler," he said, looking keenly at her, but she flashed her eyes at him, pleading.

"It's Marguerite. I swear. I am sorry I lied to you then, but I couldn't help it. I had no choice. Please, Fergus, let me explain why I did it, why I left—"

"What?" he yelled at her, "Explain? That you are a liar, a fraud! A gold-digger! A floozie!"

"Please, Fergus—"

"Quiet, I don't want to hear it." He manhandled her in his arms, dragging her a few steps.

She shrieked. "Please—"

"Silence!" He shoved her again, not quite sure what he

wished to do with her, though his traitorous cock knew exactly, given a chance... and was telling him loud and clear.

Another shriek escaped her mouth. "And you..." she blurted out, struggling to find the right words, finally losing it. She couldn't help it. "You... you are a miserable ape, Fergus!" She spat at his obstinacy, his stubbornness infuriating her.

"Drop the reformed slut act; it won't work. Highly unlikely, in the circumstances, don't you think?" he said sarcastically.

Marguerite struggled to free herself, but he kept her tight to him and put his other arm around her, thus keeping her crushed against him, locked in his arms. Their faces were an inch apart, breathing in the scent on each other's skin. She tried her utmost to liberate herself, kicking him too, when a string of French improprieties left her mouth.

He got most of them; he was proficient in French, but some were unknown to him. By her tone, her vehemence, he was sure none of them were of any repeatable nature.

He laughed. Her irritation at being immobilised in his arms aroused him even more. His cock was throbbing by then.

"Our first lover's tiff, hmm, my lady? Hey? Rather exciting if I am honest," he said, and he roared again, which vexed her the more.

"Let me go," she cried out, trying hard to free herself.

As they scuffled, her remarks were uttered in English now. So he couldn't misinterpret her sentiments with his heavy-handed tactics, establishing the flood of vulgarities as unequivocal out of her pouty little mouth. Though he found her mouth dainty and cute, and oh so kissable, the vulgarities gushing out of those sweet lips were atrocious. They hurt his ears!

As they wrestled, she stamped on his foot forcefully, twice. He cursed and limped for a moment on one leg, yet he didn't let go of her. Unbalanced on his foot, he tumbled to the floor, taking her with him, but he released her. She tried to run on all fours, but he caught her ankle and pulled her hard to him as she squealed in panic, and as they tangled and scuffled, he ended up on top of her on the floor. She couldn't move, his grip on her fierce.

He glanced at her with a smirk of victory while she was still imprecating against him. The curses had returned to her native language. He gave her a devilish grin, as if saying to her in no uncertain terms, *'I am in charge now,'* before his mouth crashed on hers, silencing her.

Fergus took her lips with the combined force of anger, lust, and desire mingled, his entire body behind it. His tongue slipped into her mouth, owning it, ravishing her. Her mouth tasted sweet and chocolaty, her tongue soft and delicious.

Within seconds, she ceased fighting him, went limp under him, and kissed him back with the same want and desire, and her tongue danced with his in a singsong of passion.

They explored each other's mouths with fervent yearning, his hands roaming her body. They kissed long and voraciously. One kiss led to another, as they savoured each other in a fever of lust. He was like a starving man finally appeasing his hunger. The kisses had them breathless when they came up for air. It was at that point, he relented his grip on her when his arousal was at its highest and his guard at his lowest after the kisses.

"I wonder if a fuck with you is worth two million pounds? Um…" he whispered with a low, guttural tone in her ear, between ragged breaths.

"What?" she asked, still in a daze of lust.

"Overpriced, if you ask me," he went on, snorting, half in amusement and half in arousal, in anticipation.

Suddenly, she understood what he said! It was then, she freed a leg from underneath his weight. Her knee hit him between his legs, in his groin, crashing his dick hard. It hit his bollocks so forcefully that it had him rolling off her in pain.

He swayed on the floor, spinning in agony, holding his crotch in misery, while she rose from the floor. She stood there for a second, dishevelled and still panting from his kisses, and looked at him with contempt, a triumphant smile on her lips.

Then she fled and locked herself in her bedroom.

Chapter 7

Fergus got up earlier than usual the next morning and hovered about in his study, not really focusing on anything. He was in a foul mood. He had not slept. His bollocks were still tender, *the bloody minx!* It wasn't just his sore dick that kept him awake.

He couldn't deny he had been horrid to her and ruined her wedding day. Not even his dark conscience could overlook that. The words he uttered to her were humiliating and despicable, and he felt a pang of shame. In the last two days, that sentiment—guilt—he'd thought long lost, resurfaced in his soul because of her, and he hated himself for it.

He still blamed her for everything! Six years ago, she'd left him without a word. *She gave me a false name for goodness' sake! Lisette! The minx, the floozie!* At the same time, her phone was disconnected when he had tried to reach her. She was gone. He searched for her high and low in Nice and surrounding places for two weeks. The chit had disappeared from the face of the earth without a trace. So he returned home to England, disconsolate and hurt. What justification could she possibly have for such a deception?

Now, she was again in his world, to haunt him, to make his life a misery once more; and for his sins, his father had chosen her as his wife, no less. *Bollocks to him, I hope he rots in hell!* He cursed liked a trooper for all of his mishaps.

It was her own fault if he had been despicable to her. She pushed all his buttons with her enticing little shorts and flimsy camisole, with her pouty, fleshy lips, sweet as honey, and with her lilting, sexy accent that made his cock throb. *The temptress! The sorceress! The witch!*

Besides, she got herself into the present situation. She could have refused to marry him. Instead, she went along with it to make his life hell. He guessed the money his father offered her in exchange was too strong of a temptation to refuse. Ultimately, this predicament was her own doing. She should have left him well alone. It had been hard enough to recover from her leaving him that first time…

He must keep away from her! It was his only salvation, to keep her at arm's length.

In Marguerite's defense, he knew how persuasive his dad could be when he wanted something. The old man wouldn't stop until he got what he wanted, like a dog with a bone.

His brothers would say he was an identical personality to his father.

"Like two peas in a pod!" his sister once said.

His father had the last laugh. He had wished Fergus married. His choice was either to marry the girl, or he would give up his fortune. It had left him with no alternative!

Though he couldn't dismiss the hurt he had seen in Lisette's eyes, or was she Marguerite now? Who the hell knew? Why would she lie to him about her name? He'd better get used to calling his wife by her proper name, assuming she wasn't lying again. But his words were unforgivable, regardless of what her name was, or who the devil she was and what she did. Besides, she might have a good explanation for it. Possibly... He doubted it, but he had not given her the chance to explain.

In a moment of tenderness, he smiled at her indomitable spirit, though. She had not taken his insults lying down. Oh, no! She had matched him pound for pound, and his sore dick was a testament to that spirit.

If he had to be honest, he deserved the kick in the nuts. He had been awful to her, said unspeakable things to her. It surprised him she had not done it straight after the ceremony. He laughed aloud. He couldn't deny a hint of admiration for her. The silly wretch!

She had added a deluge of insults to him, a dozen of them, in French and English, in case he doubted her intent when he manhandled her. *The stubborn hussy,* mostly unrepeatable! Hers won over his own more conventional, subdued ones. Hers were ahead in quantity and in ferociousness. *Not a competition, man! Grow up! She is your wife,* his more mature inner voice censured him. He was astonished at her filthy mouth! He would have to do something about that.

She was willful, unruly and wild. He would have to tame her... *but I wouldn't have her any other way.* He suspected these traits were part of her years ago if he had to be honest. *Obstinate as a mule, the headstrong girl!* He would like nothing better than to master her.

Fergus smiled at the challenge at hand. Oh, he would embrace the test in a second, to make her his, to sway her to his will.

Patience... she will... Marguerite will come to me willingly. He grinned at the alluring thought. Though every time he moved, his bollocks hurt, and his mood soon dimmed again. So he avoided her all day. He wasn't sure if he avoided her because he was furious with her, or he felt guilty at his remarks, or because he still desired her with all his soul.

One thing flashed in his mind, over and over—those kisses.

No doubt he had taken her mouth hungrily, deeply, ravishing her, and she had responded in kind. Her plump, sweet lips had kissed him deliriously. She had wanted him. Marguerite had kissed him back, unashamedly, passionately, until he had gone and ruined it all by opening his mouth with those words. Few women had excited him like this with just a kiss. His cock had throbbed when kissing her. She had sparked a desire he hadn't felt in years. Even now, it stirred just by thinking of her, despite the soreness. Perhaps it was best if they cooled down for a couple of days.

She was a liar and a gold-digger! A floozie! There he was again. *Stop, man! She is your wife now.* He couldn't get away from it, no matter how much he tried. *It is a fact!*

He had to figure out how to deal with her during these eighteen months of the contract, the time required to stay together to get what was due to them, hopefully, *without killing each other.* Fergus was sure she wanted the two million pounds his dad had offered, and he demanded his inheritance. He had grown up to be the next Earl of Buckley. He expected it; it was his birthright. He wouldn't relinquish a title for which he had worked so hard all his life, learning the ropes from childhood, and growing into the earl he was supposed to be. Lives depended on him.

He must devise a plan to make it through this. He cursed darkly, abundantly at his father, too, wishing the old man was doomed and burning in the bleakest pits of Hell for doing this to him. For turning his life upside down, *and of all the women in the blasted world, he had to choose her!* Fergus still couldn't believe it.

He must calm down before he spoke to her again, to avoid a repeat of their undignified argument. He wasn't prepared to have such a demeaning situation again. Though, he wouldn't mind the kisses!

Marguerite stayed in her room, avoiding him. Then she thought the whole thing was ludicrous. They were adults. This impossible situation couldn't go on for eighteen months. They had wed, and they must live together for that time. If he coveted his inheritance, as stipulated in his father's will, they had to make it work. They would have to compromise. It was down to her to change this position. *I bet the hellish lord is too proud to do anything!* So she took it upon herself to make an effort without antagonising him, whatever he threw at her. It would be hard, and she wasn't sure she could do it, but she must give it a go.

She went down to the dining room for lunch, thinking to make amends, to have an adult conversation with him and try to find a workable solution for both of them. She waited for him.

"Bancroft, where is my husband? Is he not coming to lunch?"

"No, my lady, he is having lunch in his study."

"Does he have a message for me?"

"No, my lady."

"I see."

But when he avoided her the whole afternoon and didn't turn up to supper, either, having gone out to his club with not as much as an apology or a message to her, she flew into a temper. *The rude bastard! I am a human being, and I deserve at least his courtesy. I'll show him.* She went upstairs and dressed in one of her new, fashionable, pretty dresses. She made a phone call, and fifteen minutes later she was out of the house.

Fergus was on his second brandy at the club, when his soul felt another twinge of remorse. It was no use; it hit him. He wasn't listening to his companions or participating in the conversation. He couldn't get her out of his mind. The bloody girl had woven herself into his brain again.

She'd been on his mind for years, on and off. He had always struggled to push her out of his head, but he wasn't one to dwell on spilt milk. So through the seasons, every time her image reappeared, he tried to quash it. But for the last two days, since he wed her, he thought of nothing else but her, with all the stirring emotions a man could feel.

He looked at the time; it was 10:00 pm. He debated for a few minutes with himself. It was no use. He downed the rest of the amber liquid in his glass in one go. The burning felt good, warming him.

He had to do something about her. So, he stood tall and mighty with a deep in breath, said his goodbyes, chanced his luck, and went home.

"Good evening, a perfect warm day today. Crazy weather this month," the butler said, easing him out of his coat.

"Good evening, Bancroft, you are right, crazy indeed. Is my wife in the sitting room or upstairs?" Fergus asked, and when the man hesitated, he glanced at him perplexed.

"What?"

"She is not at home, my lord."

Fergus stared at him like he had spoken in a foreign, incomprehensible language. He tilted his head on one side, frowning. "What do you mean?"

"She is out, sir," Bancroft replied with a hint of smile.

Fergus shook his head, wandered a few steps into the hall, then turned on his footsteps back to the man, stopping right in front of him. "Out? Are you sure?" His head flinched slightly back in confusion.

"Yes, sure."

"Out?" he repeated, darting his pale blue eyes around as if not believing what he was hearing.

"I'm afraid so." The butler became uneasy, and when he

saw his young master blink rapidly, rubbing his chin, he knew they were in trouble. It was never a good sign.

"Out where?" Fergus yelled explosively in an outburst the old man had not seen him display since his lordship was a teenager.

"I couldn't guess, sir."

"What? You don't know?" Fergus spat, beyond exasperated.

"She didn't say, my lord."

"Call Mrs. Briggs," he commanded. A nerve twitched in his jaw as he tried to contain himself.

When the housekeeper came and told him she didn't know, either, his already shaky control was short-lived. His temper flew. "What the hell do I have you for if you don't even know where my wife is?" he raged with a guttural roar, his fists clenched and unclenched like they were on springs.

"My lord, I asked her, but she didn't say," the man replied calmly, knowing full well he had to let the storm pass and the young earl would apologise eventually.

"She didn't, did she? Let me tell you something. I wish to know everything she does—if she eats, if she drinks, if she reads, or if she walks. Where she goes, when and with whom, understood? If she sneezes, I want to know about it, is that clear?" he growled, pacing the hallway with long, deliberate strides, back and forth, like a caged animal, his temper flaring. Fergus was in a panic at Marguerite being away from him. He wouldn't be able to stand it if she left him again.

"Yes, my lord!" his faithful staff said in unison, glancing at each other and rolling their eyes when the young man wasn't looking.

"When did she leave?" Fergus' eyes flashed fire at them.

"Two hours ago."

"Mrs. Briggs, check upstairs in her room, see if you can

find a clue?" Somehow, his control was reining in his temper somewhat.

"If it is of any help, Mrs. Sorensen picked her up. I saw her from the window. I think it was Mrs. Sorensen, can't be sure, it was dark."

"Mrs. Sorensen?" He growled at her, losing it again, with a vein straining in his neck.

"Yes, sir." The housekeeper turned red like a beetroot, with Bancroft giving her a sympathetic nod.

"Why didn't you say so? Never mind! Thank you, I'll take it from here," he barked, waving a hand as he picked up his mobile phone, while they scurried away with relief.

He dialed, still pacing the hall.

"Sorensen?"

"Yes?"

"Fergus here, where the devil is my wife?"

"Have you lost your bride already? That was quick, even by your standards."

"Where is she, Zac?"

"What the hell do I know, she is your wife, man, not mine!" His companion snorted.

"She is with Mollie!"

"Ah… I see. She is out, girls' night out."

"Where?"

"Listen, I am Mollie's husband, not her bodyguard. They went to a cocktail bar."

"A bar?" Fergus cried out. "Where? I am going to pick her up. It's late, anyway, time to come home."

"Wait, before I tell you, let me speak to Mollie first. Now that I think of it, she said something about Marguerite being upset. What did you do to her?"

"None of your business!"

"Buck, you'll drive that girl away," Zac replied, remembering Mollie saying she had a teary new bride on the phone.

"She was crying. I suppose you know nothing about that, do you?"

"Well, I-I—"

"Let me talk to her before you go bull charging in there to make matters worse."

Zac had a point, Fergus reluctantly agreed.

In a trendy cocktail bar across town, the girls were sitting at the counter, talking and sipping their drinks. The mood was somber.

"I don't understand, Marguerite. Why is Fergus so horrible to you? It was his father who dictated this condition, not you. If he hadn't selected you as his bride, it would have been some other girl. He would have done it with or without you. I'm surprised that after two days, your husband has not uttered a pleasant word to you. I mean, you are so lovely, it would delight any man that he had chosen you," Mollie said, shaking her head in disbelief at the situation, feeling guilty, too. She sipped at her Espresso Martini. Perhaps this time she had miscalculated the entire situation, *my plan a total pants.*

"He should relent by now, don't you think, and be civil? There is no justification for rudeness. Besides, his father would have paired him with or without our app. Your husband should know better than anyone. At least you scored ninety-five percent; you were his 'top pick.' Our app was so clear on the choice. The old earl counted on this fact for you two to get along. Anyway, Fergus is a well-known ogre, so ill tempered, he scares everyone in the office. Perhaps it's going to take a little longer for love to work its magic on him," Kathryn emphasised, having a good gulp at her Cosmopolitan cocktail, sympathising with the girl and squeezing her hand.

"Love?" Marguerite cried out. "He hates me!" She burst

into tears, then gulped down her Death in the Afternoon cocktail, a deadly concoction of Champagne and Absinthe. If she had to be honest, Marguerite felt like death.

Mollie ordered her a second drink to calm her down. She was still sipping on her first.

"Hey, hey, you are a bride, you should be happy, not crying. I can't believe he is doing this to you. The bloody awful man," she said with vehemence. She put an arm around her, trying to console her friend. She blamed herself, seeing Marguerite so upset. *I should not have meddled in this, oh sweet Jesus, too late now…*

"Steady on, Marguerite. You don't want to get drunk," Kathryn warned her, when her companion almost finished her second cocktail in one go.

"I am sorry, girls. I have a confession to make. You have been so good to me, I can't lie to you anymore," Marguerite said, while another sob escaped her.

"A confession?" The girls glanced at each other.

"What is it?" Kathryn asked with a crease on her forehead.

"You see… I haven't been completely honest with you."

"What do you mean?" Mollie asked, her baby blue eyes big in surprise.

"I met Fergus six years ago. He is not a stranger to me. I know him well," Marguerite mumbled, finishing her drink.

"You do?"

"Aha! We met in France, when I settled in Nice for a while," she said and blushed to the roots of her hair.

"Well, I never! How? What happened?" Kathryn said, as her eyebrows shot up.

"How shall I say this?" Marguerite took a deep breath and began her tale, "Let me start at the beginning before I even met Fergus. I was in my last year in high school when I lived in Lille; that's where I grew up. Lille is about 140 miles northeast of Paris, it's where I met a man called Alain Basset. I was eighteen years old, and I fell in love with him. The following year, it was time for me to go to University. I got a place in Paris and enrolled in the 'Sciences et Lettres,' studying Literature. Alain followed me to Paris and found himself a job. It was fine at first; we were happy. We moved in together, to save money. It made sense instead of paying for two accommodations. Then it all turned into a nightmare, an ordeal. I don't even know how it happened. Alain became jealous, suspicious, and controlling. As time passed, he turned violent. I became his prisoner. He wouldn't let me see anyone, go anywhere, not even go to classes, and when I did, he hurt me. Even if I had done nothing wrong." Marguerite paused for a moment, taking a sip of her drink.

Then she went on, "At one point, I thought he was going to kill me, I was so scared. So, I left him, moved into my own accommodations, but he pursued me. I had to request a restraining order on him, but it was no use. The police did nothing about it. He persisted. Ultimately, to cut a long story short, I had to run away from this man. So, I changed my appearance and cities, assumed a false name. I ran to the South of France. I hopped between cities, under different names at least three times, to escape him. Alain had the knack of finding me." Marguerite sobbed and dried her tears with her fingers.

"Oh, dear me! It's horrid! Come on, darling, don't cry," Mollie said and rubbed her friend's back soothingly. She couldn't believe her ears. She felt heartbroken for her.

"It was when I moved to Nice, in the South of France, and changed my name again that I met Fergus. I was working there. I went under the false name of Lisette Lacroix then. I fell in love with him, though reluctant to have a relationship given the circumstances. But Fergus drew me in. I spent the best three weeks of my entire life with him. Then Alain found me again, and I had to run away, suddenly, with no time for as much as a goodbye to Fergus." Marguerite took a deep breath, but tears were flowing down her cheeks.

"Oh, dear God. I am so sorry," Mollie said, wide eyed. She couldn't hide the distress in her voice. Her baby blue eyes were enormous, and she was shaking her head in astonishment at the revelations. She caressed her companion's hair, her mouth turned down at the corners while her bottom lip quivered at her friend's anguish, but she stayed strong for her.

"Good heavens, I can't believe this." Kathryn's dark eyes stared at her. She patted Marguerite's arm, asking her if she was okay to continue.

Her companion nodded. "I came back three weeks later, when I expected it was safe to visit Fergus, to explain, but he had left. He had gone home to England." Marguerite continued, "I didn't want to put him in danger, you see. Alain had been violent with any man he thought was my boyfriend, real or imaginary." She gave a little sob. "So I let it go, and I did nothing to contact Fergus, to keep him safe. I had fallen in love with him, but it all had to finish abruptly because of Alain. Fergus knows nothing about this. I never told him, to protect him from my ex-boyfriend. My husband thinks I left him so callously six years ago, without even the guts to break up with him. He knew me as Lisette. Imagine the shock at the wedding, knowing it was all a lie. Well... now you know why he hates me, and I cannot blame him, either."

"Oh, darling, I am so sorry," the girls echoed. They hugged her in turns, trying to comfort her, their hearts going out to her. They ordered another round of drinks, much needed following the sad account from their companion.

"Oh, but there is more."

"Go on, darling, what happened next?" Mollie said, sipping another Espresso Martini. "Are you okay to continue?" She squeezed her companion's hand, who nodded in agreement.

"One day, my ex-boyfriend battered one of my male colleagues, almost killing the poor man. It took my dear colleague so long to get better, but he recovered. Then, I was finally free of Alain when he was locked up in jail for attempted murder. Alain even knifed me on the shoulder," Marguerite said, watching the look of horror on the girls' faces. She inhaled and sipped more of her drink. Somewhat, she had recovered her composure.

"And I won't tell you what my poor mother had to endure! Alain's menaces, my furtive visits when he wasn't around. Not knowing where I was or when she would see me next... So, when Alain went to prison, Mother and I finally spent some time together, properly, after years of sorrow. Though, after my mother died, I had no reason to stay in France. I came to England, to Oxford, to start a new life, knowing I was safe now. I put my old life behind me." She paused for an instant. "Fergus knows nothing of all this. He thinks I am a floozie for the way I behaved with him. He called me a fraud, a gold-digger! A liar! He believes all I want is the money his father promised me in the contract," Marguerite said, but she couldn't help another sob, and a tear came down her face.

"Oh, for God's sake, it wasn't your fault. How dare he call you that. You poor thing," Mollie added, patting her friend's back, trying to ease her pain. "Come on, darling, don't cry."

"He can't blame you for that, surely. You must tell him the truth," Kathryn interjected.

"He won't let me explain, and even if I do, he won't believe me, I am certain," Marguerite said with a frown, recalling the previous night's outcome when she tried.

"Of course, he will," the girls replied in unison.

"I am sorry, I feel awful for not telling you this before. But that's a part of my old life, a past I'd rather forget. Fergus hates me! And to be honest, I am not sure I can blame him."

"No, stop saying that. I won't have it. Besides, don't overlook this. You scored ninety-five percent on our app. You still matched to him. He is your pairing. Deep down, he must love you still—" Kathryn said triumphantly, drying a tear on Marguerite's face.

"Ah, maybe the results are wrong," she interjected, doubting the app was correct as far as Fergus and she were concerned.

"No, they are not! You paired up perfectly," Kathryn replied with a confident grin on her face.

"Well, I don't think it'll work with him."

"Give him time. Perhaps, it will…" Mollie replied sheepishly.

Kathryn looked at her companion with a frown.

"Dear God! When his father came to me with the proposition, I hoped… well, I don't know what I hoped. I couldn't believe it, but Fergus thinks I did it for the money. I don't care about the money. I swear! I would have said yes, even without the cash. Of course, I had doubts about it all, given our past, but I believed it was fate giving us a second chance. Our destiny to be together! Foolish, ha?" Marguerite said and cried disconsolately.

"Are they in there?" Fergus asked as he joined Zac outside the cocktail bar.

"Please don't blast in there like a bull. Mollie tells me she's been crying, and she is very upset."

"Fine, fine!" But he charged into the bar as if he were a gunslinger entering a saloon in the Wild West.

"Fergus!" Kathryn cried out with enormous round eyes, as he steered across the bar toward them, and Marguerite, who had her back to him, spun around in horror.

"Hi, Zac." Mollie gave her husband a harsh look for

bringing in the culprit of Marguerite's most recent distress. "Do you guys want a drink?" she went on with a frown, her tone higher with a hint of rebuke.

"No, thank you. I've come to pick up my wife. It's late," Fergus said.

Returning a strained smile, Marguerite flushed. "I don't remember asking you, and I am not sure I want go home just yet," she said as a waft of alcohol came his way. "Back to that lonely mausoleum…" she murmured this last sentence under her breath.

But he heard her and raised an elegant brow, sucking in a sudden short breath, as an instinctive grin formed on his lips. "Well, I have, and we are going home. We need to talk. It is important."

"Talk? No inclination of doing such a thing right now. Thank you! Perhaps tomorrow," Marguerite said flatly, then she shifted to the bar and ordered a new drink with a haughty expression.

"I think you've had enough cocktails for one night. We must go home and talk," he reaffirmed with deliberate diction, his pale blue eyes flashing fire at her.

She was in her plain faculties, but a third drink had made her braver than she was.

The girls and Zac darted their eyes from one to the other, watching the exchange as if in a tennis match.

Fergus grabbed Marguerite's elbow, but she shook him off and waved a dismissive hand at him.

"I'm not going anywhere with you, not until I am good and ready! I am not done yet." She lifted her chin to him in rebellion, calmly, and when the waiter gave her the cocktail, she directed a strained smile at Fergus. "Cheers," Marguerite said, raising the glass to him with an insolent smirk, and drinking it in one go.

He closed his eyes for an instant, his nostrils flaring. Fergus turned to glance at Zac and the girls, then back to Marguerite. He leaned toward her for a second. "Get your ass off that seat. Now! Or I swear to God, I'll drag you out," he murmured into her ear.

As his dictum registered, she narrowed her eyes on him. "Sod off, Fergus!" she whispered back, the words in a singsong voice with a sigh fanning his ear like a soft breeze, and with the breeze, another waft of alcohol reached his nostrils.

A thunderous expression seized him.

The girls and Zac were observing the scene unfold, holding their breaths. A storm was brewing in front of them, and they didn't fancy the outcome!

"I am going to count to three... one, two..." Fergus said, his lips caressing her ear, then he stood tall and upright like a Viking readying himself for battle. He rubbed his chin.

She watched him do this and gulped. She chickened out! Marguerite left her seat swiftly, settled next to him, picked up her handbag, and kissed the girls goodbye.

Mollie put a warning hand on Fergus' arm. "Do not upset her again, or I swear, you'll have me to answer to. Let her explain," she warned him, and Marguerite gave her a sweet smile.

Fergus rolled his eyes and peered at Zac in commiseration, as if to say, *you poor man!*

Sitting in the car, Marguerite looked straight ahead. The more she thought of it, the more incensed she became. His silence irked her even more. "You have ignored me for the last two days, called me a liar, a fraud, and a gold-digger, insulted me," she said at last. "The moment I go out with my friends, you come to pick me up? What for? I waited for you at lunch, and at dinner, but no! Not even an apology, and you have the temerity to boss me around?"

"And I apologise, okay? I am sorry," he said in a huff.

Her head spun to him, not sure she had heard him right. "What?"

"I said I am sorry, I apologise!" he sulked.

"Oh, yea! That sounds like a sincere apology," she pouted, and he rolled his eyes.

"How much did you have to drink?"

"Not enough."

"Don't push your luck," Fergus replied calmly.

"My luck! Married to you! That's a joke, isn't it?" She was incandescent when a curse, in French, found its way out of her mouth. With the slurring of her words, he hardly got any of it, though what he understood was not good.

"And whose fault is that? You've got a dirty mouth on you, do you know that? Unacceptable. That's a filthy habit of yours."

"Moron," she mumbled under breath, and she followed it with another curse.

"Quiet! Enough," he yelled, and for an instant, he flashed fire at her with his blue moons before returning his eyes to the road.

"Beast!"

"Shush, I said. I apologised to you."

"Don't bloody shush me. Who the hell do you think you are? Don't play the lordly man with me," she cried out. By then, she realised they had entered the tree-lined, long driveway of his home. He was slowing down to park, but before he could stop the car, she flung herself out of it. In her haste and her present state of inebriation, as the car was still moving, she lost her balance and crashed to the pavement on her hands and knees violently.

It was his turn to swear. He became furious at her action.

He watched her get up and rush to the house. He stopped the car quickly and went after her.

Bancroft, watching her burst into the hall and charge up the stairs swiftly pursued by Fergus at the speed of light, didn't know what to do.

She dashed to her bedroom, but she was too slow. He cracked the door open with his hand, before she had time to close it, and pushed in.

"Are you out of your mind?" Fergus howled at her, standing in the doorframe with a thunderous expression. He went in.

She gulped and stepped back. "Get out of my room."

"Are you bloody crazy, launching yourself out of a moving car? Are you hurt?"

"Leave me alone, get out."

"Let me see. Sit down. You're hurt," he said, pointing at the bed.

"Out," she screamed, pushing him back with both palms. As she did so, a grimace on her face showed the pain. She left bloodstains on his jacket. She had scraped her hands and knees on the pavement.

He grabbed her by the wrists and glanced at her hands then at her face. Their eyes locked for an instant, and a spark of pure desire surged through his body and exploded uncontrollably along his frame and limbs, touching every cell. It fired his heart with a bang, as if Cupid himself had thrown him the celebrated arrow. He put her arms behind her back, tightly, and drew her to him.

"Ah, you silly man, leave me alone."

"Now sit, silent! Let me see your palms and knees; you are bleeding."

"I said—" she tried, but he didn't let her finish and crashed his lips on hers. Her needy soul expanded with love for him.

He claimed her mouth in a delirious, intoxicating kiss, and

she opened up to him. She stopped struggling. His mouth owned hers utterly, voraciously, until she was breathless. He cupped her face in both hands, the kiss enveloping them completely, long and hard.

"Now relax, sit down, and not a word. Let me look at your hands and knees. I won't tell you again," he repeated in a tender tone when he parted from the kisses.

"Why do you care, anyway?" she mumbled with a flush.

"You are my wife, aren't you? Now sit!"

Slowly, he walked her back with him until her heels hit the bed. He pushed her slightly and she landed on the bed on her backside. She sat there as quiet as a lamb.

He took her hands and looked at them; they were scraped badly, her raw flesh bleeding. He kneeled to see her knees, and they were just as bad.

"You silly girl, look at what you have done to yourself. Never do that again. Do you understand?" His pale blue eyes were spitting fire at her, but his tone betrayed his concern at her injuries. "Jesus, I could have crushed you under the wheels of my car. This happens when you drink one too many. You do stupid things."

"I am not drunk!"

"You could have fooled me. Stay there and do not move," he commanded and stepped to the door. He called out to Bancroft to bring antiseptic for her wounds. Fergus stared at her without a word while he waited for the butler. He opted for silence since every time he opened his mouth to her, he said something regretful that got them into a scrape.

She was silent, too, but the glimpses they were throwing at each other, which had started belligerently, mellowed, and they turned into longing looks. Yearning spilled out of every pore for both of them. His eyes intense on her, unabashed, not leaving her for a second, he kept himself still, tall and imposing.

Tension left his body, and a rush of some indescribable emotion flooded his senses. He had an overwhelming desire to get close to her, to hold her in his arms and kiss her senseless all over again. But he didn't, though his eyes never left her until the butler came in with the necessary items.

"Thank you, I'll take it from here," he said to Bancroft.

***

She darted furtive glances at him but opted for silence, too. Besides, she was feeling somewhat dizzy after his powerful kisses. The air around her was electric with his intense eyes on her; she didn't know what to do. She kept repeating to herself, *keep your mouth shut, don't look at him.* So she didn't say a word, but her eyes couldn't stray far from him, peeking repeatedly. At one point, she couldn't avoid a shiver.

He sat on the bed next to her, but there was a space between them. So, he tugged her toward him. He gently extended one of Marguerite's long legs from under that pretty, flowery dress of hers that was so becoming, onto his lap, to have better access to her knee, to medicate her.

She gave a brief, short squeal at his actions but didn't resist. Her breathing lowered, her bosom heaved, and she licked her lips. Heat burst into her body, his hand on her leg making her gulp.

Fergus medicated her knee gently. He did the same with her other leg, changing sides, while he couldn't help a slight caress up her thigh with one hand, while seeing to her knee with the other. A second sensual massage up her thigh made her yell, a brief, sharp little cry.

His caresses drove smouldering hotness to her core. She was sure that if he caressed her any higher up her thigh, he would meet with the tiny dribble that had gushed out of her gleaming wet pussy. Another touch from him shook her. She shivered. To break the silence, and the alluring, titillating moment down below, she spoke. "Ouch, it stings," she said, referring to the administered medication on her raw knee, trying to withdraw her leg from his lap.

He held on to her firmly but stopped caressing her. "Stay still, let me do this," Fergus said in a soft, velvety voice.

"But it hurts."

"Stop being a baby."

They threw brief glances at each other. She even launched a small smile at him, and his mouth curled up on one side.

He medicated her hands, and she let him work on them without a complaint. When he finished the job, their eyes locked again. They stared at each other. Fergus' lips brushed her wrists, first one, then the other, kissing them gingerly, deliciously, while his eyes never left hers.

It caused her to shudder. She gave out a tiny, almost inaudible wail. Her eyes went wide. It wasn't the passionate, lustful, ravishing, perhaps angry kisses of a few moments ago or of the night before.

These kisses were a tiny gentle brush of his lips, loving and tender, playfully teasing her, reminiscent of those he ran over her body six years ago. The way he used to kiss her all over, sending her into a frenzy of passionate delirium.

He pulled her close to him by the wrists, and he wrapped his arms around her, while his lips moved onto hers. This time, the kiss was sweet, soulful, slow, and dreamy. They were reacquainting themselves, remembering how it used to feel, rediscovering the sentiments for each other.

"A good night's sleep will do you good. Relax tonight. I want you in my study at 10:00 tomorrow morning. We'll talk then as it's late now, and you've had too much to drink. Goodnight," he said after he ended the kissing.

Despite his desire, he rose and left her room.

Chapter 8

That same night, after Marguerite and Fergus left the cocktail bar, Finley joined his companions. The atmosphere became more relaxed, and they chatted pleasantly.

Finley reminisced about when he'd won a scholarship to Eton, and with Zac also studying at the school, they had a great time.

The lifelong friends first met with Fergus at the school, an introvert kid, but the boys soon had him out of his shell. The three youngsters ran into many scrapes during their stay there, often landing in the headmaster's office for reprimand.

The girls delighted in the stories, chuckling at some of their outlandish escapades, and snorting with witty comments.

"Will Fergus mellow? I mean with Marguerite? What do you think?" Mollie asked them with a nervous laugh.

"Well, he was reserved when he was younger, sensitive, quite compassionate if you ask me. Not the irascible fellow he's turned into in recent years. But your guess is as good as mine," Zac replied.

"I don't think he's a bad lad. His mother died when he was

about fifteen years old. He had to grow up fast after that. He and his siblings lived in the care of nannies then. With four young children, not exactly angels at that, not a single nanny lasted more than six months. Once, he told me it was down to him to watch over his siblings. His father was busy working, with little time to dedicate to them. It's difficult to say, but he has a good heart. You know, when he was thirteen years old, he refused two additional aristocratic titles, as first born, titles coming from his mother's side of the family, to bestow them instead on his younger brothers. He said that his own father's title and lands were more than enough for him, that he mustn't be too greedy. So, Marguerite will have to find his good side and bring it out again. She will; that's a determined lady if I ever saw one!" Finley said.

They all sipped at their drinks mulling this over.

"Jesus, two days and not a civilised word between them is worrying, though, even by Fergus' standard," Zac stressed with a frown.

As the evening progressed, the guys talked shop, and the discussion moved on to business. With the girls on one side, the boys on the other, the conversation continued separately.

Kathryn noticed Mollie's agitation all evening; the issue with Marguerite had upset her. She patted her companion's shoulders in sympathy. "Don't worry, darling, you'll see, Marguerite and Fergus will work out their differences. I am sure of it," Kathryn said with a sip at her cocktail.

"What if they don't?"

"Oh, Mollie, you shouldn't say this. I know what you mean, though. It was our app that put them together. But I don't blame myself. Sometimes, the personal chemistry isn't there, and no science can replicate that. Or individuals may not answer the questions truthfully, or other extraneous factors can block them getting closer, impede the relationship. In this case, we didn't realise they had a past, did we? A difficult one it was, too, and influencing the present situation. There is nothing we can do about that. External elements are just as important in the pairing, and those we can't foresee," said Kathryn in encouragement to her friend, patting her hand.

"Oh, I blame myself," Mollie replied in agony, rolling and unrolling a strand of her hair in her fingers, looking around about her aimlessly, everywhere but at her friend.

"Don't be silly. You cannot go blaming yourself every time a couple in our app won't make it. Besides, don't forget, with Marguerite and Fergus, aside the troubled past, there is also the unsettled present. What I mean to say is Fergus' father making it mandatory for him to marry her. That's painful for anyone, especially for someone like him. Even if his dad had good intentions at heart. So, a difficult pairing, regardless."

"But that's just it. Old Buckley would not have done it if our dating app had not suggested it was a ninety-five percent pairing, a top pick, would he now?" Mollie stated in a shrill voice, blushing fiercely.

"Who knows, maybe not. But, darling, you mustn't think this. It is so coincidental all these outside circumstances are hanging over them. Not our doing."

"It is our doing!"

"How? What do you mean?"

"Well, not yours… but mine!"

"Don't be stubborn, Mollie! How can it be your fault or your doing? You stop saying that." Kathryn flicked back a long lock of black hair with her hand to emphasise her words.

"But it is my fault! Not the app's, but mine!"

"How?" Kathryn sighed; she was getting irritated with her friend's stubbornness and rolled her eyes.

"It is! Oh, dear Lord! What are we going to do now?" Mollie smoothed her palms on her dress and sighed, a crest-fallen expression on her face.

"I don't follow you. What the hell are you saying to me?"

"Oh, for crying out loud, Kat, I influenced the damn results between Marguerite and Fergus. Don't you understand?" Mollie said, while her nostrils flared.

"I beg your pardon?" Kathryn mumbled, turning white as a sheet. She stared at her companion in disbelief, taking a huge breath in.

"I did it! There! Now you know." Mollie's shoulders sagged, and she gulped down her drink.

"What?" her companion repeated, her jaw dropping and her eyes blinking rapidly, striving to comprehend what Mollie had just told her.

"I switched the results. Don't you see? The app had chosen that sweet girl, Imelda! Could you imagine that delightful thing with Fergus? Good God, no! She would not have survived ten minutes, I tell you. He would have strangled her just because she giggles too much, or thrown her out of his house because she is always happy. Mind you, Imelda was a fifty-five percent match, so not much of a pairing, either, anyway. You see my position? I made Fergus and Marguerite my secret pairing."

"No, I don't blooming see!" Kathryn cried out, turning red with irritation to the root of her hair.

"Oh, Kat! The girl was totally wrong for him. I couldn't figure out how Imelda and Fergus would get on. Marguerite scored fifty-three; not high, either, only two percent behind Imelda. But with Marguerite, yes, there was something in it. A proper match for the feisty Dark Lord. Oh, God! Yes, I thought, she was far better suited to Fergus than that irresponsible scatterbrain, as sweet as Imelda is," Mollie said, shaking her head. She hesitated for a moment, then went on, "Besides, George likes Imelda, and she adores him, you know that. This dancing business between them, if you ask me, is foreplay. They fancy the pants off each other. All that stuff about teaching him to dance Mambo... You have seen

Imelda and George dance together, haven't you? And—"
Mollie blabbered convolutedly, realising she had screwed up
big time.

"What? Stop!" Kathryn was perplexed, her hands clasped
her face, flabbergasted. She deposited a furious scowl on her
friend, even more alarmed by her companion's spine-chilling
confession.

"I am sorry, Kat!" Mollie mumbled sheepishly.

"Are you out of your mind? Flipping heck, Mollie! This is
crazy!" Kathryn's nostrils flared with a harsh puff of air out.

"So sorry. How was I to know about Fergus and
Marguerite's past, or that his father intended to mandate
matrimony on him? I would have never done it if I had known
these things."

"Oh, my God! Do you realise what you've done?"

"How was I to know? Hey, you tell me that? All I expected
was for them to have a date or two for an evening, nothing
drastic. That was all. If they didn't get on, well, no harm
done. Then, I would push on Imelda, even though George
would kill me if I did. I am sure of it. But I figured Marguerite
should be first choice. The pairing made more sense. I
switched the pairing around," Mollie said, trying to defend her
action, not very successfully.

Her companion was having none of it. "Did you change
anyone else's results?" Kathryn asked her calmly, but her chilly
tone would have frozen the seas, her eyes chastising Mollie.

"No, of course not! I am sorry"

"Are you sure? Don't lie to me!"

"I swear! None! Never!"

"Then, what the hell possessed you to do that with
Marguerite?" Kathryn spat as she inhaled deeply, feeling the
start of a big headache coming her way.

"I told you, Imelda—"

"Don't be ridiculous; we had more unlikely matches than

Imelda and Fergus. I am sure that's not all the truth. So, let's hear it, Mollie!"

"Well, I-I…" her companion started, unsure how to begin. Her stomach tightened with anguish at her dismal, inappropriate intervention in the matters of the heart between other people. But what's done, was done! She couldn't help it.

"Mollie! Out with it!" Kathryn fixed a hard stare on her friend, seeing her hesitate.

"Oh, I don't know. A few months back, before we even completed the work on our app, a weird thing happened."

"What?"

"One late afternoon, I had just finished a class and was going home. I saw Marguerite walking near the Radcliffe Camera, by the All Souls College on the left, coming toward me. But she didn't spot me, totally blanked me. Something distracted her. It was odd. The place was crowded, though. I was about to call out to her, but she suddenly retreated behind a doorway. Surprised and intrigued by what she was doing, it looked to me as if she was hiding. She gawked at three men talking on the opposite side of the street. It felt strange. She had an odd expression. It was haunting, a sadness that had clouded her face. I wasn't sure what to make of it. Then when one of these men broke off from the group and went in the opposite direction, she followed him with her eyes. She ran a few steps farther after him to take a better look. It was Fergus! I don't know what I expected. The man is often in the papers, anyway. Perhaps curiosity, I told myself. But that night, I couldn't get her from my mind. But I dismissed it. It wasn't until months later, when I analysed the results for Fergus, and Imelda and Marguerite showed up as picks for him, her expression got to me. What I had seen that day, it was longing in that look. Understand? I had to pair her with him."

"Blimey! But you said it was a ninety-five percent a match.

Couldn't you have left it at fifty-three? We could have had a way out if things don't work out."

"Dear Kat, I would be a genius if I knew. I have no answer for that."

"Crazy! You are totally bonkers. Do you realise what you have done?"

"It seemed a good idea at the time. Besides, don't forget, we had deleted everything on Fergus from the app. Nothing was to happen as far as I was concerned. Never thought his father was going to find her to make his son marry her," Mollie tried in her defense. She rubbed her temples in distress and sighed.

"When I think about it, you mentioned Marguerite's name to the old fellow. Did you do it on purpose?" Kat asked, furrowing her brows.

"Yes, but I believed the worse that could happen was a date between Fergus and Marguerite. Just a date! See what I mean?" she pleaded in her defense.

"No, I don't see, Mollie. You must stop meddling in people's lives. Zac is right."

"Oh, please say nothing to Zac. He'd kill me if he knew." Mollie flushed. Her husband had warned her several times not to meddle in his friends' affairs.

"I should tell him, so you learn your lesson," Kat spat, primly and proper, rolling her eyes.

"Don't you dare! Come on, darling. It worked with you and Finley, didn't it?"

"Good Lord, you didn't manipulate the results between us, did you?" Kathryn asked in disbelief, her eyes round and big, disconcerted.

"No, of course, not. You and he, my dear, are the perfect pairing. That's undisputed. What I mean is about giving Fin a little push to declare his love to you. That worked!" Mollie gave her a sweet smile of contrition.

"Umm... You are a nut case," Kat said. She finished her drink and muttered under her breath about her companion's irresponsible behaviour, while Mollie slapped her hand on Kathryn's thigh, and a grin lit up her face despite herself.

"Oh, sweet Jesus! Fergus will kill me if he finds out. What are we going to do? We shall have to tell them."

"No! You must keep this to yourself, Mollie. You mustn't say a thing. It is our secret. Besides, everything is irrelevant now. Fergus' father made it a matter of wife and wealth or nothing. It must remain a secret."

"But don't you see what's happening between them? It's cruel."

"It'll be worse if you tell them. He must stay married to her for eighteen months, anyway, if he wishes to have his inheritance, but then knowing it was all a sham to start with, you'll give him ammunition to fight her. Or worse, he'll find a loophole in the law with this news. He'll ditch the girl, who loves him more than ever, with a grain of hope in her soul. It would break her heart. So, Marguerite will end up worse off, understand? Besides, who knows, they've only been together two days, umm... matters may change. She is a determined lady. She is like a marshmallow on the outside and pure steel on the inside. She'll take him on. So, no!"

"We'll say nothing?" Mollie launched a dubious look at her friend.

"Nothing!"

"Are you sure?" she asked, mystified, rubbing her cheek, anxiously.

"I am sure! Not a word about this to anyone. Nothing!" Kat sentenced.

"Oh, dear God! So be it."

Chapter 9

The next day, Bancroft brought in a tray with coffee and placed it on his desk. Fergus was in his study, and it was almost 10:00 am.

"Thank you," Fergus said. He shifted to glance at his faithful butler, hesitated and inhaled, "I am sorry, Bancroft. I apologised to Mrs. Briggs at breakfast, too. I mean, I apologised for yelling last night about my wife having gone out. It was disgraceful of me. I have no excuse, but these last couple of days have been a struggle. The last few weeks have been hideous, you know. I..." A pinkish burn crept up his neck.

Bancroft smiled. He had never known the young lord to flush as an adult. Though he had become aloof in recent years, Fergus had always treated his staff fairly and with respect. That morning, he sounded like the child Bancroft used to scold after he did something naughty.

"Don't mention it, my lord. I understand."

"Do you, Bancroft?"

"More than you realise. Besides, Briggs has a soft spot for you and your siblings. She'll forgive you anything."

"Umm… Yes, she did, the sweet woman." He sighed and rubbed a hand at the back of his neck.

"You see…" Fergus paused for a moment, clearly pensive, somewhat lost in thought. "Do you think my father was crazy doing this? Wife and wealth or nothing?"

"I dare say, no. I don't think so. It's perfect if you ask me. You need a good wife, and you got one. The loveliest and the sweetest a fellow could wish for. Look at her. Isn't she a dream if I may be so bold?" Bancroft said, pointing at the floor-to-ceiling windows behind his desk looking out onto the grounds.

Fergus turned toward the garden. The morning was so bright, he was almost blinded with light. He saw Marguerite strolling in the gardens on the most glorious of spring days. The sky was a brushstroke of blue to the horizon, the sun blazing a warmth that made the birds chirpy, the grass greener, blossoms spread their scent, and filled every human heart with happiness. He stared at her through the glass.

"Anything else you need, my lord?" the butler asked behind him with a small grin.

"No, thank you," he replied over his shoulder, his eyes staying riveted on her, and Bancroft left him to it.

Fergus marveled at his wife. Funny! Three days after his wedding, and he should consider her as *his wife* when he had not even bedded her, not uttered a single nice word to her, if he had to admit. *Well, at least it's a step forward.* He followed her every move as she strolled. He shook his head. A slight smile curved upon his lips, and he muttered under his breath, "Look at her." He snorted. *I can't believe it. My wife!* The thought that he was a married man hit him with the force of a gale in an instant. His chest tightened for her. He couldn't take his eyes off her. Fergus was hypnotized, spellbound.

She seemed not to have a care in the world, as she roamed leisurely in his garden while he watched her every action, even if he had said to her the previous night, 'We'll talk in my study at 10:00 am.'

He peeked at his wristwatch. It was two minutes to ten. *Unruly woman!*

Marguerite stopped to smell the scent of a flower blossom, cut it off from the low branch, inhaling its sweet perfume again, and put it behind her ear with a smile, proud of herself.

He noticed her black hair in that tight bun at the nape of her neck... God, she had looked so enticing when he saw her that first night three days ago, with her long and lush ringlets to her waist, but he had ruined everything. She sure looked prettier with dark hair. It suited her better than the short blonde he recalled her with years ago. Suddenly, he had the overwhelming desire to run to her and undo her chignon, let those dark locks cascade and flow freely about her body. He sighed at his unorthodox momentary lapse of passion.

Her figure was so familiar. Her round hips so enticing, as he remembered, beautiful as ever, sexy, her sensual curves a sublime sight for sore eyes. *It must be destiny.* He laughed at his foolishness. It shocked him having the thought; he had no business thinking these half-witted sentiments.

She was a liar and a gold-digger. He had to withstand the storm, namely Marguerite, for eighteen months, and it would liberate him of her. He would soon be back to his normal life then.

Easier said than done... Do I wish to return to my old life? Get rid of her? Umm... He muttered an oath under his breath for having doubts. The sight of her was confusing him, his feelings mixed and in a turmoil. *What the hell, man up, stand firm to her,* his inner voice said to him mercilessly. *Jesus, those kisses last night, though.* His cock stirred at the image. *Bloody minx!* He would have kissed those sweet lips until the end of his days.

He opened the doors to the garden, and a warm breeze blew in with a thousand scents from the grounds in bloom. He inhaled, closed his eyes an instant, with the warmth of the sunlight caressing his skin. It felt as if a tender hand was stroking him and pushing away all his worries. It was as if the scented breeze had intoxicated him and cocooned him in a soft embrace, lingering, weaving around him, seducing him and whispering, *it will be all right.* Only the blue sky, the sun, the birds, the myriad of scents, and Marguerite were alive for him that morning. Nothing else mattered.

He shook his head at the strangeness of his mood. His sister's words came to mind. *'No matter how hard you wish to appear, harsh and morose, deep down, you are an incurable romantic.'* He had scoffed when Belinda had said it. Sadly, at that precise moment in time, in his foolish state of mind, he would have to agree with his sister. *This is all nonsense!* He shook his head. *Stop this load of bosh, man!* He got irritated at his own spurious, witless feelings!

He was about to step out, call out to Marguerite, so they could finally have that coveted talk, when she suddenly sat on the lawn. Then, she lay there, outstretched, sprawled on the grass, her limbs spread out by her side. She flapped her limbs in and out on the grass as if she were a butterfly about to take off. She soaked in the morning sunlight and the fresh air, delighting in the propitious moment.

Despite himself, it made him laugh. Now, a laugh on him was rare, but lately becoming less so. Watching her, he had smiled these three days more times that he cared to admit, not overtly, but his heart had danced with joy, despite himself. To glance at her at this moment, he would think she was the happiest woman on earth. Well… She was in this marriage for a reason, and it was not him. But it seemed cruel to stop her enjoying this snippet of gaiety, and another unusual pang of guilt surfaced in him.

He had a calendar full of appointments for the day, and he had to run like clockwork to satisfy them all. Everybody must have their fair share of him. As he looked at his wristwatch, she had wasted over ten minutes of his time. He sighed, with his hands on his hips. He closed his eyes, debating with himself, his chin on his chest, pensive for a moment. *What to do with her.*

Then Fergus stepped outside into the garden and walked toward her. His sight never leaving her for an instant, he considered himself a lucky man, having a wife so pretty. *You foolish idiot,* was his next thought.

He stopped by her side, careful not to stand in the sun's way, at the rays of light stroking her face. "Marguerite?" he called out softly, beguilingly, her name purring out of him despite himself.

Her large almond-shaped grey eyes opened.

Fergus stared at her peachy complexion and her sweet face. She had never looked so charming as she did that day. His insides clenched, and a swell of passion for this woman struck his soul. He had to refrain himself from saying something passionate to her, but his heart was soaring.

The sun was in her eyes. She lifted a hand to cover them, to look at him, and a faint grin lit up her face. She was trying to gaze at him in the hazy sunshine. "Yes?" she answered chirpily, sitting up on the ground to have a better view of him, and when their eyes locked, she lowered hers.

He gazed at her intently without a word.

Marguerite's head snapped up, feeling his eyes on her. This time there was a tender smile on her pretty face, inviting. The sudden movement dislodged a ringlet from her severe chignon. It was flapping in the gentle breeze, in and out of her face. She took it with her slender, elegant fingers and placed it behind her ear gently.

He watched her movement, mesmerised, and his gaze intensified on her. Right then, he would have given away half his wealth to caress her too.

She beamed at him.

His heart raced in his chest, pounding, thundering, ready to explode. She overwhelmed him. She looked so adorable and pretty that he swore he heard church bells ringing in his ears in a singsong of love and happiness. His soul flooded with tenderness for the bewitching creature. A powerful force was taking him over, and he felt enamoured with her. If he had not learned to master his self-control long ago, he would have gotten her into his arms and made love to her there and then, on the grass. He inhaled and exhaled. Fergus closed his eyes, shaking his head to get rid of the visions of her in his arms that assailed his mind. He struggled to wipe out the nonsense that had won over his heart in the last half hour.

Snap up, man! This dainty, beautiful little hussy has treated you with disrespect and called you all sorts of unrepeatable names for the past two days. She lied to you then, and now she is after the money your father promised her. Never forget that! Don't be taken in by her sweet demeanour. Don't get silly ideas or confused... She'll pretend passion and love to you to get to the cash. His inner voice was merciless.

"Get your backside off the grass and into my office. This minute. You are late!" he voiced in a commanding tone, turned on his heels, and walked back to his study.

Typical of him! For once, she was enjoying herself, and he ruined it with his imperious command. But the way he'd called out to her at first, *'Marguerite,'* he had said in a deep silvery voice, in a silky and melodious tone, as if singing to her. Thus, tenderly, her name had floated from his mouth into the air, and Zephyr had carried it off in a flurry puff of wind, as if in a wondrous dream, to her. No doubt, the enchanted, velvety sound came from his lips, from Fergus *and ah... how those lips had kissed her last night!* Albeit briefly, but they had, and the first night too, despite himself.

She dabbed her lips with her fingertips, reliving his mouth on hers. There was passion in him; she couldn't deny it. He had kissed her, like he used to. The way he had looked at her just now, there was no mistake. He still wanted her, she was sure of it. She had butterflies in her stomach, but he was denying it to himself and to her.

A smile curled up on her face at the realisation. *Oh, Dark Lord, you are mine! You were then, and you are now, like I have always been yours. The sooner you grasp it, the better for both of us.* How could she make him understand he felt that same way? *He must acknowledge it to himself.*

As usual, he ruined the moment with his peremptory command. When he waved his big hand at her from the office, beckoning her in his urgent, imperious fashion, she snorted.

He is incorrigible!

The delightful day had put her in a good mood. She was in a chirpy state of mind, and not even his lordship's ill temper was going to ruin it for her. Life was too short to stay angry at one another. They had to overcome that stage.

As she reveled in the gardens on this glorious spring morning, she had lost track of time and forgotten about having an appointment with him at 10:00 am. Anyway, it wasn't a job interview. She was his wife, for goodness' sake! So, who cared if she was a few minutes late.

But he beckoned her with another agitated wave of his hand from the house, and Marguerite scurried along. She joined him in his study. Entering his sanctuary had the opposite effect on her. It was his place, his domain! Her agitation took hold of her again. She glanced at her wristwatch, cursing under her breath. She was so late! He wouldn't like that. She felt as if she were a naughty child in the headmaster's office, waiting for her punishment.

Her apprehension resurfaced, not knowing what to expect. She bit her bottom lip. *What does he want to talk about? Is he going to tell me off? For jumping out of the car? Or for swearing?* He hadn't liked her swearing. *More likely both.* She sighed with a sonorous puff.

She had launched at him an indecent oath last night, and a few the night before that, in French and English. He didn't appreciate that. He had been furious, too, when she threw herself out of the moving car. She fretted.

Marguerite's knees and hands were still painful from her fall, so she'd embraced the few minutes of relaxation, but she had a hunch she would regret her blunder. Now she felt the mist from the grass on her back, her clothes damp on her skin.

He locked the glass doors to the garden and spun to her. Fergus glanced at her up and down but gave nothing away. His face was unreadable.

She shifted on her feet, hesitant, restless under his scrutiny.

He gestured to the chair in front of him with a wave of his hand. He sat behind his desk. "Marguerite, you are over twenty minutes late. This won't do. I'll overlook this today, given your fall last night, but I insist on punctuality. Lateness is quite a peeve of mine. So you must be on time, always. Do I make myself clear?"

"Yes. I am sorry. I was… I was…" She realised she had no excuse. He had caught her sprawled on the magnificent lawns in the sunshine.

"You were sunbathing and gathering flowers?" he added with an ironic tone, arching his eyebrows. His face was serious, but there was amusement in his eyes.

"Well, I-I…" she stammered.

He put a hand up that read, *I don't need an answer to that.*

She blushed and yanked the blossom from behind her ear.

"You don't have to take the flower off on my account. It

looks pretty on you," he whispered in the same tone he had said her name, with half a smile.

She glanced up. If her face was already red, now it turned scarlet to the very roots of her hair, and her heart melted for him.

He pretended not to notice and went on about her lateness. As he talked a minute or two about how he wanted people to deal with his orders as instructed, she couldn't help watching him, not listening anymore to what he was saying. He'd looked so magnificent earlier when he was out in the garden, in his beige chinos and white polo shirt with the sun and the sky as his backdrop. He was a tall, handsome man. When his pale blue eyes searched hers, she felt it at her core. Fergus was dashing, with harmonious, aristocratic manly features. His powerful body rendered him so masculine in that casual ensemble of his. It gave him a bearing reminiscent of when they were in Nice, reminding her of the young lad she had known all those years ago.

Suddenly, she missed the man she loved then, terribly! *Is he still the same man?* She didn't know. Why couldn't he realise he felt the same way about her as she felt about him?

For three days, he had ignored her at best, and at worst, they had argued or said horrible words to each other, with the exception of the passionate kissing interludes. She inhaled, wishing matters were different between them, longing for more of his kisses.

Is this how it's going to be? Then her lips thinned, pressed together in a veiled scowl. She refused it! *No, this won't do!* She hadn't survived those desperate years with Alain on her tail for nothing. Not if she wasn't a determined girl, a tough person. In her darkest moments, the thought of Fergus had kept her going. Even if she thought she might not see him ever again.

Marguerite was strong. The resolute lady wanted Fergus with all her soul. He had to understand she loved him, let her explain why she left him. She had to get through to him, and he had to admit to himself he felt the same way about her. *Dare she say he loved her? Is this what I saw a few minutes ago? Love?* Perhaps… but she shivered at the daunting task ahead of her. It felt as if she was scaling a vast mountain, the summit unreachable, with in-between a steep, unrelenting, hard climb in front of her if she wished to get to him.

I must conquer that climb! Give it my best shot. He must understand we belong to each other. His father understood this, why can't he?

"Are you all right? You seem distracted. Are you listening to me?" he asked, irritated, taking her out of her reverie, when he realised she was absorbed in her own thoughts.

"Sorry…" she mumbled and flushed.

"That won't do. You are not listening to me. What the hell were you thinking about, hey? I bloody wonder… oh, forget it! Now hear me out. We must learn to communicate without going at our throats. No more insults. Do you understand?" He paused. "It's not healthy, and we cannot keep this up for a year and a half. And do not launch yourself out of a moving car ever again, understood?" he concluded, still burning at her escapade last night.

She lowered her eyes, pressing her hands on her lap. "Well, you started this," she said in her dogged willfulness. The minute she uttered the words, she realised it was the wrong thing to say. *I am supposed to be conciliatory, not on the warpath! Silly girl!* The mistaken way to go about it. Not what she had in mind to say. She swore silently to herself for her stupidity. She had promised herself not to antagonise him, but the moment she opened her mouth, that was exactly what she had done. He was right; they must learn to communicate without getting their backs up. *I am an idiot!*

"Me?" he replied with his eyes big. "How? When I raised your veil three days ago, I had the shock of my life. How is this my fault, hey?"

"Well, you called me a floozie, a gold-digger and—" she said in her defense, trying to smooth things over, but she was only making it worse.

"And I apologised in the car last night, twice. I tried, but you wouldn't let me. You threw an insult at me, not to mention the unrepeatable improprieties in French and English two nights ago, I might add. In case you have forgotten, and some quite shocking for a lady."

"Well... I am sorry! Besides, I am not a lady," she murmured, shaking her head. She looked at her hands on her lap, fingering her wedding ring relentlessly.

"You are now, whether you like it or not," he said, scowling at her. "I am sorry for the horrid things I said to you. It was uncivilised of me," he went on in one breath. He wasn't used to apologising, and here he was with a third apology to her in two days. So to divert from this, he asked swiftly, "How are your hands and knees? Are you feeling better?"

"Still a little sore, but I'll survive. And your... your..." She didn't know how to refer to her knee crashing hard into his groin a couple of nights ago. She just waved her hand, pointing at the middle of his legs, embarrassed.

"You mean when you nearly disabled me for life? Which brings me to—"

"Hm..." She couldn't help an unladylike snort, which stopped him mid-sentence.

"What's so bloody funny? I tell you, if your knee had hit me any harder, any higher, there would never be another heir in my line. You almost killed me!" he said in all seriousness. "So let's get down to the rules before you get any more silly ideas," he concluded.

"What rules?"

"Rule number one, never jump off moving cars. I want you safe and not hurt in any way. Rule number two, never slap me, kick me, knee me, or hit any part of my body again, understood? Whether you think I deserve it or not. Are we clear on that? Rule number three, no insults."

"Aha!" But she chuckled. She couldn't help it.

"Incredible! You think this is funny?" he asked, astonished at hearing her laugh.

"I admit, it was amusing," she snorted some more. "Seeing you rolling on the floor holding your... you know, it was funny," she repeated through bursts of giggles.

"Funny! I was in agony," he cried out in dismay.

"See you hop on one foot when I kicked your shin, well..." she carried on undeterred, with another burst of mirth coming out of her mouth. "Besides, you deserved it! All of it. Did you understand what I said in French?" She mentioned some of the unrepeatable words she had lashed at him, through fits of giggles. "It was funny! You should have seen your face, not used to this, are you? Everyone fears you, but I am not scared."

He frowned at her, winced, and muttered an oath under his breath. "Perhaps you should be, you minx," he said, but she chortled uninhibited.

She struggled to halt herself from laughing. *Stop giggling you silly woman,* she told herself, *enough! Or you'll get his back up again.* Thinking she had gone too far, though, she couldn't contain herself. "Oh, Fergus!" Marguerite mumbled and kept on snorting, unladylike, as if it was another person laughing and not her. She fought hard to control herself, to school her features. She knew this would antagonise him even more, so she tried to stop herself but to no avail. The problem was, sometimes, when she was nervous, like at that moment, this happened to her. She laughed. A fit of laughter would take over, and the more she tried to block it, the worse it grew. The more she tried to stop it, the more she was incapable of it.

He rose in all seriousness, glaring at her, his face a solemn mask.

She ceased giggling abruptly when she watched him in his full height with his hands on his hips.

Her childish behaviour mortified her.

"Funny? You think this is funny, do you?" he added, he rubbed his chin with his hand, outstaring her with a wolfish smile.

"Sorry, F-Fergus…" she stammered with a furious blush.

He moved around the desk, grabbed her upper arm and pulled her out of her chair, none too delicately.

"F-Fer—" she yelped, not expecting it, blinking fast.

He pressed her hard against him, his arms wrapped around her. Adrenaline flowing in her body, his touch was electric. Her heart thumped in her chest. It had the desired effect; it silenced her. He gazed into her eyes for a few moments. Her breathing quickened, her bosom heaving against his chest. Her blood whooshed, pounding in her veins.

He smiled, a slow, wide, wicked smile. Then Fergus' mouth captured hers. Their lips melded, and she opened up for him in a dreamy, engulfing kiss. Sparks flew around them and scaled up to the stratosphere, it was so intense. He kissed her savagely, fiercely, and she wouldn't have it any other way. She returned the kiss with a burning and all-consuming passion of her own, a deep, soulful kiss as her hands held his face.

He stopped the kiss abruptly, his eyes blazing with ardent longing. "Was it fun? Let's see how fun you'll find this, then," he rasped, his breathing still low from the frenzied kisses. Suddenly, he released her and moved away from her. She mourned the loss of his touch with a sigh, but she was still dazed by his close encounter. He went to the sofa and sat there.

She followed his movement, and when she recovered somewhat from the passionate kisses, she wondered what the hell he was doing.

"Come here," he said to her coolly, beckoning her with his index finger. He seemed to have regained his self-control.

"Why?" she retorted, suspicious, uncertain of his intentions.

"Did you hear me?" he asked, once more beckoning her with his finger, but she was rooted to her spot. "Move, here! I am not telling you again," he commanded, his voice imperious in his demand. He looked in complete control, his composure suddenly agitating her.

Oh, bloody hell! She recalled a similar circumstance all those years ago, with her on his knees… In an instant, she understood his intention. She was dreading it and relishing it, just like that time long ago. But his sharp gaze never left her.

"*Now!*" he repeated in such a mighty command that she jerked on her feet on the spot and moved to him as if he had pulled her with an invisible rope.

"Fergus," she said, standing next to him. "I am sorry. I'm nervous. I didn't mean to laugh, to offend you—" she mumbled, hoping she had not made matters worse, but he didn't let her finish. She had done the exact opposite to what she had intended to do, astonished at her own impudent laughing behaviour. *Why do I always end up irritating him!* She hoped he was not mad at her again, but he grabbed her wrist. It was so sudden that she shrieked. He flung her over his knees, face down.

"You are way out of line! This situation does not grant you the privilege to be rude. I must stop this nonsense before you get any more silly ideas. You can't behave wildly with me, I won't have it," he said with a scowl.

"What the hell are you doing?"

"Well, if my rules make you laugh, you are not taking this seriously. Perhaps a good spanking will restore your senses that this is no joke. In particular when it was you who agreed to marry me."

"You are not serious!" she cried out, and she thrashed about, struggling to liberate herself.

"Oh, trust me, I am, my lady!" He gave her such a smack right on the crest of her buttock over her dress.

"Aw, aw, are you insane? Put me down!" And she wrestled some more, trying to get off his lap. He grappled with her until his firm hand kept her steady on his lap, while with his other, a whack fell upon her backside.

She couldn't move. There were tears in her eyes, but with the dazzling kiss which had already melted her core, his spanking only added a delicious fuel to an already mighty heat, warming her body.

"Let me go! This instant, do you hear?" she shrieked against the deliciousness that was engulfing her frame, mortified that she was enjoying and dreading this at the same time.

"Quiet!"

"You idiot!" she screamed, cursing him.

"You see? I am telling you no insults, and here you are disregarding me straight away."

"Autocratic moron," she whimpered.

"Again? For each insult, I'll add an extra ten spanks. So, if you want me to do this all day, by all means, keep them coming. I'll do this for as long as it takes. When I say no more insults, I mean it. And in any language. Understood?" he said, with another set of smacks thrashing her backside.

"Fergus, please—"

"I have apologised to you three times now, but you keep on the same path. Not listening to me, insulting me. Endangering yourself, throwing yourself out of a moving car, too. Not to mention laughing at me. So disrespectful! You are under my care now. You are my wife, by your choice, no less. And you'll respect me, whether you like it or not," he concluded. He whacked her bottom over her dress.

"You started this, you silly!" she yelled. As much as she struggled, she couldn't move, making any action impossible.

"Right, that's it, had enough of your nonsense." He pressed her down in this position, keeping her from fighting him. She sought to defend herself, but it was useless.

He pulled her dress up to her waist, her panties down to her ankles. He proceeded, without preamble, to smack her bare backside.

***

Her beautiful derrière was a vision to him. He had missed the warmth of her body through the years. Now there she was, his wife, and on his knees. This might just turn out a memorable day!

At her raucous protests, he swung his arm back as if he were about to hit a tennis volley, with her ass as the intended target. When his hand connected with it, repeatedly, it was with strength and speed as if he were on one of his fastest, powerful tennis serves. Each spank was executed to perfection. The raw power of his palm, the perfect placement on the crest of her buttocks, made her eyes water, the imprint of his digits on her peachy skin glowing scarlet.

The heavy sting brought a flow of tears to her eyes. Her ass was on fire, like a blazing, roaring log in the hearth. "Ow, stop! Someone'll see us... the garden..." she gasped through tears, but words failed her as another bunch of swats fell on her backside. As she dangled on his knees, tears were flowing.

"Don't worry, they'll pretend it isn't happening!" He smacked her hard.

"Stop now!" she begged.

"I have apologised to you, but you insist on your path. This won't do."

"I'm sorry."

"Are you going to sit and listen to me, seriously? No more nonsense? I don't want your safety at risk, either, like last night. No more crazy things, and no more insults, no more disrespect. No more swearing at me, no more kicking me, understood? No more knees crashing in my groin. I won't have it! Umm…" He traced her red hot skin tenderly with his hand.

The warmth of his palm on her fiery backside had a cooling and delirious effect. Butterflies fluttered in her tummy as he rubbed the skin of her already hot, aroused body. She stopped fighting him. Her pussy was drenched.

"Please," she pleaded. He thrashed her butt a few more times until it scorched her, the booming impact of his hand on her skin reverberating in the room. Tears abounded in her eyes. She felt embarrassed, placed on his knees like a naughty child. "I promise, stop," she begged. She was mortified, very sore, and very aroused. Her body lay limp on his lap, exhausted, sniveling, and whimpering.

"No more lies! Above all, no more deception, is that clear? No more false names like in Nice. And how on earth did you think it was safe to marry a stranger, hey?" He smacked her butt again with great big wallops.

"But I know you!"

"From years ago!"

"So? Aw, aw!" she said, as another whack fell upon her shapely ass.

"I could have turned out to be a murderer for all you knew. I don't want any more nonsense out of you! Understood?"

"Fergus!"

"Will you behave? I was giving you an olive branch. I apologised to you, and you threw it back at me. Laughing. Disrespectful. We must learn to communicate without insulting each other. Without being horrid to each other. We have to be respectful."

"I promise!"

"Fun, was it? Not giggling now, are you?" He raised his hand for one last smack!

"I won't. I won't. I promise." The sting on her butt was unbearable.

"I hope you learned your lesson. When I am telling you something it is not a laughing matter. In particular when your behaviour and your safety is concerned," he said and then stopped spanking her. He kept her on his knees with his hand warming her posterior, rubbing the glowing red skin.

Marguerite hissed a sigh of relief, limp, even though the stinging was still flaming her.

He massaged her butt cheeks. They felt more like caresses. The warmth that had been latent resurfaced and spread across her body with the intensity of the heat on her buttocks. Her insides flared, her pussy throbbed.

He raised her up and sat her on his knees. She still had tears in her eyes. He took one or two away with his fingers.

She rested her head on his chest. A tiny tremor shook her.

He wrapped his arms around her. "Are you all right?" he asked, his voice gentle now. "We must stop making each other mad. Do you understand?"

"Yes," she mumbled, limp in his arms as he caressed her face.

"We must learn to live together," he said. He lifted her chin with his fingers to look into her eyes. "You do want to stay with me, don't you? I mean, for these eighteen months." He only added the last sentence for appearance's sake…

She nodded.

Their eyes locked, and invariably, as the longing in each other's eyes scorched them, there was only one way to go. His lips crashed on hers. It was a raw and sensuous passion.

His hand went to her chignon. He kept her head steady, kissing her utterly, with all his body and soul behind it. She was delighting in his mouth, butterflies danced in her tummy about this man.

His hand found her hairpins and began to take them out, one by one.

"What are you doing?" she whispered breathlessly after his lips left hers.

"One more thing! Don't choose this hairdo again. I want to see your hair loose about you. Promise?" he murmured in between kisses to her eyes and chin, while he was getting rid of the dainty barrette in her hair, thus her long ringlets cascaded about her.

She nodded, making cute little movements of her head to let it fall freely.

He held her dark locks in his hand and let them loose between his fingers. They felt luscious and silky at his touch. Capturing her lips with a ravenous kiss, he fisted her hair.

Her stomach flipped in anticipation.

"You look prettier as a brunette. It suits you," he said when his mouth left hers.

"I thought you might not like it," she mumbled and lowered her head briefly, but her heart thundered at the compliment.

"I love it. Is this your natural colour?"

"Aha." She flushed. Her head tilted on one side with a prolonged grin, and she put a hand lightly on his shoulder.

"You are so beautiful, girl!" he whispered. He kissed her again, blood flooding to his manhood in such great rushes, it was throbbing inside his chinos.

Marguerite could feel his enormous hard-on sitting on his lap, and her womanly parts pulsated, wishing he would touch her there... but he had other ideas.

His hand went to the buttons at the front of her dress. When he couldn't undo them because they were fake ones, she giggled and pointed at the zipper on her back.

He undid it. Then he pulled her panties, already on her ankles, down and off her, tossing them on the floor.

"We should go upstairs, the glass doors to the garden—"

"There is a button on my desk, on the left. Go press it," he said, "but switch on the lamp before you do." His voice was hoarse, looking at her in anticipation.

She stood, with the zipper of her dress undone, and went to it. Flashes of the silky skin on her back gleamed at him as the nirvana he had been awaiting.

She switched on the lamplight on his desk with a trembling hand, then she found the button on his desk and pressed it. The curtains over the glass doors moved electronically and closed. The unexpected noise and movement made her jump. She turned coyly to him with a small smile, trying to keep her dress up.

"Lock the door," he mumbled, motioning to the other side of the room with his head, and his eyes followed her. He took his mobile phone out of his pocket and called his secretary.

"Perkins, cancel all my appointments for today," he whispered into it, then put the phone on the console table behind the settee.

"Why don't we go upstairs?" she said, inhaling with a little gasp. She had not made love for a long time and she was apprehensive. She massaged her backside with her hand, and a grin appeared on his face.

"I want you here, now," he replied with a deep breath. His cock was hard and pulsating; he could hardly contain himself.

She locked the door to the study and returned to him. She was about to sit on his lap again, but he shook his head.

"No, stand in front of me; take your dress off."

She stood facing him, hesitated, and a little awkwardly, she complied. Her dress slid off her shoulder and down her frame to her feet. She stepped out of it. Her naked pussy gleaming, and her curvaceous, delicious body appeared in front of him like he had dreamed of many times, her large bosom heaving for him. The difference, it was more beautiful than in his dreams, turning him crazy with desire at the sight of her. He licked his lips, and a rough grunt left his mouth. *And she is mine.*

She returned a coy smile, too, feeling somewhat mortified standing there almost naked for his enjoyment.

"Take your bra off," he commanded.

She was nervous and couldn't undo the back with his eyes riveted on her.

"Come here," he said. When she did, he sat her on his knee facing away from him. He undid her bra and let it slide from her. As she turned to him, his gaze moved from her face to her beautiful globes. He took a nipple in his mouth and sucked it roughly. He had always loved her breasts. They were now his, as all of her was his.

"Fergus…" she mumbled as he picked up the other and gorged on her nipples to his heart's content. She was panting, her pussy beyond wet.

"Now, stand in from of me," he demanded. She hesitated, but she stood in front of him, her breathing in small bursts, her pussy throbbing and gleaming.

The view of her sex made his cock pulsate inside his boxers, with the wet head pushing into his chinos. His eyes feasted on her, slowly, taking all of her in. "Come here. Now undress me, sweetheart," he whispered, his voice hoarse and rough.

She obeyed him. Marguerite kneeled on the floor between his legs, stark naked. She took off his shoes. One sock was off, then the other. She was throwing little fleeting glances at him while he stared at her, unabashed.

Marguerite massaged his foot in her hands, while he placed the other on her pussy, rubbing her clit with his big toe.

Her eyes popped open wide, and she threw her head back,

her legs parting of their own volition as he massaged her there for a moment. Her wetness was growing exponentially.

"Unzip my trousers," he commanded, taking away his toe from her clit, and she moaned its loss.

She moved up on her knees and reached out. She undid his belt and took it off, then it was his trousers. She dragged them off, but he helped her with that. It left him in his boxers and polo. When she pulled his boxers down his legs and off, too, his massive cock popped out to say hello to her, bright and cheerful in its full, hard length, and ready to play.

She knew what she wanted to do. She took him in her mouth. Her lips wrapped around the tip of his wet shaft as she licked and sucked him, her hand clasping the length to keep it steady.

He growled, a sound so deep and guttural that it reverberated in the room. She remembered how wonderful it was with him, and how he liked it, so it aroused her even more.

He pulled his head back, enjoying her mouth on him. Soon he stopped her. Fergus wanted to be inside her and yanked her up on the settee. She lay back along the length of it. He was over her in a flash. He nestled between her legs. In one pull, his polo shirt went off over his head and down on the heap of clothes on the floor. His powerful chest muscles were a delight on view. He put his hands under her buttocks, and she whimpered, still sore after the spanking.

He lifted her, so his lips moved to her clit, and he sucked, his tongue bursting inside her. She gave tiny cries of pleasures. She was soon panting in little bursts. His tongue was king inside her. She was mumbling his name, pleading for release, her back arching.

Then he released her, going over her. He trailed a finger down from her neck and over her nipple to her belly button, slowly locking his eyes on hers as his cock slid inside her. "God, you are a gorgeous woman!"

She hissed with delight.

Fergus stood still, allowing time for her to adjust to him, savouring the moment so long wished for. He relished having her as his eyes never left hers. He plunged in and out of her. Her walls clenched around him, and more blood flooded his manhood, while she purred his name in little cries and moans until her orgasm hit her powerfully.

He followed suit; they shivered and rocked until totally done in. He crashed on top of her, spent.

"You are mine!" he whispered in her ear.

She put her arms around his neck and brushed his cheeks with random tiny kisses. He delighted in them.

A sweet smile spread on his face.

"Bloody hell, Lisette, I missed you!" he said when he recovered and was able to speak again.

"I did, too, Fergus. It's Marguerite now. Or Margot," she whispered.

"I know, love. I've got to get used to your real name. For a moment, I thought we were in Nice," he said, and he looked just like then to her.

"Marguerite," he whispered her name, over and over, with eyes full of love.

She delighted in the sound of her name coming from his lips, in that same singsong tone she liked so much. It was then, she sent a brief prayer to the heavens. She prayed for his father, hoping the man would be in Paradise for restoring Fergus and joy to her existence.

"Marguerite, it is then," Fergus murmured. He doubted he would let her go in eighteen months, or ever again...

Would she want to stay? He dismissed his doubts in this glorious moment; time would tell.

Unbeknown to her, Fergus had the same idea. He wished his dad a pleasant afterlife in Heaven, thanking him for giving him a second chance at happiness by bringing Marguerite back into his life. He pleaded forgiveness, too, for doubting him, for wishing him in Hell.

It seems, after all, the old man knew what he was doing! He shook his head and kissed her ravenously again.

Eventually, they moved upstairs and spent the rest of the day in bed, lovemaking. Not even food stirred them away from the rediscovered pleasures of their bodies until late that night. They fell asleep in each other's arms.

The love in their hearts, until that day lying dormant in the depths of their souls, made a comeback, engulfing them in the land of passion, and liberated, it poured out freely.

Chapter 10

He had awakened with a start; he felt crumpled and couldn't move. Fergus looked about him. Then he realised why. She was fast asleep. He had forgotten for a split second.

Fergus smiled, enchanted. He caressed her naked back lightly.

He wasn't used to women staying the night after lovemaking. Waking up with Marguerite sprawled with half of her body over him, was a new, charming experience. *My lovely wife!* It felt right, pleasurable, like coming home after a lengthy absence. It was cosy and satisfying. He relaxed and enjoyed it, delighting in her warmth.

Marguerite had an arm wrapped around his chest. Her head lay on his shoulder and one long leg across his groin, nude in all her glory. A goddess! His heart overflowed with joy at having her with him.

Her beautiful hair hung loose all over the place like a mantle, messy, rumpled and so very sexy. They were in her room, so he darted his eyes about him. He extended his free arm and grabbed his wristwatch from the bedside table, trying not to wake her. It was 5:00 am. He put it back and lay there savouring the moment. He moved her hair to one side and kissed the tip of her nose.

She wrinkled it in a funny way that made him smile. She stirred and turned away from him. Within seconds, she returned in position and snuggled up to him again, her body half over his once more.

"Can't stay away from you," she mumbled through a sleepy yawn. Then, she placed a kiss on his chest.

"Can't you?" He laughed, caressing her cheek with his fingertips.

"What time is it?" she asked, brushing her lips on his nipple, and her pink tongue gave him a tiny lick.

It tickled him, and he snorted. "Early, go back to sleep."

"Sleep? Really, husband!" She raised her face to him with a mischievous smile, now fully awake.

He chuckled, pulled her fully on top of him, and kissed her languidly. "Good morning, sweet lips!" he said through tender little nibbles of her lips.

She giggled through it. "Morning, husband," she mumbled as he continued his tiny bites on her lips. Her hand strayed to his cock.

He stopped the kissing at her touch, raising an eyebrow and giving her a wolfish grin.

"Ooh, this big already, ha? Is he saluting the new day or is it me?" she said half in merriment.

He chortled. "You, sweet lips, you!" He grabbed her hips with his enormous hands, raised her up, and then lowered her on his shaft. She hissed a low, languid moan of pleasure as he entered her.

She sat up, straddling him, with his manhood deep inside her.

He adjusted his hands, to get a good grip on her hips, and

started moving her up and down on his length, directing the tempo.

She was a vision, with her head back in ecstasy. Her hair flowing long and loose, she was riding him, hissing little sounds of pleasure that made his dick throb inside her. They were reliving the thrilling pleasures of their bodies—long lost all those years ago, and rediscovering new ones too. They couldn't have enough of each other.

Fergus' upper body half rose toward her, and he pulled her to him to get close as his mouth reached for her nipple. He sucked, and she moaned.

She placed her hands flat on the bed, on either side of him, riding his cock at her own pace now, while he savoured her breasts to his insatiable delight, greedily sucking her. Then he turned her over, flat on the bed. She shrieked with delight. He was on top of her.

He lifted her legs on his hips to get better access. Then he slammed into her with intemperate yearning and unappeasable craving as if he wanted to mesh with her, demanding her, taking her—until their lust, love, and passion were quenched, and they hit their climaxes in great clamour.

"Are they not coming down today? It's 9:30 am. Shall I remove breakfast then?" Mrs. Briggs asked Fergus' valet, who was hovering in the breakfast room having a coffee.

"And how should I know? I haven't seen the man since yesterday morning. He's been too busy with her—" he replied, but he couldn't finish his sentence.

"Crispin, take your cup to the kitchen; you shouldn't lie about in here. They might still come in," the butler ordered.

"Yes, Mr. Bancroft. I doubt it, though." The valet winked at him and left the room.

Bancroft shook his head at the coarseness of the young man.

"I'll wait another half an hour. Then I'll ask Cora to take everything back to the kitchen," Mrs. Briggs said. "I guess the honeymoon has started. It was overdue if you ask me and about time," she continued with a loving smile. She was so fond of her young lord and his siblings, having seen them grow up.

"Not even his lordship could resist a pretty and sweet girl like her. His father might have taken a bit of a gamble in doing this, but he knew what he was doing. He made an excellent choice; she'll make him happy."

"Yes, I think so, too. B-but——"

"What?"

"Yesterday morning, in the study, I am not sure, it sounded, as if they were, ahem… he was… I don't understand. How shall I put it…" she blabbered, unsure.

"Do you mean spanking her?"

"Why, yes! I think so."

"Yes, some couples like a little spanking now and then. It spices things up. Have you ever tried it, Mrs. Briggs?" Bancroft said, deadpan, with amusement in his eyes. He realised the woman would think him forward and rude for saying such a thing, but he couldn't help it. She had started the conversation in that tone anyway.

The auburn-haired woman in her early fifties, slightly plump but youthful looking housekeeper's dark eyes grew out of orbit. She turned as red as a beetroot at the pearly-haired butler's insinuations.

They had worked together for almost twenty years, both now widowed, Bancroft long ago and Mrs. Briggs three years ago. They had become good friends as time passed. Still, both were rather reserved.

"Well, I never!" The housekeeper's furious blushing went on for at least thirty seconds.

Bancroft thought, *well, what do you know! She looks as cute as a button when she flushes.*

"Cora, Cora!" she called out for the maid, embarrassed. A safety net between them was sometimes necessary. Frankly, she didn't mind the attention from him. Things were hotting up, and she was rather enjoying the attention.

———

Fergus had noticed the scar on her shoulder. *This is new!* He didn't remember seeing it before. It was long and thin. He counted the stitches with his fingers and there were many, just below the shoulder blade.

"How did you get this?" he asked her, fingering it delicately. He brushed his lips along the length of it.

She smiled, but her eyes were hard, and a sudden shiver took hold of her.

He wrapped his arms around her. "What is it? How did you get this?" he repeated when she didn't answer.

She placed her head on his shoulder, took a deep breath, exhaling slowly. "A knife," she murmured, so low, he wasn't sure he had heard her right.

"What?" He froze, his fingers still on the scar.

"A knife," she repeated, clearing her throat nervously.

He lifted his head from the pillow and stared at her. This time her face had taken a hard countenance. He had not seen that expression on her before. "Bloody Hell! What happened?" he asked in disbelief when it sunk in. His pale blue eyes were big and round, so shocked that anyone could do such a thing to her. His mouth was agape as he sat up in bed to gawk at her, bewildered. At first, he imagined perhaps she had resisted a robbery.

When her long story on Alain, her violent ex-boyfriend began, his jaw muscles visibly tightened. His mouth went dry. He rubbed her arms as she spoke in short, small strokes relentlessly, encouraging her, taking her hand to his lips several times to ease the pain, to comfort her.

As her tale went on, a sudden heaviness expanded in his heart. The tightening in his chest felt painful. His soul cried out to her, but he kept his self-control. He wanted to know it all, and he regretted not being there for her in the worst moments of her life.

She told him everything in a distant, aloof, dull monotone, the only way to go through it without feeling all the horrors of it again and burst into tears. Her stare was far away, as if it wasn't she who lived through the savagery and fear.

She told him everything about Alain. A relationship established at the end of high school in Lille where she lived. Her early days at University in Paris with the man. But there, the liaison turned noxious and almost saw her dead. She briefed him on how she moved to the South of France to elude her ex-boyfriend, but he would always find her.

The reason she had run away and left Fergus so unexpectedly in Nice, without saying goodbye. Her ex-boyfriend had tracked her down once more. This was now clear to Fergus, and a pang of guilt surfaced in his soul. He understood why she did it, why she left him. She had to disappear again.

Her hands trembled as he caressed her. He brought her palms to his lips to soothe her.

"Oh, darling, I had to escape Alain as much to protect myself as to keep you safe. Alain would have killed you if he knew we were together."

"Keep me safe? Oh, sweet lips..." He kissed her tenderly, softly. He held her in his arms, caressing her hair, but then he asked her to go on with her tale.

She told him why she couldn't avoid the relentless changes

of cities, names, and jobs, to hide from Alain. She spoke about her torment of living in fear and about her anguish at her ruined life. The grief and suffering at having to live looking over her shoulder, at a life of running away that was no existence at all, at her shattered dreams. The awful feeling her ex-boyfriend had ingrained in her that she was useless, worthless.

Fergus listened to her in silence, occasionally asking a question, not to interrupt her flow. He flinched at her tragic tale, at the violence she had experienced, at the harm and the perils an obnoxious man had submitted her to throughout the years.

Suddenly, she wept. He snuggled her into his arm for a long time, until she was ready and willing to continue her story.

He wished he could wipe out her past with a magic stroke. Though nobody could do that, only time would diminish the horror of the memories.

"What I regret the most was having to abandon you and run away without you knowing why I left. But it was vital for your own safety," she said with a sob, while Fergus held her in his arms and kissed the top of her head.

Notwithstanding the perils, she told him how she disregarded her own safety and came back to Nice three weeks later to search for him, to explain, but Fergus had returned home to England. So, reluctantly, she decided it was for the best to protect him from Alain. She would have to let him go. He would be safe that way.

"You should have told me! When you disappeared, I looked for you for two weeks. There was no trace of you. I thought I had lost you forever," he said, caressing her tenderly.

He craved to take her pain away. His heart tightened at her hurt, at his not knowing of her past, and most of all, at his remorse for thinking the worst of her, while all she had known was suffering. And he wished he could turn back time.

"Oh, Fergus, I couldn't tell you. Alain would've killed you!" she said. She threw her arms around his neck. "I would have never forgiven myself if he had harmed you. As it is, I cannot forgive myself for what Alain did to my poor colleague. He battered him so badly with his fists and knifed him several times. My friend almost died, a miracle he survived, you know. He cut me, too, in the process, as I tried to stop the attack," she sobbed and hesitated for a moment, touching her scar below the shoulder. "All my colleague was doing was giving me a lift home one night, that's all. He is lucky to have recovered. After that, the police caught my ex-boyfriend. They charged him with attempted murder. He is now safely behind bars, in prison, where he deserves to be. He won't harm anyone anymore." She gave a final sob.

"Nobody is going to hurt you again. I promise you. No one! Ever!" he uttered with conviction. He was trying to stay calm for her, not to upset her any more than she already was.

Perhaps she had been right. The tale made his blood boil, and Fergus would have killed the man if he had known. A surge of protectiveness came over him. He must ask Perkins to investigate the background on her ex-boyfriend, on Alain. He needed to know for sure she was safe now.

"Promise me one thing?" he said to her.

"What?"

"You'll hide nothing from me, ever again?"

"Oh, darling?"

"Please," he urged her.

"I promise," she whispered.

He took her into his arms and sealed the pledge with a kiss.

Chapter 11

Belinda was in a state of semi-consciousness, between awakening and sleeping. She floated into this drowsiness for a while. The surrounding noise sounded muffled to her, as if she were in a dream. But she was not dreaming, causing her to jump in her sleep and suddenly awaken with a start. When she opened her eyes, she heard a loud tap at the door. She sat up in bed, flashed around the room, and panicked.

For a split second, in her confused state, she wondered, *where the hell am I?* Then it hit her! It all came crashing back to her. *The damn clinic!* That's where she was, in the bedroom assigned to her several days ago, when she first arrived. The horrid police officer, the one who always got her back up, advised the court it was the best solution for her. If her family wanted her out of prison, she had to stay out of trouble. The judge issued a court order, so she could learn to control her temper, *not get into trouble again,* as they had put it.

Her brother, Fergus, had chosen this place for her, but effectively, she thought of it as a punishment, no more, no less, just as the penitentiary was.

She breathed a heavy sigh, and her hand slid over her face in a jerky action. *Damn!*

For Belinda, it was either the clinic or remain in the dreaded prison. She even spent three dreadful months in jail, witnessing a murder in the midst. She wasn't sure which was worse, a clinic full of discipline, or a penitentiary full of regulations.

What the hell. No difference, it was all the same to her. She loathed them all. Belinda had found herself between a hammer and a sickle. She had no option, the clinic being the lesser of the two evils.

Sweet Jesus! That's what happens when you behave wildly, and your mind wanders in crazy directions. When you do obnoxious things! Like she had done with her last boyfriend and battered his ridiculously expensive Ferrari. Criminal damage was on her record now. Two boyfriends, two fancy cars gone to the dogs. *They deserved it, though.* Why she kept doing that, she didn't know.

God, what am I going to do? She had been sorry to have marred her father's last six months on earth with all the court proceedings and ending up in jail. *Poor Daddy,* she thought with regret. Belinda had made it up in extremis to him two days before his death, fresh out of prison on compassionate leave, holding his hand and reading to him.

She had been the apple of his eye, and he had given her everything she asked. Spoiled her, she had to admit. Her mother died when she was just a baby, so her dad poured all his love into his daughter. Even her older brother had been too gentle with her, and in his own way, sad for his little sister who would never know their mother's devotion. So Fergus had spoiled her too.

That morning she felt miserable. The last conversation with her father flashed through her head. She missed him terribly; she had adored him.

'I wish you were always this lovely, Belinda. You have a good heart,

like Fergus does, but both of you must show it more. Please promise me you won't go crazy when I am gone.'

'Don't talk this way, Daddy, you'll outlive me, I tell you.'

'Promise me you'll find a good man, marry him, and be a perfect wife and wonderful mother. You'll need a family of your own when I am gone. Your brothers will be busy with their own, and I don't want you to be alone.'

'Poppycock! Oh, Daddy, stop talking like this,' she had replied, but he insisted. He had talked on and on about it until she had to promise him. Her father went happily to his grave with her commitment to marry a "good man," to the point of reminding her of her pledge at the reading of his will.

When had he done that? When had he added this to his message for the family? she wondered. Or had he planned it ahead of time? Knowing her father, he had probably done it ahead of time. Her father always had a knack of surprising her somehow.

The recording of her father's address to the family, from beyond the grave, was a revelation to the siblings. Her dad's speech about her promise had even brought Fergus into his plea—as if her big brother didn't have enough surprises and troubles of his own that day— to vouch for her to deliver on her agreement, on her promise to marry "a good man."

Her father had known she always kept her promises to him. The old fog had tricked her into it with his sorrowful look. She seemed safe in that one thing he said, 'find a good man' and there were no good men around she could tell right now. So I am okay for now!

Another loud tap on the door drew her out of her reverie. She closed her eyes. Perhaps she should stay in bed forever. I can do no harm if I don't get up. Thus, she lay back and covered her head with the blankets, trying to suppress the continuous knocking sound at the door. Whoever was hammering on it now, she wished them gone, for them to leave her alone.

But the thumping did not cease; it got louder instead.

"Belinda, get up! You wanted me to wake you up. You are running late for your session!" Erin's voice came through. She recognised her friend's lovely melodious tone.

The charming lady overlooked to mention for your *'anger management sessions...'*

At that exact minute, the woman wasn't pleased, though. As time went on, her tone took on a commanding cadence she was not familiar with.

Belinda met Erin Blake on the first day, soon after her arrival. She had shown her the ropes around the clinic. Erin was in therapy herself, and they had become close in that brief space of time. She had taken Belinda under her wing. The woman was always in the company of Goran Marshall. A handsome guy, not her type, but she couldn't deny he was hot. She would bet her life on it, *Goran is Erin's bodyguard.*

Though no one told her anything, Belinda assumed he was a bodyguard. She'd had a few herself over the years, enabling her to recognise the type, the style, the behaviour. If she had to admit, Goran felt more like Erin's jailer than her bodyguard. The girl wasn't certain what the story was, but Erin must have done something more than ruin a few stupid cars.

Damn and double damn! Today, I am not in the mood.

"You know they hate lateness here. Come on; get up," Erin said, thumping harder.

Belinda reluctantly got up from bed and opened the door.

"Good morning," Erin said, poking her head in with a big smile.

"God, you are so chirpy today. I don't like chirpy people in the morning," Belinda replied. Her companion scoffed, but she went on, "Thank you for waking me up. I should buy myself an alarm clock. It would be easier if we kept our mobile phones in this damn place, though." Phones were not allowed in the clinic.

"Well, I'll leave you to it. You'd better hurry, see you at

lunch. I don't want to be late for my session," her companion said.

"Okay, thank you, Erin!"

***

She made her way to the table. She grinned at Goran with an intake of breath and glanced at the ladies. Erin and Lily had assembled with him in the dining room, as agreed.

"You look done in," he said with a chuckle. He stood for her, as his companions mumbled their hellos.

"Oh, hell, I cannot stand another one of these damn sessions." Belinda was irked, plopped her backside on a chair with a groan, then she propped her head in her hand on the table with a pout.

"Come on, darling, surely it's not that bad?" Lily asked with mirth.

Belinda shook her head and glared at her.

She had met Lily Banks with Erin on her first day, too, and with Goran, the four of them had become inseparable. She had recognised Lily at once, a rather willowy girl with lovely, long auburn hair. Belinda knew who she was.

'Hey? I would have known you anywhere! I saw your movie last year. It was fantastic! I was at your premiere. I attended the launch party after-wards, too,' she had blurted excitedly at the girl on her first day.

'Oh, were you? That night was a bit of a blur to me, I'm afraid, but thank you. Though, I am surprised anyone remembers me now. It seems so long ago! It all sounds like it was in another life,' the young actress replied with a gentle but regretful smile on that first day, her green eyes twinkling at the obvious compliment. She flicked her gorgeous auburn hair back, and her slender figure shuffled childishly.

Lily Banks had risen through the ranks to the spotlight in the film industry three years ago. Her acting roles as the girl next door were much in demand. The public adored her. She was youthful, successful, and admired until notoriety struck. The willowy young woman had fallen in with a dangerous crowd. Drugs, alcohol, and scandal had ensued, until the film studio forced her to take refuge in the clinic to kick the habits. They ordered her to stay away from the limelight until matters settled down.

"It is, though! These damn sessions are a pain. I hate this clinic," Belinda replied, when her thoughts came back to the present.

Her companion smiled with a light pat on her shoulder. "Are you hungry? I am starving. We should get some food before there is nothing left," the young actress said, pinching Goran's arm next to her.

"Ouch!" he cried out, "what did you do that for?" He slapped her hand playfully, and she laughed.

"Come on; I am famished," Lily repeated, pulling him by the arm and pointing at the mouth-watering delicacies. Goran stood up, and the two moved toward the buffet, "Are you coming?" she launched over her shoulders at her companions, still seated.

"We'll wait until the queue is empty," Belinda said, staying at the table. When they were out of earshot, she turned to Erin. "God, Lily has it bad!" she said with a mischievous smile.

"What?" Erin looked puzzled, not knowing what she was talking about.

"Lily's got the hots for Goran!"

"What? Surely not!" Her companion's eyes grew big with a scoff.

"I say the two of them are quite in love. He fancies the pants off her!"

"Really?"

"Come on, Erin, don't tell me you haven't noticed?" Belinda rolled her eyes.

"I guess my mind is on other things and," she smiled, "I can't believe it! They fancy each other? Well, what do you know!"

"Quite so!"

"I guess they suit each other. Young, beautiful, in love with life. Yes, they'll fit in well together," Erin replied in empathy.

"Like you suit Dr. Stewart. You fancy him, I know. I've seen the way you look at him," Belinda said without hesitation, leaning into her with a shoulder bump and a smug smile on her face. She patted her companion's arm.

"Don't be ridiculous! The rules-mongering doctor? Of course not! And I don't look at him," Erin denied vehemently, blinking and pursing her lips.

Her friend smiled and launched her a dubious look. "Well, a rule mongering despot he is. That's certain. I guess you like that sort of thing." Belinda snorted.

"The man is good-looking, but from there to fancying him, that's quite a leap," Erin answered. "I am still mourning my family. These thoughts have no place in my head right now."

"But you fancy him all the same, Erin. You'll make a cute couple. And don't deny it!"

"I most certainly do. Besides, Dr. Stewart runs this clinic as if it were a military garrison."

"Yes, I know. I am tired of this place," Belinda replied with a sigh, "I really am."

As her day progressed, her mood had gotten worse. She wrinkled her nose in a grimace.

"Come on; you have been here a week. I am on my fourth week! You've got at least six months to go in here, remember, so you'd better get used to it," Erin replied.

"Hell! Don't remind me of it, six months. I tell you, I don't know how much longer I'll be able to take this. The session this morning was excruciatingly boring."

"They are supposed to be useful, not fun."

"To think my brother's estate is only an hour away from here. I could be there in no time. There is no one there. My brother is in Oxford, trying to deal with his new wife. He got married last week. I feel sorry for the poor girl, you know, taking him on. God knows if she'll last. My other brothers are abroad, Sebastian and Frederick. Oh, you'll like Frederick, Erin! He'll be your type."

"Frederick? My type? What makes you think that?"

"He goes for women like you, reserved, pretty, languid looking, with a brilliant head on her shoulder."

"If I had a good head on my shoulders, I wouldn't be here. How old is your brother?"

"Twenty-five, and he is a dish. He'll give you a good run for your money. Ditch the rules mongering doctor," Belinda said, laughing, and her pale blue eyes lit up with mischief.

"Sweetie-pie, your sibling is a babe, I am thirty-three."

"So? He'll adore you. He adores fully fleshed women, not silly girls like me. I have never known him to have a girlfriend younger than him, always older by a long shot. Oh, God, there he is, the damn man, Dr. Stewart. I hate this clinic. I won't stand six months in here."

"Darling, time will go fast, and before you know, it is gone."

"I doubt it, Erin. If I have one more session like this morning, I'll die."

"Rubbish!"

"I wish I was at Penningbrooke Hall, away from all this. There is a lovely little pub in the village, and I really fancy a drink. Hey, what do you say? We could get into the boot of a visitor's car and be out of here in no time, and none the wiser until probably tomorrow."

"Don't be a fool. You'll go straight to prison if you were to leave without permission."

"Yes, I'll be breaking the court order. What a palaver! I am not sure I can stay, Erin. I really can't."

"You are under the weather today. Let's walk in the garden after lunch. It'll do you good."

"I am sick of this."

"Well, well, well… I am sure you'll cheer up now. Look who's coming? Your gorgeous police officer." The table faced the big window overlooking the front of the house. A man was riding up on his motorbike, a huge, vintage Harley Davidson.

"Inspector Wendell! Bloody hell, that's all I need today. What the devil does he want now?"

"If you ask me, the man finds all sort of excuses to interview you, to come here. You'd think an inspector had better matters to attend to."

"It is a murder enquiry, you know. I was a witness to it when I was in prison."

"Still, in a week, he's been here three times. I had a brief chat with him the other day, while he was waiting for you. He is a nice guy. I think he is a good man. You could do much worse, so give the man a chance," Erin said, wriggling her eyebrows.

Belinda's body shivered violently. She blanched as Erin's words unsettled her.

'*He is a good man.*' Her words kept ringing in her ears. Belinda's promise to her father came to mind. She believed in these little signs, and it made her suddenly dizzy. She gulped an intake of breath to calm herself. "Oh, stop that nonsense, I hate the man. Remember, he is the one who sent me to prison. He insisted with the judge to issue me with a court order when Dad tried to get me out, for me to be in here. The weasel!" She spat, once she had recovered her senses, and scowled.

"He wants to keep you out of trouble. You cannot deny the man is charming and attractive, though. He looks like a model, not a policeman. He asked me to look after you while you are in here if you must know. Look at the big motorbike under him," Erin said, and Belinda laughed, but it turned into a nervous laugh.

But not even Wendell could restore her mood that day. When she decided something, she seldom looked too deeply into the consequences.

Chapter 12

They spent the next four days in bed, sampling the spellbinding delights of each other's bodies. Only hunger caused them to resurface from the room. Sometimes, they even had a dinner tray in the bed. Fergus cancelled all of his appointments for the week and dedicated himself to her.

When the weather was glorious, between lovemaking interludes, they stayed out on the lawn, lying next to each other in silence. They held hands, just delighted to be together. One afternoon, they went for a drive in the Cotswolds countryside and had a picnic. Like young lovers, the enchanting surroundings gave a magic sparkle to the dreamy outing as they enjoyed themselves. They visited Belinda for a couple of hours at the clinic, too. These were blissful days for them.

Marguerite was buoyant that she had told him about Alain, the reason she had left him abruptly six years ago. She felt liberated, finally free from her past, and optimistic. Perhaps now they could have a future.

Fergus regretted not looking after her. He went through guilt and remorse about her suffering. He promised himself he'd make it up to her. He had the rest of his life to make her joyful again. From then on, he wished only for her happiness and to protect her with his life. Nothing else mattered.

They hadn't bridged the subject of the contract ending in eighteen months and what they would do about it. Nor had they discussed whether the marriage had suddenly become a real one, though, it felt so genuine to them as they filled in the gaps of the past. They didn't want to rock the boat about this niggling and disturbing thought. The happy days were too precious to unsettle them.

It had taken no time for the emotions they had harboured long ago to come to the surface again. These feelings erupted in their hearts without warning. They found themselves more in love each day as they rediscovered the joy and passion of being together again.

He was conscious they had not had a proper honeymoon, either, but she laughed.

"All I need is you, Fergus. I don't care where I am. Your home is just as wonderful as any place."

"You mean this mausoleum?" he said with a playful grin, lifting his eyebrows.

"Mausoleum?"

"That's what you called my house the night you were drunk."

"I did not say that! And I was not drunk, perhaps, a little tipsy," she retorted, turning crimson.

"You did. And you were."

"You do realise there are parts of this house that call for urgent repairs, don't you?" she suggested, drawing him elsewhere in the conversation. She wished him to forget the word she used for his home.

"Yes, I know. You can work on this now, your ladyship, your duty, as my countess. What the hell have I married you for, then? One less thing for me to worry about," he said with humour in his eyes.

"Fine, I'll do it. You'll see, faster and cheaper than you." It thrilled her he would trust her with it.

"Not a competition, darling. But I'll hold you to it. In time, you can change this mausoleum to your liking and make the house homely for us," he replied in all seriousness, but he couldn't hide a hint of a tender smile. She kissed him longingly.

They were growing familiar with one another again. Even the banter was turning easy. Their love was restored, flying high in their hearts like a banner.

Though Fergus had an insidious, niggling thought throughout the past few days. It grew larger by the day. It worried him. He should have said something sooner, but he couldn't bring himself to it. While his wife filled in the gaps of her past for him, he had not mentioned everything to Marguerite. He'd omitted a major detail out of his life. It felt awkward to approach the subject a week after the wedding, when they had already filled in gaps of their lives up to now. But he must, and the sooner, the better. He had let the days pass by and now… *damn!*

Besides, Lucy didn't know yet. He had to break the news of his nuptials to her first, before telling his wife. He realised it would bring him trouble with Marguerite. He cursed silently. Who could anticipate how Lucy would react? He couldn't help it. He would have to solve the situation before telling Marguerite. But first things first; he had to tell Lucy he had wed, ease her into it.

Fergus took that moment to address the subject. "I must go to my estate in Gloucestershire, to Penningbrooke Hall. I have urgent business I must attend to. It's only for three days," he blurted, trying to avoid her eyes. She looked at him, but he placed a kiss on her forehead.

"I'll come with you," Marguerite replied without hesitation, not even flinching.

"No, my love. I'd rather you stay here; you'll distract me from my work."

"I'll do no such thing."

"You can look into the repairs for the house while I am gone. You mentioned these were urgent. I promise, I'll take you to Penningbrooke next time."

"Oh, Fergus, three days? No, impossible. I'll miss you awfully. I'll come with you." She got up from bed, gave him a deep scowl, and stomped a foot on the floor.

"And I'll miss you, too, but I can help it. I'll be too busy around the estate."

"I don't care. I could make phone calls to the various tradesman from there. Do things online, and—" she went on, trying to convince him.

"No! You stay in Oxford and get started here. Three days will fly by. Besides, it'll give your pussy a rest; it *is* a little sore." He got up, too, and whispered the last sentence, leaning into her ear in a naughty tone.

She giggled and became scarlet from head to toe. She was a determined lady, and she would not desist. "Oh, darling." she pouted, "I'll be as quiet as a mouse, I promise. I won't bother you. Please, can I come?" Her face was in a grimace.

"Don't be such a baby. Enjoy a night out with Mollie and Kathryn while I am gone. Tell them how I don't drive you to tears anymore and how your pussy is sore with love." He wriggled his eyebrows to her. "But not getting drunk this time." He chuckled.

"I wasn't drunk! And I want to come with you." She would not give up and frowned at him.

"No, I said. You start on the house repairs, so when I am back, you can show me details of builders, estimates, and the rest. Trust me, these things take a lot of time, and you won't even realise I am gone."

"Oh, Fergus, how can you say that? The bed will be empty without you."

"I know, sweet lips," he added in a velvety singsong. He grabbed her by the waist, drew her to him, and kissed her ravenously. Then, he slowly dragged her back to bed, as they slumped on it, without breaking the kiss.

"When are you going?" she asked, as they stopped the kissing.

"Tomorrow."

"Tomorrow?" she yelped and was about to get out of bed again, but he stopped her, pulling her back to him. "Oh, Fergus, you are a naughty man, telling me this at such short notice and taking advantage while I am in bed with you. I can't believe it," she said in a scowl.

"Hey, hey, no scowling. You don't wish to ruin our last night together for three days, do you?"

"No, but you—" she tried. He didn't let her finish and kissed her. One kiss led to another. Things invariably went on further and they made love again.

She woke up early the next morning. Fergus was ready to leave. She accompanied him to the front door of the house and put her arms around his neck, clinging to him.

"God, I'll miss you so much. Please take me with you?"

"Darling, we've been through this five times already," Fergus said gently, caressing her face with his knuckles, and then putting a rebellious lock of her hair behind her ear. He held her with his arms around her waist, then nuzzled her neck.

"Ooh…"

"I'll be back before you know it," he said and nipped her bottom lip gently with his teeth. He kissed her plump, sweet lips in a delicious languorous kiss. Then, he was gone.

She stood there, watching the car go up the long drive out of the house until it disappeared from view.

The next two days were busy for Marguerite. She stayed in Oxford as her husband wished. She scheduled appointments with tradespeople to inspect the repairs for the house and give their opinions on what was needed. Bancroft provided her with a list, and she was glad for the help. It wasn't easy to select the person for the right project, as she soon discovered.

It would have been the butler's job otherwise, but the estimates for the repairs would sit on his lordship's desk for weeks, as he was always busy. So her husband had given his blessing for her to speed up the proceedings. She reckoned she would be hectic well beyond Fergus's return and cracked on diligently with it, but she missed her man terribly.

Marguerite sent to his mobile phone a saucy photo of herself in the bath, but it made her nervous when there was no reply to it for hours. She wondered if she had upset him. She heard Bancroft mention the mobile phone coverage on the farmlands was sketchy, though. The response she eventually got from Fergus late that evening, what he wanted to do to her in that bath, caused her to laugh and blush with joy.

On the afternoon of the second day, an appeal came through on the telephone.

"The doctor requires his lordship on the phone, madam. It is the clinic where Lady Belinda is staying. He says it is urgent. Would you take it?"

"Sure," she said. She took the call and learned that her young sister-in-law had disappeared from the place with no one's permission.

"I am sorry, Marguerite, but Belinda is in violation of her court order by leaving the premises," Dr. Stewart stated. "I am worried about it. She must come back. By law, I am required to inform the court. She will be arrested and marched back to prison if she doesn't return promptly. The judge won't like it."

"Oh, dear God!" she said. She had met Dr. Stewart at the clinic when she visited Belinda with Fergus one afternoon.

"A patient informed me she wanted to reach Fergus' country house. I'm uncertain if this is the case..." he said over the phone.

The likelihood, Marguerite thought, *Belinda estimated with Fergus in Oxford entertained with his new bride, she would be safe to run to Penningbrooke without raising the alarm or her brother's wrath, at least for the night. Silly girl!* She had no time to lose. Marguerite had to go to the estate.

"When did she disappear?"

"We believe half an hour ago, or more. We searched for her, but she's gone."

"Good Lord!"

"I am sorry to bother you with this. I tried to call Fergus' mobile, but there is no answer. Otherwise, I would have told him."

"Please do not worry. I am glad you did."

"I can pretend we won't notice Belinda's absence until tomorrow morning, but if she's not back by then, I must inform the court. I am so sorry. I don't want to do it. But I'll have no choice," Dr. Stewart replied.

"Leave it with me. Don't trouble yourself. She'll be back," Marguerite affirmed with a confidence she didn't feel. "Bancroft," she called out, once she ended the call, "would you be so kind as to get a car ready for me. I am traveling to the estate."

"But my lady, you can't, his lordship stated—"

"Bancroft, my husband will go mad when he learns Belinda has left the damn place. She is on her way to Penningbrooke. She must return to the clinic by tomorrow. If not, she'll end up in prison again. If I am there when she gets to the estate, perhaps I can convince her to go back voluntarily."

"But, my lady, his lordship said you are to be here and—"

"My dear man, you have helped me all the way since I married Fergus over ten days ago, and I am very grateful to you. Don't fail me now. I'll go there with or without your help. Please, get me a car and directions to the estate."

"Yes, of course, Lady Buckley. The driver will take you," the butler replied reluctantly, with resignation in his voice.

"Oh, I can drive myself."

"Let Jones drive you, please. His lordship would insist on that if he were here," he replied. He wanted to add, '*otherwise, I'll be in trouble,*' but he reckoned he would be in the doghouse anyway for letting her go to Penningbrooke.

"Fine. But don't inform Fergus on anything yet. There is no point in upsetting him now. I'll tell him when I get there."

"Yes, of course, madam. As you wish," he concluded.

Cora, the maid, helped Marguerite pack and she was gone within twenty minutes.

Bancroft seemed uncomfortable, but he owed his loyalty to Fergus. Though he liked his new mistress much, he felt guilty about betraying his promise to her, but he'd had no choice.

He couldn't let her descend unannounced on Penningbrooke with Lucy there. Fergus had to know.

Chapter 13

Meanwhile, in Baumettes, a massive prison in the 9th arrondissement on the outskirts of Marseilles, in the South of France; a young man returned to his detention cell. As he entered the place, he forcibly launched a newspaper onto the table at the centre of the cramped up room. He missed. The paper flung into his cell-mate instead, striking his arm, and it dropped to the ground.

Alain Basset looked up with a start. He was sitting at the table finishing his crossword when the paper struck him. It took him out of his reverie with a bang. As it fell, the pages of the newspaper scattered on the floor. He was losing patience with his new young roommate. He glared at the fellow.

The Englishman, as they called him in the slammer, though his roommate's name was Ross, had recently received a prison sentence to serve nine months for drug possession, and to his misfortune, Alain thought, they now shared the cell.

Alain's old placid mate, with whom he had shared the unit for the past three years, had been released. To his further calamity, as if a jail punishment was not enough, this young untidy, mad youth, The Englishman, had taken his place.

The Frenchman released an oath under his breath.

He was the messiest person Alain had ever come across in his life, and in a small cell, it was the worst quality possible to him. The Englishman was chatty, friendly, and not even prison dimmed his sociable spirit, his chirpy outlook. It was so annoying to a loner, to a silent, guarded man like Alain.

"Sorry, bro," the young chap said. "My mother came to visit this morning, poor thing. She travelled all the way from home."

"England?" Alain asked, trying to keep his calm so not to throttle his cellmate.

"Cried buckets, the wretched thing. I told her not to worry, that I am fine, but no use, poor mother. I tried to encourage her. I explained nine months will soon pass, but it didn't work. I sat there watched her weep for an hour."

An annoying young man! Alain didn't understand all what he said in his fluid English, but it irritated him. He put up with the young fellow. The Englishman was a diversion to his constant thought, to that one notion that would never leave Alain alone. *Marguerite is somewhere out there. Without me!* He harboured one hope in his heart, that someday they would reunite. This hope kept Alain sane and focused.

He wasn't sure when he would get out of the prison. His sentence for almost killing Marguerite's colleague and knifing her had been eight years, of which he had already served three. He had been lucky. He could have gotten twenty instead. His lawyer played the diminished capacity card at the tribunal, feigning momentary insanity.

He had been contrite and penitent at the trial, voicing his remorse in public. This helped his cause, and the judge had been lenient. But the court issued him with a ban never to land near Marguerite again. *Rubbish!* It was of no consequence to him. All Alain had to do was bide his time and be patient. He would find her again. He always did.

"Paper, floor, clean!" he cried out to Ross in his pidgin English instead, annoyed at the mess. He struggled to make the youth comprehend he must collect the newspaper from the floor. So he used his hands vigorously with rudimentary help of sign language.

"In a minute! I just need a rest; my mother stressed me out," the young chap retorted.

Ten minutes later, the soft snores coming from the young man in his bunk bed told Alain he had no intention to tidy up the scattered newspaper pages. He wasn't in a hurry, anyway, the mess could be in situ for ages.

Alain muttered an oath under his breath. He launched his hands up in the air in exasperation, kneeled, and began gathering the pages. As he collected them, he realised they were not in French, the reason they had allowed it in; it was an English newspaper.

He glanced at the front page of The Oxford Mail. It was dated almost two weeks ago.

Alain's English language was poor. He could get by with words here and there. It was improving with the endless chatter of his cellmate in his mother tongue. But reading a newspaper was another matter altogether, so he ignored it. But he folded the pages, one by one in order, by page number, without paying attention to the content. He was a meticulous man. As he did so, a picture on the third page of the newspaper leapt at him. It took his breath away. His head leaned into the paper as his lips parted and his eyes widened in disbelief. A photograph of her. Marguerite!

Even though she looked a little different, it was her, no doubt about it. His heartbeat rose to the nines, the useless organ almost leaping out of his chest. His backside crushed to the floor, he become still as a rock, and he stared at her for some time. At last, he traced the photo with his fingers, gingerly, and then a scowl marred his face.

He wasn't certain what the caption said. The words "marriage" and her picture in a white dress needed no explanation, though. It was the photograph of Marguerite's wedding day.

In a sudden fit of temper, Alain yanked The Englishman out of his top bunk bed. He held him by the scruff of the neck and crashed him on the floor. He dragged him up and plopped him hard into a chair with the newspaper in front of him.

He dazed the young fellow at first, but he protested, "What's wrong with you, man?"

"Read! Tell me!" Alain yelled. He pointed at the newspaper on the table, at the specific article.

"What the fuck! I was sleeping!" Ross tried to get up, but Alain crashed him back onto the chair.

"Now, read!"

The Englishman stared at him. The Frenchman had never been openly friendly toward him since he joined his detention cell, but he was patient and condescending. Therefore, the glare of fire and the contorted expression in the Frenchman's face scared him.

Ross scanned the article, but he made him read it three times. When Alain still understood only half of it and questioned him, the young man explained. Marguerite Morel had married an earl and was now living in England with her husband.

Oh, Alain had understood that well enough! But he wanted to know more about this earl.

"Do you know this woman? The earl? Oxford is my hometown," Ross asked, astonished the Frenchman had an interest in the Earl of Buckley.

"No!" Alain said flatly. He lied.

"Then why do you care?" Ross asked, baffled.

"Curiosity."

"Umm…"

After that day, Alain's attitude toward Ross changed. He was polite and friendly with The Englishman. He urged the youth to teach him English, about Oxford, and about England. He became a model prisoner and was nice to anyone around him. He became a "yes" man to the prison authorities, subservient to them and all their requests.

His goal in mind, an early release on parole, and Marguerite.

He knew where she was now!

Chapter 14

The moment Marguerite left the house in Oxford, the butler tried Fergus' mobile phone. There was no connection. Then, Bancroft called the landline at Penningbrooke Hall, but he was told the young lord was out. So he spoke to Mrs. Briggs. He was getting agitated.

Fergus had instructed him that under no circumstances should his wife go to the estate, and he had ordered him to keep an eye on her. Bancroft knew the reason, too. The issue with Belinda changed the priorities, but Fergus would go mad whichever way he looked at it. First, his sister's escapade would incense him. Belinda was defying prison again. Second, his heavenly wife would turn up unannounced if he didn't speak to him soon and warn him. Third, the earl would have some explaining to do, and he suspected the young man was not quite ready for it. This was a catastrophe! So, the butler tried his phone several times without success.

He went in the kitchen for a cup of tea.

"What is it, Bancroft?" Ethel, the cook, asked him. The fellow was hot and bothered. He related his problem to the elderly woman.

"Oh, dear me," she said in sympathy, "well, let me put it this way. I'm glad I'm here and not there when the master finds out."

"Poor Mrs. Briggs is at Penningbrooke. Oh calamity, I told her to brace herself for fireworks."

"Mrs. Briggs, glad I've got you. I've tried to call my husband, but he's not picking up. Is he there?" Marguerite asked while admiring the landscape on the road. She had phoned the landline on the estate.

"He's doing the rounds on the estate, seeing his tenants. He's not back yet. The coverage for mobile phones isn't great out there. Do I need to tell him anything?"

"Belinda is coming to the house. Is she there yet?" she asked. Mrs. Briggs was already aware, as Bancroft had told her, but she feigned ignorance.

"Really? Oh, no. She isn't."

"I'm on my way to the estate, too. If she arrives before me, will you keep her away from Fergus until I get there? Otherwise, tempers will fly." Marguerite explained the problem to the woman with heavy sighs in between.

"I understand, madam, I'll try."

"Good, thank you. Oh, Mrs. Briggs, I'll need a room, too. Fergus is busy and I don't want to disturb him."

"Yes, of course. Leave it with me. You'll have the prettiest." After Bancroft's call, the housekeeper had already started the preparations for the rooms for both the ladies on their way, though she suspected Fergus wouldn't let his bride sleep anywhere that didn't include him.

The young man likes his room on the estate, so my preparation for his wife's may not be needed after all, she mused with a short laugh.

Fergus liked to have Bancroft with him whether he was in Oxford, at Penningbrooke, or anywhere in England. He had grown up with the man and trusted him implicitly.

This time, Fergus had left Marguerite alone in the house in town, so he decided she would be safer in his old butler's care. So he took Mrs. Briggs with him to the estate instead. The housekeeper was most efficient, too, and in the family for twenty years but the old fellow was like a second father to him. So he had made an exception for Marguerite.

That afternoon, Fergus visited his farmlands. He tried to see everybody when he was out there. He was out calling on the rest of his tenants, like he had done the day before. The problem was in open farmland, his mobile phone connection was not great, practically zero. So he went on his rounds, blissfully unaware of what was happening.

He was glad, the previous day, on his arrival at Penningbrooke, he had approached the subject with Lucy. He explained about his marriage and his new wife, a difficult discussion at the best of times. But he had managed it, and he would return to the conversation one more time. He wondered how she was settling with the idea.

They'll have to meet, and probably soon.

He had also sorted the other issue this morning. Another difficult conversation, this one even more thorny. He had given closure to his past women, but he had the feeling that one or two might not take to it too kindly.

Jesus, it could all blow up in his face. Thus, he was glad he had gone to the estate alone.

The car stopped, and Jones shifted to her in the back seat.

"Perhaps, madam wishes a peek at the estate before we get to it. There is a magnificent view up here. You can see it all well," the driver stated, pointing at the window.

Marguerite turned to look out. "The house?" she said. She peered about. The low sun was in her eyes, so she squinted a few times.

"Yes, it's easier if you stand outside for a full view." Jones came out of the car and opened the door for her.

Marguerite stepped out. She stood on the road, on the high ground, looking down at the gently sloping hill, where at the bottom, the house nestled. She raised her hand to cover her eyes from the setting sun. Her jaw dropped when she had an unobstructed view of Penningbrooke Hall. She let out a low whimper, overwhelmed. She stared at it, spellbound. She glanced at Jones with questioning eyes, big and round in astonishment, then turned to the sight again.

The elegant residence was a wide, stately home, tall and impressive in a mellow limestone build, the colour of honey. It was gleaming in all its splendour under the setting sun, H-shaped and striking, surrounded by rolling farmlands as far as the eye could see. It was a magnificent house.

"A branch of the family built the original house in the late 1570s, rich merchants as they were then, they came from Scotland. Sir Ludlow Waltham inherited Penningbrooke Hall in 1588. He became the first Earl of Buckley two years later," Jones continued.

She turned to him, blinking rapidly, astonished, struggling to play it cool, then back to the view, mesmerised.

"It's a lavish house, my lady, with staterooms, several drawing rooms, a grand central hall, saloons, a chapel, and the list goes on," Jones explained with a smile. She gawked, too flabbergasted to utter a word, but he went on. "So much to see. The family are great collectors of paintings, books, and ceramics. It has a massive library with thousands of books, with valuable manuscripts and first editions, collected over the past four hundred and fifty years by successive generations of the Waltham family."

"Well, I never! It's s-splendid. How many b-bedrooms does it have?" Marguerite stammered, not knowing exactly what else to say. *Such a silly question!* She stood still like a statue, enchanted at the sight, her bosom heaving with emotion.

The driver smiled. "I don't know, my lady. Not even Bancroft knows, there are so many. But I am sure it could fit an army's regiment comfortably."

"Jesus, it's so grand!"

"It has a gallery of priceless landscape paintings and portraits of kings and queens, from James the First, to Queen Victoria, to more recent royals. Not to mention the family ancestors' portraits through the centuries."

She threw her head back. A nervous snort escaped her. She'd always known Fergus was wealthy, even when she first met him all those years ago. His elegant and sophisticated bearing was unmistakable, then marrying him confirmed it. But this… this was something else.

She'd seen nothing like this before.

Marguerite had once been to the Palace of Versailles as a youth on a school trip, and she had marveled in awe at the place. Who would have thought, years later, she would be awestruck at her own husband's estate. Though smaller, it came pretty close to the opulence of the Sun King's domain. She even sensed, when Fergus got something into his head, he could be just as autocratic as Louis XIV of France, too. No doubt about it, and with a residence to match. She was dumbstruck, trying to take everything in. Her eyes saw, but her mind could not compute the scale of the grandeur.

"Look at the grounds," she whispered in admiration.

"The gardens are large, with over two hundred acres in formal gardens, pleasure grounds, and lakes. So many places to wander along and pause, to enjoy. The bluebells and marigolds are in full bloom now. If you stroll down to the lake, the walk is stunning, with the grounds carpeted in blue and orange. There is a statue walk and a maze, too. The children loved to lose themselves in there when they were young."

"A maze! Oh, sweet heaven, I can't believe it!"

"There are 1200 acres of woodlands, too, Buckley, quite extensive, where deer and antelope roam free. If you see, to the left of the estate, they are visible. Can you see the dense woodlands?"

"Aha!"

"Over and beyond, acres and acres of farmlands surround the estate and the woodlands, which his lordship gives out to tenancy. He has a great relationship with his tenants. They all love him, as he is quite fair with them."

"My God! It is so big!" She shook her head and put her hand on her heart. It was beating so fast with emotion.

"Indeed."

"This is surreal. This is my husband's home?" she muttered under her breath to herself.

"And yours, my lady. You are his countess, now!" the driver said.

She turned to him and her eyes glistened. Her poverty-stricken childhood suddenly flashed in her mind. A tear fell on her cheek. She wiped it with her hand. She wished her mother could see this now, and she could partake of her happiness. Above all, she wished her mother knew she was safe now.

She inhaled. Her eyes swiped all over the place in reverence and awe until she recovered. "Thank you, Jones, it's a stunning view. So kind of you to stop here for me. We must go," she urged reluctantly. If she wasn't pressed for time, she would have stood there for the entire afternoon staring at the historic house. It was mesmerising. As it was, Belinda's issue returned to her mind, and she stepped into the car.

Thirty minutes later, Jones parked in front of the house.

The housekeeper came through the main entrance, down the stone steps to greet her. A valet swiftly picked up her bags from the back of the car and disappeared inside the house.

"Hello, Mrs. Briggs, this is marvelous," she blurted like a blabbering teenage, darting her eyes around the facade of the place.

"Welcome, my lady. I'm certain your husband will want to do formal introductions to staff—"

"Is he home?"

"No, not yet. Come in, have some tea, a rest and a bath. I'll call you when his lordship returns."

Marguerite entered the grand marble hall. The large central entrance of the house was, in her opinion, big enough to host a banquet on its own. It was spectacular in paneled oak and chequered black-and-white marble flooring. The grand chandelier, hanging low from the high ceiling, came down, full of sparkling teardrop-shaped crystals twinkling like diamonds.

She looked mesmerised, as if she were in Aladdin's cave. She walked through a sequence of rooms, which only increased her awe for the place. Mrs. Briggs gave her an informal introduction to several members of staff, too.

Fergus finally connected on his mobile phone and read his messages while he was in a farmhouse that had wi-fi, while taking a well-deserved cup of tea from the farmer's wife.

Bancroft had tried to phone him several times, which concerned him. So, he excused himself from his tenant and went outside to make the call. Alas, he had good reason to be worried, and he was not to enjoy his cup of tea.

The butler gave him the bad news. The issue with his sister

hit him first, and the fact his bride was en route to Penning-brooke infuriated him, too. If she was not already there…

Fergus flew into a rage at Belinda's problem. There was nothing the man could have done in the event, though his request about Marguerite was clear. *'Under no circumstance is my wife to come to the estate,'* Fergus had commanded. He knew she was not good at following orders. He had suspected she might follow him there, as a surprise.

As it was, he understood the issue with Belinda had taken precedence. The butler could do nothing about it. Still, Fergus was not a cheerful man. *I'll have a lot of explaining to do.*

Then, he phoned the estate. "Mrs. Briggs, my sister and my wife are about to come—"

"Your wife is here, my lord!"

"Damn!" He muttered several oaths under his breath. "What is she doing?" he asked once he recovered.

"She is in her room, taking a bath."

"Which room have you given her?"

"The countess' room."

"Good, and, Briggs, please keep Lucy away from Marguerite until I get home."

Marguerite had tea in the large drawing room on the first floor, feeling out of place, but the kindness of the staff soon made her comfortable. Then she went upstairs for a bath. She was hoping for Fergus to come home soon.

She was in her wonderful bedroom on the second floor, the room made out as if for a queen. It was so outlandish and divine. Briggs had said every item of furniture, from the bed to the dressing table and everything in between, was a precious antique. A delicate dusk rose blossom in damask covered the walls, while the canopy bed lashed in opulent green silk. It was an extravagant and elegant room. His massive house in Oxford was grand, but this was like nothing she had seen. She had tears in her eyes, emotion getting hold of her.

But she didn't allow her surroundings to cloud her mind for long and kept her focus. She worried about Belinda. She had asked Mrs. Briggs to warn her the moment either Fergus or his sister arrived. Marguerite feared what her husband would do. Something told her she would see his temper flare. He would not be a cheerful man.

A housemaid was helping her dry her long hair at the dressing table after her bath.

"Thank you, I can take it from here," she said to the maid with a smile. She wasn't used to people fussing over her, even with the best of intentions. She needed a few minutes alone to gather her thoughts.

"Very good, my lady. I left your dress for this evening on the bed; accessories are ready too," the housemaid replied.

She thanked the young girl again, but as soon as the maid left, Marguerite fretted. Her sister-in-law had left the clinic hours ago, and there was still no sign of her. The clinic was closer to Penningbrooke than Oxford. So according to her timetable, Belinda should have turned up at the house hours ago. *Where the hell is she?* She wrung her hands together, anxiety building up. Perhaps she had changed her mind, gone someplace else. *God, it doesn't bear thinking about it!*

The young woman had no phone. She'd left it behind—the doctor didn't allow phones on the premises, so hers was still locked up in Dr. Stewart's office. Therefore, the girl was unreachable. Marguerite hoped the estate was still Belinda's destination. She speculated what to do when there was a tap on the door.

"Come in," she said, turning to it. The housemaid returned with a tray.

"Mrs. Briggs thought you may want some more tea, my lady. I brought extra cups in case Miss Belinda or his lordship arrive."

"That's so thoughtful, thank you. I'll help myself," she replied with a nod of the head.

The girl placed the tray on the low table by the settee. "Do you need me to help you dress, my lady?"

"No, thank you, I am fine," she said. The maid nodded and left.

Marguerite was about to do her usual chignon when she recalled Fergus' instructions about her hair. She smiled, smoothing her long locks with her hand. She was going to humour him tonight, let her natural ringlets loose about her, fashionably.

She dressed up, choosing a flattering silk, red wrap dress. It featured her small waist, highlighted her voluptuous bust, and framed her body elegantly. High stiletto shoes completed the ensemble. She looked divine, simple, sexy, and refined! She had not seen her husband for two days… she wanted to look her best for him. Besides, she desired something nice for this sumptuous house. Marguerite was glad she had followed her instinct in selecting that particular dress.

She proceeded to the green damask settee at the foot of her bed and poured herself a cup of tea. As she was preparing this, the door opened. She hadn't heard a tap on it, but there was none. She turned to it.

A child poked her head through the small opening of the door and darted her eyes around the room, then landed them on her.

"Hello!" Marguerite said to her with an inviting smile.

"Hello," the little girl mumbled back with a shy grin, turning red. She was now standing in the doorframe, shuffling on her feet. Her eyes shifted from Marguerite to the tray on the low table.

"Come in; would you like some tea and biscuits?" she asked the young one.

The child was sweet, with a rosy complexion, dressed in jeans, a pink sweater and pink Wellington boots.

"Yes," she replied and nodded but didn't move.

"Come in; I'll pour you a cup of tea. Sit with me," Marguerite said, patting the settee.

The girl came in and plopped herself down next to her.

"You have this cup. I have not touched it yet. Careful, it might still be hot," Marguerite said, looking at her. "And who might you be?" she went on, raising her eyebrows questioningly.

"Lucy," she replied, "and what's your name?"

"My name is Marguerite. Pleased to meet you, Lucy," she said sweetly. "Are you lost, darling?" She caressed the girl's hair and gave her the most charming smile she possessed. In such an enormous house, it would be easy to wander.

"No," the girl retorted, shaking her head and glancing at the biscuits.

Marguerite thought there was something familiar about her. She picked up the plate of biscuits, offering them to the girl.

"So, who are you then?" she asked again, while the child picked up a biscuit from the plate and munched on it.

"Lucy, I told you," she replied with her mouth full.

"Oh, yes, you did. What I mean is what are you doing up here?" Marguerite asked, pouring herself a cup of tea.

The girl shrugged her shoulders and took a little sip of tea. A charming child, but she couldn't guess her age.

The curious daughter of one of the staff, thought Marguerite with a smile.

"How old are you, Lucy?"

"Almost six."

"How lovely! You look big for your age." She moved back

a strand of hair from the girl's face. "What's your mommy's name?"

"Natasha."

"Does she work here?" Marguerite asked, sipping her tea.

"No," the girl replied with a shake of her head while pieces of biscuits landed on her pink sweater. Marguerite brushed the crumbs from the child's sweater with a grin.

"Is she on the estate?"

"No."

"Where is she, then?"

"Mommy is dead."

"Oh, I am so sorry, sweetie," Marguerite murmured and put an arm around the child's shoulders, cuddling her. She felt guilty for having mentioned it unwittingly to the poor creature. So she held the girl close, caressing her gently. "I didn't know."

"Sometimes, I live with Granny. But Daddy and Olivia look after me, too," the girl said.

"Oh, I see. On the estate?" she asked, and the girl nodded.

"But I don't remember my mom."

"Oh, pumpkin, I am sure your dad has photos of your mommy, doesn't he?" She hugged her, caressing her face.

"Yes, but I have a new mommy now."

"Have you? That's wonderful."

"Aha!"

"I am sure, honey, she'll be an amazing new mother for you."

"Yes, Daddy said so."

"You'll like her; you'll see."

"I like you."

"Thank you, darling," Marguerite mumbled and paused for an instant, not knowing what to say.

"You are my mommy," Lucy went on with a proud smile.

"Oh, sweetie…" Marguerite's heart tightened for the

charming child. She felt flattered, though. *Poor Lucy,* she thought, and she wished she could find a mother for her. Her heartstrings pulled for the child.

She was about to explain to Lucy, *'I am not your mother, darling,'* but the door opened before she could speak. Fergus stood there, tall, straight as a pillar, and he gulped.

For an instant, Marguerite grasped the look of horror on his face.

Does he know about Belinda already? was her first thought. Though he did, that was not the reason he was horrified.

"Daddy!" The child's screams of joy reverberated in the room. She jumped off the settee and dashed to him, hurling herself into his arms.

He scooped her up and threw a small smile at Marguerite, while she looked at him like he had suddenly sprung two heads.

"Hello, princess!" Fergus said to the girl.

"Marguerite and I were having tea, Daddy."

"Were you, darling?" Fergus asked in a sweet, singsong voice, gently caressing the girl's face, then tickling her tummy. Rashes of raucous, high-pitched laughter erupted from his daughter's mouth.

The unfamiliar man standing in front of her did not resemble the Fergus Marguerite knew. This was a gentle and loving father. It was easy to pick the resemblance now, the reason the child had looked familiar to her. The russet hues in her dark hair, the pale blue eyes, the aristocratic cheekbones.

Yes, she's his daughter all right!

"Can Daddy have some tea, too, Marguerite?"

"Sure," she mumbled, barely able to breathe. She poured tea in a cup, her hands trembling, and she spilled some on the tray. But she was happy to have something to do, avoiding his gaze. She realised his scrutiny was on her.

"Come, Daddy, sit with us?" The child wrestled him until

he put her down on her feet again. She took his hand, pulling him toward the settee to Marguerite. "Sit, Daddy!"

He obeyed. Fergus darted a glance at his wife, who pretending to be busy with the tea, staring at the cup instead, but she couldn't avoid a blush.

Lucy stood in front of them. She grabbed a hand from each, contented. All the while, his eyes skimmed between the child and Marguerite.

At times, she was sure Fergus deserved the moniker of the Dark Lord. If there was an occasion Marguerite justified it, this was it! *He should have told me.* But why had nobody mentioned the child? Told her about Lucy? Not a word about his daughter from anybody, not before or after the marriage. *Was Lucy a secret?* Not even his dad had pointed out a thing to her!

A thought flashed to a fleeting conversation with his father. *'He needs a strong lady to push him on the right path again, and an heir. I need an excellent woman for him, a loving one. He must have children… from the proper side of the blanket. Not sire them as if…"* She remembered the old earl saying something on those lines, but he soon moved his conversation to the proposal instead.

Marguerite had been so overwhelmed with the proposal to marry Fergus, she hadn't grasped what his father had insinuated. Perhaps he tried to tell her. Did he change his mind? Did he think it would put her off and held her back? *You stupid girl!* she told herself.

His siblings had said nothing to her, his staff even less, and his friends, zilch! It was obvious. The blackguard must have given them all the "silence" order on the subject. Who would have dared Fergus's wrath?

The girls would have told her if they knew, though, she

was sure. Oh, he was the infamous Dark Lord indeed! *Silly woman! No wonder he didn't want me to come to the estate. Wicked man, what a blow!* He bedded her for ten days, professed his passion to her, and mentioned nothing about his daughter. *The damn man!*

Her lips were in a thin line. She kept her eyes from him, not daring to show the fury rising in her. Her scowl deepened as her thoughts were whooshing around her head. *Does he love me at all? Was it all a lie?*

But by the anxious expression on his face, she was running away with herself. He loved her, in his own contorted fashion; he did. She knew. But he had to do things in his own way. God only knew why Fergus decided not to tell her. *Moron!*

She shook herself, ignoring his scrutiny on her. Those pale blue eyes, with an uneasy gaze on her, had been on her since he entered the room. *The damn Dark Lord!*

Naturally, she had been ecstatic to meet the sweet child. *Such a beautiful little girl. Look at her, a miniature version of Fergus. How did I miss the likeness, not realised it at once? It is so strong!* She loved the child already, effortlessly because she was part of him.

When he dared a small smile at her, she just shook her head. She launched a scowl at him instead, as if to say, '*don't you even try to justify yourself!*'

A pang squeezed her heart. For a minute, she had no air in her lungs. *Breathe, Marguerite, breathe.*

A woman stopped at the door, left open, and peeked inside. "There you are, Lucy. I've been looking all over for you. You must come, get dressed for supper. I am sorry, my lord, she—"

"That's okay, Olivia."

"I don't want to get dressed," Lucy complained with a pout and crossed her little arms on her chest with a frown.

She is his daughter all right!

"You wish to have supper with Marguerite and Daddy in the large dining room tonight, like a big girl, don't you?" he said sweetly to her, moving a lock of hair from her face.

"Yes. But like this. I want to keep my jeans on." Lucy shook her head resolutely.

"Well, see how lovely Marguerite looks. Don't you want to show her how pretty you can look in a dress, too, hey? What about your new dress, princess?" he continued.

The child smiled again and rocked on her feet shyly. "Aha!" She nodded with a blush.

"Then, run. Off you go with Olivia."

"Okay, Daddy." She kissed him and gave his wife a kiss, too, then she was off.

Chapter 15

He waited for his daughter to leave the room, then he spun to his wife. She was staring right ahead, avoiding him, trying not to look at him.

"I'm sorry you had to find out this way, darling. I was waiting for the perfect moment." Fergus reached out for her hand. She yanked hers away, rose from the sofa, and stepped aside from him, quickly placing some distance between them. She stood with her back to him, her palms on the dressing table, her breathing laboured in confusion.

"I was going to tell you—" he said.

"Tell me? Exactly when were you going to tell me?" Marguerite asked him with composure, spinning to him and stopping him mid-sentence.

The regret in her eyes told him everything.

"I was. I swear." He remained seated and blew out a noisy breath.

"No, don't lie to me. You never intended to," she spat, her lips in a thin line.

"Of course, I was. I grant you, not at the beginning. Not at first, you are right. Think of it, please. I didn't know who the hell I was going to marry. When you turned up… the woman who had disappeared so abruptly from me, the one I had known by a different name. Well? Can you blame me for not telling you? For all I knew, you'd be gone in a year and a half."

"Yes, I believe that."

"My daughter lost her mother. I won't let her go through that pain again, not if I can help it. How could I introduce her to someone who would be gone in months?"

"You mean a woman like me! A gold-digger, don't you? That's what you are saying. Deep down, you still believe I married you for the money, that I am not part of your life."

"You know that's not true. That was at the beginning. Yes, I admit, but not now—"

"Then why did you lie to me?"

"I didn't lie to you. I just omitted a fact," he said steadily, without flinching.

"Omitted a fact?" she cried out. "Don't start your fancy talk to confuse me. You didn't wish me to meet her. You had no intention to bring us together. That's why you didn't want me at Penningbrooke with you." She paced the room and went to the window with her back to him. A tear ran down her face. She cleared it with her hand and turned to him again with a sorrowful expression.

Fergus closed his eyes and threw his head backward, annoyed at himself for hurting her. He moved as if to rise from the settee, but she put her palms up in warning, and he stilled.

"I came here to tell Lucy about you. I could not introduce you to her, without telling her how matters had changed for me, what would change for her, too! That you were now in our lives. She is a child, and children don't like changes. I had to explain things to her. It works better that way," he said with vehemence.

Even in her upset, she could see he was a wonderful father concerned about his daughter.

"But I am not a child! Why didn't you tell me about her?"

"I am sorry, I know I should have. It was remiss of me. I should have told you first, I realise that." He ran a hand through his hair and hissed a breath out.

"Remiss? No! That doesn't even cover it. I'll tell you how it is. In order to get your inheritance, you must stay married to me for eighteen months. So you decided you might as well enjoy yourself, to roll in bed with me for the duration. I am a floozie! You said it." The word 'floozie' gritted out of her teeth. She tugged at her hair disconsolately, as if she was about to pull it out, and turned away from him.

"Oh, for God's sake, darling. That's not true! Grant me the shock at seeing you again after so long. Suddenly, I find myself married, forced to marry you. You cannot ignore my shock and my anger at this. But not after the week we just had. Things are different between us now, and you know it."

"Are they? They don't seem like that to me. Deep down, you still think I am a gold-digger, a floozie."

"Oh, Marguerite, please. We are fine together. We are part of each other; you can't possibly think I meant those words. I won't let you. You hurt me all those years ago when you left, and I was angry at you. I didn't know the truth about you, which you skipped from me!" Fergus added with heartfelt vehemence.

Despite herself, a smile curled up on one side of her mouth at the raw emotion on his face, but she ignored his little dig at her. Effectively, she had done the same thing to protect him when she fled all those years ago. So, Fergus had now protected his daughter from an unknown woman, and she could understand that, though she would not make it easier for him. The fact was he had hurt her by not telling her about Lucy. Besides, she had a niggling doubt about herself...

Whether she was enough for Fergus. An aftermath from Alain's insecurities, her self-doubts were so easy to resurface at her lowest moments.

"You won't let me? Well, you are doing your best to make me believe you meant every mean word!" she lashed at him, "You are a Dark Lord. They are right." Her lips flattened and her nostrils flared as she clenched and unclenched the sides of her dress. She paced the room back and forth without looking at him.

Though he was still seated, seemingly calm on the settee, the anxiety in his eyes and the expression on his face gave him away for once. "Ah, no! Remember, we said no more insults. Otherwise, as God is my witness, I'll put you over my knees right now," he replied, unnerved at her obstinacy at not wanting to accept his apologies.

"Well, we said a lot of things, but you meant none of them. You have different rules for me, double standards, no intention for me to become part of your life. You don't think of me as a permanent addition to your family, as your wife. You cannot deny that." She stomped a foot on the floor.

"Please stop that! I don't have double standards. Hell, no! I was wrong in not telling you about Lucy, I admit, and I said I'm sorry. I have apologised. What more do you wish me to say? Of course, you are part of my family. Marguerite—" His stare fixed on her while his words ripped out firmly.

"Typical of you! A silly answer, just because you have apologised, it doesn't make it fine, does it? You are a despotic husband. You want things always your own way."

"I said no more name calling. You are my wife." He moved, as if to rise from the settee to approach her. "Darling, please," he pleaded with her, but she put her hand up, stopping him in his tracks.

It conveyed to him, *'don't even try!'*

"I don't begrudge the girl; let's be clear about that. She is the sweetest child ever. She's lovely, but you should have said something. My irritation is with you," she spat and crossed her arms on her chest with a scowl.

He stood, in his full height, and rolled his eyes, his hands on his hips, and she gulped.

"I know, and I apologise. We are going in circles. But…" he hissed. He rubbed his chin. She could see he was beginning to lose his patience. But she was proud and felt offended.

"That's why you didn't want me to come with you to Penningbrooke," she replied, another tear staining her cheek.

"Darling, please…" He moved closer to her, his heart tightening at her tears, but she stepped away from him.

"I have explained. I wanted to tell Lucy about you first, whether it was right or wrong. You've got to understand that was all, no other motive for it. I needed to see her reaction. Anyway, it delighted her when I told her—" Fergus said, but a knock on the door interrupted them. He swore at the interruption, black curses flowing out of his mouth.

"Come in," Marguerite said.

His eyes blazed at her, too, for allowing someone in when they were arguing.

She dried another tear with her hand, welcoming the interruption instead. She was mad at him, though, deep down, she realised he was right. In his place, she would have done exactly the same. She would have waited until sure of their feelings first. To see if they had a future, if the marriage had a chance, before telling him something so delicate. In his shoes, she would have acted in the same manner. So why was she holding it against him? She couldn't think straight. So, she welcomed the interruption.

"I am sorry, my lord, but you wanted to know when Miss Belinda was home. She has just arrived. She is in her room," Mrs. Briggs told them when she came into the room.

He glanced at his wife, then at the housekeeper, and finally stared ahead. He swore. Curses as black as the night dropped from his mouth. It was not his day…

"Thank you, Mrs. Briggs, I'll see to her in a moment," he said, and the woman left.

"We'll discuss this later. I have to talk to my silly sister before she ends up in prison once more." He went to move toward the door.

"You are doing it again; you are shutting me out," Marguerite cried after him.

He stopped dead in his tracks and turned to her. "No, I am not! If you mean my sister, you don't know Belinda. It is best if I deal with her alone. She is stubborn as hell—" But she didn't let him finish.

"Well, I wonder who she reminds me of?" She glowered at him.

"I'll see you at dinner," he replied coolly. He turned on his heels and left.

When he left the room, she cried tears of rage and sorrow. She was doomed to lose him again; he didn't want her. All her insecurities were assailing her again. That's why he had not told her something so vitally important. She fretted. *Breathe, Marguerite, breathe!* She tried to calm herself. *Think, woman!* She took several long breaths.

Fergus said he was sorry. He apologised, recognised he had made a mess of things, but he wanted to protect Lucy. In his place, she would have done exactly the same. He didn't wish to upset his daughter; she came first. *Oh, he's a noble father.* A delightful side of him which caused her heart to melt. Marguerite reflected on that.

What they'd had these last few days was a genuine senti-ment. She couldn't deny it; she felt it in her bones. Yes, the first three days of their marriage were hell. But this past week had been amazing for them. Their kisses, their caresses, those were real. He meant every lovely word he'd said to her, each endearment. *This is what I must focus on!*

What of it if he made a wreck of this one thing? It would not be the last mess he would make during their life together. She was certain there would be other mistakes on both sides. She was prone to them, too, and it was early days in their marriage. *For God's sake, we've been married for less than two weeks, with a brief relationship six years ago! We need to learn more about one another and our life together.* If he was willing, so was she. She would not bear it if she were to lose him again. Marguerite resolved that she wouldn't let this matter come between them. She would forgive him. She loved him so much, she would forgive him anything, anyway. *I won't give him the impression I am a pushover, though, no sir! He'll have to understand that.*

But she would not let this impede her overall happiness. Besides, the child was a delight to her. She already loved Lucy. She was adorable, the feeling almost immediate.

Marguerite gulped. With a child in the midst, the pressure on her was bigger. She had become a wife, but also a mother. Lucy was part of Fergus. By default, she would be part of Marguerite, too.

Fergus was right. He had acted responsibly toward the girl. Perhaps not so much toward Marguerite, but she would over-look this one time. So, she dried her tears. She smoothed her dress, fixed her makeup, had one last glance in the mirror, and went out of the room.

Once in the hallway, as she closed her bedroom door, yelling struck her ears. *Fergus!*

Her husband and his sister—she assumed the woman's

voice to be Belinda's—reached her loud and clear from the other end of the hallway. It seemed the siblings had lost their cool.

She breathed in. He would be in a terrible mood. *Breathe, Marguerite, breathe,* she chanted her mantra in her head, *there is nothing you can do.* She hated people screaming at each other since her dark days with Alain. She inhaled and exhaled a few times to calm herself.

Mrs. Briggs approached her along the hall. "Supper will be served late tonight, madam. You can guess why," the house-keeper said with a concerned expression on her face.

"Where is Belinda's room?" she asked.

"Follow the yelling! I beg your pardon, I shouldn't have spoken—"

"No, please don't apologise. Everyone on the estate will hear them soon." Marguerite rolled her eyes.

"They have been at it for ten minutes. Perhaps you could make some peace between them… it won't end well if they keep like this." The housekeeper wrung her hands in agitation.

"What can I do? I offered, Mrs. Briggs. But my husband told me, categorically, he wanted to deal with his sister alone."

"If I may be so daring, my lady, sometimes a wife doesn't need to follow what her husband says to the letter. If it is for a higher good, of course," Mrs. Briggs replied.

Marguerite raised her eyebrows and scoffed, but the woman went on, "I have known his lordship and his siblings for almost twenty years. Belinda was a baby when I came to the house and in this case—"

"Marguerite!" A light shrill voice reached them. They glanced up. Fergus' daughter was standing midway up the stairs to the next floor. She was all dressed up and making her way down at a trot.

"Don't run, darling, or you'll fall," Briggs said to the child, "come down gently."

"Yes," replied the nanny behind the girl. "You know that well enough, slowly now. Off you go down," Olivia reinforced the point.

Lucy paused and stepped down the stairs in grand style. She looked every bit like a lady, the offspring of an earl.

Marguerite had an idea.

Fergus had been reticent to speak around his daughter, and rightly so. She'd found the way for brother and sister to stop screaming at one another.

"You can go, Olivia. I'll watch over Lucy," Mrs. Briggs told the nanny who had the night off.

"My… look at you, so pretty, darling," Marguerite said, kneeling to her eye level, and the girl turned pinkish. "Come. Let's call on your father and aunt." She took her hand. "I'll take care of her," she went on to the housekeeper.

"As you wish, madam." And the housekeeper went downstairs on her errands.

"Daddy gets mad at Auntie Bella sometimes. Can you make them stop, Marguerite? It makes me sad when they argue."

"I'll try, sweetheart. You want to see Belinda, don't you?" she asked, pausing, somewhat uncertain.

"Aha!" The child nodded eagerly.

"That's right, Lucy. They shouldn't be yelling like this. It is not acceptable, not proper. Let's tell them." Marguerite's last sentences was meant rhetorically, and she mumbled to herself. She would soon learn not to express her thoughts out loud with a child.

"Oh, but Daddy says not to enter a room when adults are talking."

"Well, they are not talking, are they? They are yelling. That's different, darling. Let me worry about that. Come along now, let's go."

They stood outside Belinda's room, and the voices inside, arguing with each other, struck them high and pitchy.

"Are you sure Daddy won't get mad at us, too?" Lucy mumbled with wide eyes. The girl was rather a mature six-year-old.

Marguerite gulped. The child had a point. He'd be furious at her for interrupting. But they weren't going anywhere like this. So she had to try her own way, she resolved.

Marguerite nodded with conviction, even though she didn't quite feel it. She tapped on the door with the sweetest smile she possessed.

"What now?" she heard his irritated voice shout from the inside. She knocked once more, then she pushed the door open without waiting for a reply.

She entered the room defiantly, her head held high.

"Auntie Bella," the child screamed and dashed to Belinda. She threw herself at her aunt. The young woman scooped her niece up into her arms and, perched on her hips, twirled her around with joy.

"Oh, I've missed you, Lucy!" Belinda smothered the child's face in kisses. "I am glad to see friendly faces." She declared, "Hello, Marguerite, have you not run away from this brother of mine yet? God knows why not! He is a bear!" his sister said lightly, kissing her, and they turned when a growl escaped him.

Fergus threw a stare with fiery eyes at his wife that stated, *'I warned you! I know what you are doing and it won't work.'*

"Daddy, you shouldn't argue with Auntie, you were shouting! It is not proper," Lucy uttered, all composed once she was back on her feet.

"Not proper?" he echoed. He tried to sound calm. The girl nodded vigorously.

"Yes, Marguerite said so," Lucy replied, like saying *'if Marguerite said it, then that's damn right!'*

"I see! And I told you not to enter a room when adults are talking in private," he said quite gingerly, with a serious face.

"But, Daddy, you were not talking, you were yelling! That's different; Marguerite said so!"

"Did she now?" he asked, looking at his wife, lifting his eyebrows, while she blushed furiously. But there was a hint of amusement in his eyes, which made his shoulders relax.

So, Marguerite seized her chance. "Now, Fergus, darling, why don't you go ahead? Have a shower, a brandy, go dress for supper. Wait for us in the dining room. Leave us girls together for a few minutes, hey? Belinda needs to get ready too, or we won't have dinner tonight. And I am famished." She took her husband's elbow, and with a delicate hand, she firmly pulled him toward the door.

***

His wife astonished him.

There was no resistance from him. By the time he realised what happened, he was in the hallway while the girls shut the door behind him.

Fergus looked at the door, amazed. He scoffed. He'd yelled at Belinda for the last ten minutes and now he was out of the conversation! His wife had taken charge.

Let's see if she can do any better with that headstrong girl! Well, he had nothing to lose. He wondered what the hell was happening in his household. *Bloody hell! Who is in charge here?* But he shook his head with a laugh.

"Is everything okay, my lord?" the housekeeper asked, appearing next to him. He inhaled and shrugged his shoulders. "What am I to do, Briggs, hey? My six-year-old, who is going on eighteen, it seems, tells me off because I screamed at my unruly sister. My wife despises me because I omitted to tell her I have a daughter and bundles me out of a dispute with my own sibling, whom I was about to strangle… not to mention, Belinda hates me anyway because I am sending her back to the clinic. Whether she likes it or not. Women, hey? They all hate me." He huffed a puff of air out forcefully.

"No, my lord, they don't."

"I tell you, they do. Frankly, I never thought I would say this. My father was a master at dealing with damn nuisances in the household. Nothing ever worried him."

"Oh, that's where you are wrong. Many things bothered him."

"If you say so…"

"Will you say Grace at dinner, my lord?"

"What?" Fergus glanced at her as if the woman had lost her mind.

"Bancroft told me the way your father used to say Grace to ingratiate your mother when you were children, when the poor woman was at the end of her tether with you all, remember? Or when your dad had made some big mess and upset her, he said Grace in a certain way… well, perhaps you should try it tonight."

Mrs. Briggs had taken up a role of a parent to the young brood when Fergus' mother died years ago. Bancroft and Ethel always told her the stories about the old earl trying to ingratiate his beautiful wife when she was alive and he or the children had made some big blunder. So, the housekeeper reminded Fergus of this.

He laughed.

"Oh, yes, indeed," he said, shaking his head.

Suddenly, he knew what he should do.

Chapter 16

He helped himself to a brandy while he was waiting for his family to dine. He was in everybody's bad books. *I must try to win them back.*

His sister would end up back in prison if she did not return to the clinic.

Marguerite was going to give him a hard time for not telling her about Lucy. God forbid, if she were to find out about Chloe, right here, on his doorstep. The woman had always known it was just a casual relationship and been happy with the arrangement. But when he told Chloe that morning he was married and he couldn't see her anymore, she had not taken it lightly, if her rather exasperating and unrepeatable text message on his phone was anything to go by.

This was the other reason, besides Lucy, he had wanted to go to the estate alone, to make this clear to Chloe in no uncertain terms.

With an upset Marguerite in the house at the revelation he had daughter, a rather volatile ex-lover close by, well... he could be in for a rough night!

Jesus, women! He couldn't bear thinking of it. *My wife may even decide to leave me.* No woman had meant much to him other than Marguerite. He wasn't proud of it, but it was a fact. He would not survive losing her anew. He wanted her for keeps now. His father had given him a second chance with her. This time, by hook or by crook, he would not waste it.

He gulped another mouthful, the warm liquid radiating inside of him. He inhaled. His shoulders relaxed.

"Daddy!" the child chanted as she ran to him. He set the glass on the table, picked her up in his arms, and kissed her cheek. Then, he looked up toward the door.

"Can I say, ladies, how beautiful you look tonight? Lucy, you look like a princess, my dear sister, like an angel, and my wife, well… Marguerite is a goddess!"

The women glanced at each other in the doorway. They burst out laughing, coming into the room.

"Good try, Fergus," Belinda scoffed.

"Come on, girls, please take your seats. Marguerite on my right." He pulled out the chair for her. "Bella, next to my wife." He did the same for his sister. Lucy took out her own chair on his left before he could get to her.

He smiled at them. He sat at the head of the table. It was Mrs. Briggs' cue to come in.

"Shall I serve, my lord?"

"We'll say Grace first, Mrs. Briggs. Girls, let's join hands," he said, turning to the woman briefly with a furtive wink. The old woman could hardly contain her satisfaction.

"Grace? Are you feeling well, Fergus?" Belinda said with a snort.

"Please…" He shot a chastising look at her.

"Fine!" She giggled, trying to steady her features.

They all joined hands.

Marguerite had never heard him say Grace. But they had taken most of their meals separately for the first three days. Since their reconciliation, in between lovemaking, they had taken a tray with food to bed. She wasn't certain if this was a routine at meals when the family got together, but judging by the amusement on Belinda's face, she decided perhaps a new habit. She was intrigued.

He closed his eyes, and they all followed suit. He opened one to peep at them, and he smiled. "Bless us, Oh Lord, and these, Thy gifts, which we are about to receive from Thy bounty," he began solemnly. "Bless, Oh Lord, my adorable daughter, Lucy, and Thee, for giving to her a new lovely mother," he said with his eyes closed. He couldn't help a peek at Marguerite, whose eyes popped wide open. She glanced at him with her grey ones flying out of orbit, while he heard Lucy give out a squeal of delight, still with her eyes shut.

"Bless my sweet, dear sister, Bella, Oh Lord," he continued. "Allow her peace and strength throughout her stay at the clinic—" he went on, peeking at her, to see she shivered in her seat.

"Cut the crap, Fergus! I have already agreed with Marguerite, I will go back to the clinic tonight, after dinner. Jones will drive me. Just give the poor man a raise. Driving everyone around at odd times of night and day! So, rest easy and spare me the prayer," Belinda scoffed.

He paused, lifted his eyebrows, but didn't take the bait.

Mrs. Briggs coughed loudly in a rebuke. The young woman blushed. Briggs was the closest to a mother Belinda ever had, and a small smile curled up on her face.

"Sorry," she said. "Ooh, all right, go on, then." She understood it was his attempt to make peace with her.

"As I was saying," he resumed nonplussed, "bless my little sister and avoid any more troubles for her, and bless, Oh Lord, my beautiful wife, Marguerite, for having found her way to me. I thank Thee for bringing happiness to my life again. May she always be our sweet guiding light, through Christ, our Lord. Amen."

The women stared at him like he was deranged. The least religious of the siblings, he had never been one for prayers or church. So Belinda snorted, but she couldn't deny his sudden religiousness had opened up a joyful and serene atmosphere in the room.

"Amen," they all repeated after him.

Lucy talked, overexcited, not really understanding much of it. Sensing it was a good thing, she darted her pale blue eyes on everyone, finding it a novelty and a thrill that adults were in harmony. She felt all grown up. It was her first time partaking of her evening meal in the grand dining room at Penningbrooke.

Marguerite glanced at her husband with misty eyes, in awe, as if he were a God sprung from heaven.

It was then she understood. Fergus had told her, in a roundabout way, in front of the family, she was his and there to stay.

After the prayer, dinner was a charming affair.

The pepper-crusted beef tenderloin with chocolate-port sauce was mouth-watering. It made their taste buds swell. The chocolate aroma spread around the place and worked on their brain cells too, taking them on a high as if they had just accomplished a marathon with a world record. There was a jolly atmosphere, the earlier animosity of day gone to dust.

They witnessed a glimpse of a harmonious family. How it could be! How they wished it to be.

Belinda delighted Marguerite in old stories of when the siblings were young. His sister made them laugh on past escapades that had not amused their father or the nanny of the moment much.

"Lucy, don't get ideas at being naughty like my brothers and sister," Fergus said and winked at her.

The evening went on cheerfully until it was time for Belinda to return to the clinic.

"Please, darling, stay out of trouble. You must remain at the clinic for as long as the court order requires it, no more bright ideas!" he warned his sister.

"Yes, my lord," she replied facetiously with a scoff and kissed his cheek.

Marguerite and Lucy said their goodbyes, too, with big hugs.

"Briggs, look after them for me. You know they get into trouble if I am not here to keep them in check." Belinda gave the housekeeper a kiss on the cheek, who smiled indulgently at her young charge.

Chapter 17

As they watched the car with Belinda in it move down the long drive to leave the estate, another car, coming in the opposite direction, narrowly missed it. It sped along until it stopped short of crashing into the stone steps leading up to the house with a full screech of wheels.

"Bloody Hell!" Mrs. Briggs cried out and looked at him. Marguerite gave out a small scream, while he flung himself in front of his wife and daughter, covering them with his body. Fortunately, they had hastily retreated to the top of the steps to avert a catastrophe.

"Fergus!" the woman in the driving seat uttered, leaning out of the window.

Blast! And he thought he had salvaged the evening... *oh, no!* He muttered an oath under his breath.

The attractive woman came out of the car.

"Chloe!" he exclaimed, with an icy undertone in his voice, his eyes blazing at her. But Marguerite had distinctly heard his oath.

"Darling, why don't you take Lucy up to the nursery? It is

way past her bedtime," he said to his wife. His tone was soft again; he was trying to stay cool.

"What? Are you not going to introduce me to your bride, Fergus?" Chloe blurted out, slurring her words. As the woman swayed, she was visibly intoxicated.

He turned to her, his expression one of fury. "Steady on, Chloe!" he added, whispering another oath between the teeth. "Good God, you could have killed somebody driving in that state. You are drunk!"

"No, I am not. Introduce me, then." She stomped a foot on the pavement.

He murmured another curse.

Marguerite's eyes darted from him to the woman, not knowing what to make of it. But as her initial fright subsided, she had an inkling. After all, she knew it well. Her husband had been a golden bachelor with countless affairs with women. But was this woman on the estate?

"Darling, this is Chloe Clark, one of my tenants. My wife, the Countess of Buckley!" Fergus proclaimed the formal introduction through clenched teeth, flashing eyes at the woman.

"My pleasure, please call me Marguerite," she said, going down the steps and extending her hand to Chloe.

Fergus frowned, rubbing the back of his neck. He looked at Briggs with an unspoken plea. Though her lips turned into a thin line, chastising him for bringing this embarrassing situation onto himself.

He closed his eyes and sighed. The rebuke from the housekeeper was nothing compared to the reproach his wife would unleash on him... he was sure of it.

Oh, hell, he would have more explaining to do!

The ladies shook hands.

"Would you like to come in?" Marguerite ventured with a blush, unsure how to behave with this woman—clearly, her husband's lover. She struggled to rein in a scowl at him. The surge of frustration she had felt earlier in the evening, discovering he had a daughter and not telling her about it, was taking hold of her again and growing at a rapid pace. Oh, he was the Dark Lord! The darkest of them all!

"It's late, and Chloe is in no state for civilised conversation. Mrs. Briggs, call out to one of the stable lads to drive her home. Now, please," he commanded sharply.

He launched a fiery expression at Chloe, who suddenly puked by the side of her car and moaned as bouts of vomiting overtook her.

Frigging great! It took all of his self-control to remain as still as a stone and not do anything that would make matters worse.

"God, give me strength," he mumbled under his breath and then went to Mrs. Briggs and whispered something into her ear.

"Yes, my lord," the housekeeper replied.

"Marguerite, take Lucy upstairs to the nursery. Time for her to go to bed. Now!" Fergus directed with finality, and this time it was an order.

His wife was about to say something when Mrs. Briggs put a hand on her arm with a nervous look. So, Marguerite paused, turned, and took Lucy's hand and headed for the house.

She lingered in the hall, with the excuse of taking Lucy's coat off, and heard the animated voices outside but couldn't get the gist of the conversation. The woman's words made no sense and his replies were in whispers.

Marguerite looked at Mrs. Briggs with enquiring eyes.

"I must go and fetch one of the stable lads, Chloe must go home," the woman said with an apologetic smile as she went off to do his bidding.

"Time for you to go upstairs," Marguerite said to a reluctant Lucy.

"Is Chloe sick?" The child looked up to her; obviously his daughter was familiar with the woman.

"Yes, her tummy hurts, that's it. Is Chloe your daddy's friend?"

"Yes. Chloe brings me cheesecake when she comes to the house, but I like the cheesecake from our cook best," the child said with a loving smile.

"I see," Marguerite replied, and though she had appreciated Lucy's encouragement in the child's innocent, unwitting infinite wisdom, Marguerite's eyes narrowed at her husband's behaviour. As they climbed several floors, through the long staircase, to Lucy's quarters, so did her temper.

"Can you read to me every night? Olivia or Briggs read to me when Daddy is away. You'll be here even when Daddy is out to work?" the child asked, now in her room and ready for bed.

Marguerite smiled and caressed her hair.

"Come on, young lady, you get into bed," Fergus said, suddenly appearing in the doorway, not wanting to put more pressure on his wife. Especially after the scene outside with Chloe.

"But Daddy, Bettie says her mommy reads to her every night."

"Bed, Lucy, please, in you go. It's way past your bedtime. I am sure Marguerite and I can take turns reading to you," he repeated, peeking at his wife whose scowl hit him hard. He bent on one knee on the floor to look at his daughter's face and moved a lock out of her eyes.

The girl put her arms around his collar and gave him a kiss.

Marguerite tenderly pulled over the coverlet once the child

was settled in her bed and began reading her a story until Lucy yawned sleepily.

Fergus darted his eyes between his wife and his daughter. His heart rejoiced, despite all the explaining he'd have to do. He was leaning on the wall with his arm crossed over his chest, his ankles crossed, and a satisfied smile on his face. This little blissful moment warmed his heart, and a burst of love for them ballooned in his soul.

It had been a long day.

Marguerite stopped outside her bedroom and turned to him, blocking the doorframe with her body.

"Not your room, my love," he said. "We'll sleep in my bedroom tonight. It is a ritual. It's been like this for generations. On their first night together in this house, it is a tradition for the earl and his countess to bed down in the earl's chamber," Fergus whispered to her, brushing his lips on her neck. Then, he pointed down the corridor at his room. He caressed her cheek with the back of his hand and wiggled his eyebrows with a mischievous grin.

Irritation surged and blazed through Marguerite's frame, billowing thorough her every pore. She drew back a step and stared in wrath at him. She ended up against the door. He followed on closer, totally unfazed by her thunderous expression. He didn't even blink. Instead, he waved his finger toward his bedroom farther along the hallway, with a devilish smile that turned him into the sexiest man she had ever known.

Oh, she wouldn't make it easy for him, not tonight. The damn Dark Lord. Omitting to tell her he had a daughter was bad enough and still burned her temper, but the escapade with Chloe an hour ago had her spitting bile. She was trying to control her fury and her language, but when another sexy smile from him hit her, she couldn't help it.

Marguerite narrowed her eyes on him with a stern look. "Your room? Ha!" she stated, crossing her arms over her chest with a rapid intake of breath, her scowl deepening. "Don't be so cocky just because you said nice things to me at dinner during Grace, and I admit, they were nice words. But you can't think all is fine, do you? Really, Fergus!"

"Do you want to break with tradition?" he asked, feigning perplexity mockingly. His head was at an angle, watching her. He gingerly held a lock of her hair through his fingers, "Well, I suppose there is always a first time for everything. If you prefer we sleep in your bedroom, it's cool by me," he said nonchalantly, with mirth in his eyes.

"Fergus Waltham! Don't believe for a second I have forgiven you just because we had a charming evening at dinner!" she said, yanking the ringlet of hair out of his hand. "Saying pleasant things won't make everything right. It won't do it for me. In particular after Chloe!"

"Okay, if you feel strongly about it, your room it is then," he persisted. Either he didn't hear her objections or ignored them.

There was amusement on his face; he was trying to diffuse the situation with humour, which was patently not working for her.

"No, Fergus. You misunderstand me. Tonight, dear, you'll be in your bedroom, in the earl's chamber for sure, but alone. And yes, for me, mine it is. Understood?" she cried out in exasperation. "You still have some groveling to do. Some explaining to do about dear, sweet Lucy. And by no means have I forgotten what happened outside with Chloe, not by a long shot. I can't believe you have a woman on the estate! Do you think I am stupid."

"And I'll do more groveling, more explaining tomorrow, I

promise. It's late now, and I want to go to bed, *with you*," he emphasized. "Please stop arguing with me and get into my bed. I missed you these last two days." He held a strand of her long locks in his hand and inhaled. "I love the perfume of your hair." His lips caressed her cheek. "Your scent drives me crazy! I had to resist you all night," he mumbled between kisses on her neck and shoulders.

Marguerite shivered in anticipation and bit her bottom lip, her heart pounding. Her resolve was wavering. She had missed him just as much. She would have forgiven him anything anyway.

The past was the past, and only the future mattered for her. But she couldn't ignore that for almost two weeks he had not told her about Lucy. *And Chloe? A lover? How many would eventually come out of the woodwork!* She would not give him the impression she was a pushover, regardless. So, she gave him a little impatient push with both of her hands on his chest.

"Away with you, my lord! Tonight is not your night, sir." She raised a hand out to ward him off from coming closer. But he ignored her complaints and pushed on.

"Umm..." He licked the hollow of her neck.

She gulped and closed her eyes, her decision on the line, but she would not give in. "Fergus, you are exasperating. You are used to getting your own way whether you are right or wrong. Tonight, you can't get away with it, I tell you. You lied to me! You won't win!" she blurted while her eyebrows grew closer in a scowl.

He took her hand and brought it to his lips.

She yanked it off him. "No, I said; you lied about Lucy," she repeated and stomped her foot on the floor in a tantrum, twice. "And what the hell is Chloe to you? Is she your lover? Here on the estate? Shame on you!"

He breathed in and closed his eyes for a second. "Chloe, God, no! She is my tenant."

"Tenant? Pull the other one, Fergus!"

"True, she is my tenant. But if you really must know, she pursued me for a long time, until I gave in. Yes, we had sex a few times, but she knew the score. God, if I had to tell you about all the women I had sex with before I married you, we'd be here all night," he blurted out impatiently, and she gasped in horror with her eyes flying wide and then narrowing into thin slits.

"You have bottle. I grant you that, you moron," she cried out with a snort, though she didn't feel the humour.

He paused and huffed. "I was a bachelor, remember! Unattached," he went on, "but I'll promise you, Chloe will never embarrass you or me again. Trust me when I say I have had no other woman than you since the day we married. Bloody hell, I want no other! Only *you*!" he emphasised with vehemence.

"Umm, hard to believe… and you still lied to me about Lucy," she mumbled instead, with thin lips.

He straightened up tall, his spine straight as a rod, to his full height in front of her. He stared her down. He inhaled yet forcibly expelled his breath. He rubbed his chin with his hand. His irritation was beginning to simmer now, too, more directed at Chloe for ruining his evening, if truth be told, conveniently dismissing he had not told his wife about Lucy, either.

Marguerite had to admit when he did this, he looked like a semi-god, so handsome. He was the vision of a sexy, arresting Viking ready for battle, gorgeous and a little menacing. In the last two weeks, she'd learned that this little peacock display of his was a foreplay to him losing his patience.

"Let's be clear, I didn't lie to you about my daughter! I

omitted a fact, albeit an important one, but for a good reason. I was protecting my daughter from an unknown woman then. It is not the same as lying. And I have apologised many times. And as far as Chloe is concerned, I had already told her from Oxford it was over, and I came here to reiterate it to her. I am married now, and all I want is you," he said, raising a hand in front of him, refusing to acknowledge her stubbornness.

"What? Oh, Fergus, you think because you apologise, it makes it all right, does it? You silly, beastly man. Off with you!" she replied and pushed him away.

"Beastly man? You promised no more insults, no disrespect." He frowned at her, his eyes narrowed perilously.

"I tell you, you deserve a punishment—" But she could not finish her sentence. He advanced on her. She struggled to retreat. Marguerite had nowhere to go, so she huddled up against the door. She fought him backward. She shoved him with both her hands on his chest, but he stood firm.

They wrestled for an instant until he pinned her hands behind her back. He pulled her to him tightly, searched her eyes, and they locked. Her breath hitched.

"I love you!" he whispered before his mouth crashed on hers.

She stopped struggling, melting in his arms. His words made her heart thump fast. *He loves me, sweet Jesus. Do I believe him?* But with his fleshy lips on hers, Marguerite mellowed. She was flustered, her warmth rising. She kissed him, too, with passion.

She had missed him so much, she couldn't even tell him. His tongue slipped into her mouth, overpowering her with desire and need, possessively. She moaned in his mouth and responded to him with want.

He relented his grip as she mollified in his arms. He fumbled with the handle behind her and opened the door.

Fergus pushed her gently inside her bedroom, closing the door with a kick of his heel.

But she wriggled out of his arms and stepped away, panting in quick puffs after his kisses, her heartbeat thundering. Suddenly, her complete weakness for this man irritated her. One brush of Fergus' lips on hers, sweet words in her ear, and she was gone, utterly wanting him. Though, she couldn't deny his three famous words to her had made her heart soar with giddiness. His words had mellowed her, but she would not make it so easy for him whatever he said.

She could still hear the ringing in her ears of the whispers between him and Chloe outside, and this burned her temper. *No, you must stand resolute, woman,* she told herself, *he'll think he's wrapped you around his little finger, that he can do what he wants. Don't yield to him; stay firm!*

"Out, please, get out of my room! You can be a brute of a man, a beast, sometimes. You are the Dark Lord indeed, my dear husband. That appellative suits you well if you ask me. Love me? Hmm... How can I believe you after Chloe?" Marguerite said with her head held high.

She was headstrong. She wouldn't give in. She had missed him and wished nothing better than to be in bed with him, with her sexy husband between her thighs, but she had a point to prove. She wouldn't be a pushover, regardless of how much they loved each other.

He tilted his head slightly to one side and stared at her. His pale blue moons flinched. He rubbed the back of his neck, and a devilish, hard smile curled upon his lips. "We've been together, what? About two weeks? Though, it seems not long enough for you to understand that when I say something, I mean it. You are stubborn," he said calmly. "You broke your promise with this name calling of yours. I overlooked it once earlier tonight, but you continue. A brute of a man? Hmm? The Dark Lord? You know I hate it when you do that. That's inappropriate behaviour. It is disrespectful," he went on serenely.

"Well, tough, then," she responded in a low voice, raising her chin.

"I have apologised to you. You know I love you, but you won't listen. Come here; let me remind you." He took his jacket off, and cool as a cucumber, he sat on the settee at the foot of her bed.

"What the hell are you doing?" She glanced at him in disbelief.

"You heard me, darling. And don't make me repeat it. You are having a silly fit of temper and getting yourself all worked up about nothing. I have apologised for not telling you about Lucy enough times, and Chloe is in the past, history. But you won't listen to me," he replied in full control, unflappable. He patted his knees.

She stared at him, her mouth agape. Though, if she had to be honest, she loved it when he was masterful. Butterflies flapped in her tummy; she liked it when he spanked her. Even when he roasted her backside to the nines, his simple gesture of patting his knees sent sparks flying through her frame in anticipation. Marguerite could see a mischievous glint in his eyes, but she would not give in easily. She had a point to prove. Yes, she was stubborn.

"Get lost, Fergus, go jump in the lake!" she mumbled instead, defiant.

He raised his eyebrows at her. He threw up his hands in the air in an '*I give up*' gesture and scowled.

"Now, that's awful, girl. You have a dirty mouth on you. I won't stand for it. I said no more insults, and you persist, relentless. A brute? A beast? Get lost? Go jump in the lake? Flipping heck! Oh, no, my darling. This won't do. I forbid it," he added. "Come here. Now!" The firm command was loud and clear.

Something between her legs came to life, and her pussy warmed at his demand. The skin on her backside tingled.

"You are joking, aren't you?" she asked instead. As much as she was looking forward to the spanking, she was also dreading it. Besides, he was the guilty party.

"No, I am not."

"You are at fault here, not me!" She persevered, stomping her foot refusing his order.

"At fault? For protecting my daughter? I apologised for not telling you sooner, I have already promised I will explain to you more, answer all your questions. And as far as Chloe is concerned or any other woman before you, they are all history, past, gone! Done with! Dusted! I told you, I only want you. We are going in circles. But you are stubborn and disobedient, with a filthy mouth on you. You don't listen, so you need a reminder that this won't do. You are having a silly tantrum about nothing."

"Out of my room, you big, b-boorish a-ape!" she said, stretching her arm in defiance, pointing to the door with her finger. She couldn't disguise a brief tremor in her voice, and she went on, "N-now! Fergus, I am telling you! Out!"

He stared at her then glanced at the door. A smile formed on his lips. "I am not going anywhere, darling. I am already in your bedroom when tradition dictates we should be in mine."

"Jesus, you are infuriating! Out!" She rushed the words out with an impatient snort, exasperated.

"One, you disobeyed me in coming to the estate when I told you to stay in Oxford. Even if it was for a good cause, you should have asked me first. If you'd stayed put, on my return, I would have eased Lucy on you and avoided all this nonsense, and Chloe too. Two, you persist in insulting me. You seem to be making a habit of this when you know I don't like it. Incredible how those sweet lips of yours can give sugary kisses and then can be so venomous with words.

Umm... I've got to do something about this before it gets out of hand."

"Too convenient for you, ha? You deserved them all, and more, you brute of a man. Can you blame me after finding out about Lucy and Chloe, in one evening? Were you going to fuck the woman, here in this bed, tonight, if I wasn't here. Or perhaps in the coveted earl's chamber, ha?" she said mightily, mocking him, but crossing her arms over her chest with a scowl.

He arched an elegant brow at her in disapproval and shook his head rather coolly. "That's out of order, such coarse language. I told you how I feel about you. I only want you, I love you. But your disrespect won't do. I am your husband, and you'll be respectful. This stops now!" he commanded. "Sending me to my room, indeed, silly. If you won't stop this tantrum, then I'll stop it for you. So, I am telling you, come here," he concluded, patting his lap.

"The hell I am!"

"If I have to stand and come for you, let me tell you, I'll add extra smacks!"

"Oh, no, you won't!" She made a dash for the door. He leapt from the settee like an agile panther, placing his body between her and the exit, with a wolfish grin on his lips. Fergus' eyes danced at the challenge.

She gulped. As she advanced, trying to sidestep him to get to the door, his arm outstretched, and he latched onto her. He caught her around the waist, clasping her, lifting her up by her midriff as if she were a rag doll. Her feet dangling, he hauled her to him. He moved toward the settee, while she wriggled almost double up on his arm, swinging, fighting him, protesting vigourosly.

"Let me go, you brute!" she yelled.

"See what I mean? Here we are again! You deserve this spanking, my lovely, you are very disrespectful!"

"Don't you dare! You are the one who needs punishment, not me," she squealed.

"Now, stop that nonsense. Quiet! Or do you intend to wake up the entire house? What shall Lucy think of her new mother? Psst…" he said with a smirk and shook his head, amused.

"Put me down this instant, you beast!"

"And I will, on my lap. You need a good thrashing on that naughty butt of yours." He plopped on the settee coolly, while she squirmed some more, but he pulled her over his knees, face down.

Dazed for a moment, before she realised what had happened, a bunch of smacks fell down on her backside over her dress. "Ah!" she yelped, the pain taking her breath away.

"We are bound to have a quarrel now and then. You cannot behave as if you are a street urchin when you are upset with me, yelling insults at me." He spanked her hard several times.

It made her eyes water. "Please!" she cried out. But when he pulled her dress up and her panties down, and his hand met her bare buttocks, she wailed. "Ow, ow, stop, I tell you! Put me down, right now!" she shrieked, in-between wailing.

Though he couldn't help it, he stopped to admire her gloriously shaped butt for a moment, now red like a fire engine. His cock stirred at the gorgeous sight with his palm imprints.

She took a deep breath while he paused. She felt as if a bee had stung her ass, piercing her with its stinger, the pain was so excruciating.

"My lovely, I'm not sure if this escapes you, but at this minute, you are in no position to make demands." He whacked her so hard, her breath hitched.

"Please…" she whimpered.

"Are you going to calm down? Hm? Are you going hear

me out?" He smacked the crest of her lovely bottom powerfully.

"Fergus..." she pleaded and tried to defend herself, covering her ass with her hands.

He slapped her hands off gently, but she would interfere again, struggling to protect herself. So, he caught her wrists behind her back, keeping her steady.

She raised her objections at him vigorously.

"Shush!" He raised his hand above his head and whacked the middle of her inviting derrière with several consecutive thundering wallops. He scorched her posterior to a point where her body went limp while tears were flowing in abundance.

"I promise, please stop." She sniffed. She felt humiliated that, despite the burn on her backside, her pussy was heating up, clenching with each spank, desiring him.

"I've had enough of it, no more disrespect. Let this be a lesson to you. Next time, you better think before embarking on tantrums and insults!" His hand connected with her bare buttocks several times, making the bite soar, becoming unbearable.

Her pussy throbbed. "I promise! Please, Fergus, stop."

"Sure, are we?"

"Yes. I swear!" she whined, and a sob escaped her.

"Good! I am glad to hear it. If it happens again, I won't be so lenient. No more insults. When I apologise, I do mean it, and like an adult, you accept my apology. Then we talk." He halted. His hand stayed still on her scorching behind.

The warmth took away the sting, and she relaxed her shoulders, her body limp with exhaustion, hurt, and now desire.

"Lenient!" she muttered under her breath several times in-between sobs.

He rubbed her bottom in small circles. "You see how stubborn you are. You could have spared yourself this spanking, just by being reasonable and believing in what I told you, trusting me, instead of getting into a strop and launching insults."

He massaged her butt and her upper thighs. The more he kneaded her backside, the more the pain receded and her stomach flipped in anticipation. The heaviness between her legs multiplied and awoke all her senses. With her bottom burning, her clit throbbed. Her pussy clenched, wishing he was inside her. She was wet. Her legs parted of their own volition.

He smiled and took a deep breath, seeing her like this. A tiny moan slid between her lips.

"Umm... I wonder if you learned your lesson. Or am I just indulging your fantasies, ha?" he said with a soft smile. "Above all, I want you to note that every woman before I married you was irrelevant to me. I am not proud of it, but it is a fact. You are the one who matters. Are we clear on that?"

"Yes." She nodded, adding in a little whimper as his words finally hit home, too.

Her legs parted a tad more. He groaned; his manhood pulsated for her. He was proud of his woman for wanting him, and his rubbing turned into soft caresses of her ass.

"You do realise you are naughty. Are you inviting me, darling? Tell me what you wish me to do to you?" His voice purred out of him, with a velvety cadence.

Marguerite felt humiliated in that position, on his knees like a naughty child, but even more so at having to admit to him, *'Yes! I need you to touch me now.'* She craved him inside her. She nodded. He smacked her bottom once more, hard! "Ow, ow!"

"Say it! What do you want, sweet lips?" He rubbed her buttocks tenderly, expectantly.

"Touch me, please," she whispered. Her legs moved, giving him a full view of her gleaming sex, and he licked his lips.

She craved him badly, physically, yes, but following the episode with Chloe, Marguerite wanted proof that he belonged to her now, that she was the only woman for him, that he was hers as she was his, and only his lovemaking would appease her on this.

"You are gorgeous. You see how you long for me. You should have spared your backside a thrashing." He grinned, satisfied at her desire for him.

"Fergus, please…"

"Where shall I touch you, sweetheart?" he asked, but he couldn't deny the swoosh of blood flooding his cock, making it pulsate.

"There…" she whimpered, and he smiled. He slid his fingers inside her. She hissed, stilled, barely breathing, only aware of her pleasure, her wet channel throbbing wantonly.

He thrust in and out. She moaned so loud that a proud smile curled upon his lips.

"Shush! Or they'll hear you up the hill!" He smirked, but the glistening head of his cock was pulsating and beating against his trousers. He slid his fingers out of her.

"No, please!" she blurted.

"Umm… I am giving you a terrible habit with all this pleasure after you misbehave. You'll act worse, so I can spank you again."

"No, I promise." Marguerite begged him to resume. She panted little cries when his fingertips lingered caressingly, through the length of her slit, teasing. Desire and need dazed her. "F-Fergus, p-please," she stammered.

He sat her up on his lap and tenderly wiped a tearstain from her face. His expression was soft and loving, as he caressed her cheek. Then his mouth crashed on hers ravenously. He kissed her senseless.

She puffed short breaths as his fingers glided inside her again. She looked at him, dazed. She was so aroused.

"Who's a greedy girl now? Hey?" he asked as he thrust his fingers inside her.

She grabbed his face in her hands and kissed him in a frenzy of lust. As his fingers continued to pleasure her, and when her orgasm hit her hard, she panted sweet little cries until she reached her climax. She thought she was going to pass out. Her cute, tiny cries in his mouth delighted him. She wanted him so wantonly!

"Oh, Fergus…" she whispered in a purring voice.

"Yes, love?"

"Umm…"

He unzipped her dress and slipped it off her body. Her panties, already halfway down, slid off her legs onto the floor with it. He took her bra off, it ending up on the heap on the floor, too.

He caressed Marguerite's body with long, sensual strokes. Fergus sucked her breasts. Her hand strayed to his manhood inside his trousers.

He raised his head to her. She stood, and so did he. She undid his zip and pulled his trousers off, together with his boxers.

He couldn't resist her any longer, scooping her up into his arms and bringing her to the bed. He tried to undo his shirt, but it was too much effort, and his need was so strong. So, he didn't bother, leaving it on. He parted her legs, and in one swift movement, his cock slid inside her.

"Heavenly! Wet. Beautiful!" he mumbled, pausing inside her. "I love it when you are like this." He stilled, trying to control his desire. Then he thrust in and out, struggling to make it last.

Marguerite panted his name. He took her nipples in his mouth, sucking them, then rubbing and pinching them. He repeated much of the same with each bud, until they were hard and purple like a blooming violet.

She arched her back, ready again. He pressed her down as he thrust a few more times.

His cock pulsated inside her throbbing pussy. She cried his name in soft, panting moans until her climax hit her apex, while a guttural sound, from deep inside him, reverberated around the room as his release came.

Chapter 18

He caressed her tenderly, placing small random kisses on her face. Marguerite giggled as his lips tickled the hollow of her neck.

Fergus withdrew from her and rolled to the side, pulling her with him in an embrace. They lay side by side on the bed for a while, silent and satiated.

"Hell, see what you do to me? Didn't even manage to take off my shirt," he said at last with a laugh. "Jesus, wife, you arouse me like crazy. As if I were a teenager with a sweetheart. Damn!" He continued with a love-struck, tender gaze, "But you are my sweetheart, aren't you?"

She lifted her head from his chest to peer at him, raising an eyebrow. "Are you finally going sappy on me, husband?" she snorted, but there was emotion in his eyes as he caressed her. She gazed into his eyes steadily for a moment, searching, then pressed her lips to his, satisfied and proud of his love. She sighed, contented, then playfully shoved him with her shoulder. She pushed him back flat onto the bed and straddled him.

"Let me help you then. I don't want anybody to say I am not a good wife." She smiled mischievously as she unfastened a button on his shirt. Her glorious raven hair cascaded about her in soft ringlets, and a naughty smile formed on Fergus's lips.

"Be my guest." He winked at her. "Show me, then. How good are you, wife?" He grinned, looking at her in wonderment. His nostrils flared in delight. He folded his arms under his head, satisfied with life. He enjoyed the splendid view of his beautiful, naked woman taking charge.

Marguerite tilted her head to one side, studying him for a second with a playful glint in her eyes. Thus, she went to work on him, her pulse hammering. As she uncovered every inch of his skin with each button undone, she brushed her sugary lips on the smooth, steely wall of muscles on his chest. She swiped aside the soft material of his evening shirt when she was done and nipped his nipples softly with her teeth.

He groaned.

Her enticing tongue played on his skin, licking and swirling around his nipples. She plundered down to his ribcage. She stroked and teased him like a devilish temptress. Her pink, wondrous, tempting little tongue allowed her heavenly sweet lips to kiss and taste him, too. Marguerite brushed them on his body down to his belly button.

The pleasure of her touch causing havoc inside him, his body jolted as if in an electrical storm of passion. A feeling of possessiveness aroused him to the nines, in the unequivocal thought that she was his woman, and his alone. Fergus adored the enticing siren.

He felt hot while a rush of blood swelled his cock. As if honey was pouring out of her and he was a soldier bee drenching in it, in awe of her. The difference… he had all his life to enjoy his queen, forever.

She tried to take his shirt off. Marguerite struggled with it until he helped her, and it was off. She had him naked, to admire and caress.

Then, flat on his back, at her complete mercy, he resumed his position, resting his arms under his head.

Her seductive tongue reclaimed his belly button, kissing it, licking it. The warmth between her legs grew as she slid farther down and took his cock into her mouth, tasting him.

He hissed a low growl and couldn't resist anchoring his hands in her hair, wrapping his palm around her locks, fisting them, guiding the motion of her mouth on him, until she found the rhythm he liked.

She was enjoying him, too, her pussy soaked. Her honeyed lips curled, titillating, around him. She sucked and licked up and down his manhood, until her hot lips worked their magic and his orgasm exploded, lavish and protracted.

She released him once he was totally spent. A long, drawn-out hiss of satisfaction emanated from his mouth, and it gratified her that she had pleasured him.

Marguerite lay on top of him for some time. She was still caressing him when he opened his eyes. He gazed at her in rapture. His woman. His heart flooded with emotion for her, and a sweet kiss ensued, the tenderness and devotion pouring out of him.

"God, what am I to do with you, hey? I won't be able to work anymore. All I want to do is spend the rest of my days in bed with you," he mumbled as he nibbled on her lips.

He could taste himself in her mouth and it excited him all over. Thus, he turned the tables, and in a moment, she landed on her back. He was over her.

It was his turn to capture her nipples between his fingers as his mouth met hers in a luscious and passionate exchange. He cupped her bosom, kneading them, grazing her pert tips with his fingertips, his teeth, sucking and licking them until her pink buds peaked. Her breasts swelled. A dribble came out of her pussy down along her butt. She moaned and panted his name in a soft burst of air.

His mouth moved south on her body, kissing every inch of her creamy, silky skin as he arrived in between her shapely legs. He spread them and positioned his hands on her inner thighs to keep them open. He plunged his tongue inside her. "God! Wet and juicy, my love, delicious!" he murmured to himself after tasting her pussy.

She moaned aloud, as his expert tongue was king inside her, panting his name.

"Shush, darling, they'll hear you upstairs." He beamed, proud to see her like this. He played with her soft folds, stroking them, parting them to give his tongue better access.

Marguerite's need soared. Her sex engorged; she wanted release. Her clit ached and throbbed.

"Please, Fergus," she pleaded, panting his name several times, urging him. His manhood grew hard, massive, and needy, while his mouth feasted on her pussy. He stopped.

Fergus leapt on all fours. He was all over her. Then, he plunged his cock inside her without warning, in a powerful action. She yelped her delight, and she was ready in no time.

"Wait, darling."

"Please."

"Wait."

"I can't."

"You can..." he repeated, but every muscle in her body was highly charged and pulsating. She needed release as he hammered in and out, again and again, in fiery passion.

She clenched her walls around him, and a few strokes was all it took.

"Come for me, babe!" he mumbled in ragged breaths, and she sighed in soft cries as they both reached their thunderous climaxes with a dizzying rush of ecstasy until their bodies went limp.

He slumped on top of her for a few moments, totally done in. Then he withdrew from her, lying alongside her. He drew her close to him and wrapped his arms around her. They stayed like that, thoroughly spent for some time, exhausted, not moving, not speaking, enjoying the warmth of their bodies with small random kisses now and then.

"Are you okay?" he asked at last as he caressed the scar on her shoulder.

"Aha!" She sent him the languid smile of one who was satiated with love.

He laughed and grazed at her profile with his fingertips. "And we have broken with tradition!"

"Have we?" she asked, kissing his jaw.

"Sweet lips, all Earls of Buckley's new brides have spent their first night in this house in the earl's room with their lord and master, without fail, but we haven't."

"Lord and master?" She snorted and slapped his arm playfully. "I assume they had long engagements with their wives before the wedding, ha?"

"I suppose so."

"So, there you are, we differ from them, handsome! Or are you complaining about me?" she said, looking at him with narrow eyes.

He pulled her to him for a kiss. "No, my love, no complaints. I adore you," he said.

She stilled, with tears in her eyes. She caressed his long hair out of his handsome face. "I don't think I ever stopped loving you since Nice," she replied in a mellow voice, and she placed her head on his chest.

He put her arms tight around her, kissing the top of her head. "I know, love."

"You do?"

"It's the same for me." He came back with a tender smile, stroking her cheek. They held each other close for a while, wallowing in their warmth.

"Tell me about Natasha, Lucy's mother. Did you love her?"

she asked after a while, studying him. But she lowered her eyes, a little ashamed of her blazing curiosity for the mother of his child.

"How do you know her name?" He raised his head to look at her and smiled indulgently.

"Lucy told me. Well... did you love her?"

"No!" he said flatly.

"No?" she uttered in a high-pitched tone. She peered at him with a wrinkled brow, her head back. She wasn't sure if she believed him, or not, but he reassured her.

"It was a short fling. I barely knew her. I met her in a club. It happened months before I met you. I was young, a bit of a playboy. It all fizzled out quickly. She wasn't my type. But I didn't know she was pregnant until I returned from Nice when you disappeared on me. A couple of months after I was back, one morning, Natasha came into my office and gave me the shock of my life—apart from the shock that was marrying you. God! What a thunderbolt that was. Anyway, Natasha wouldn't mind doing a test, in fact, she suggested it. She didn't want me to have any doubts about it. She was a fair girl, and Lucy is my daughter, all right, no qualms about it."

"I could have told you that just by looking at the child. She is the spitting image of you, such a beautiful girl. She'll grow into a gorgeous young woman. Oh, the admirers she is going to have."

"I'll kill any bugger who messes up with her!" he spat in all seriousness, and she snorted.

"The protective dad. I had forgotten. She'll have a hard time with you when she gets to boyfriends."

"Boyfriends? She is my little girl. I'll protect her from any scumbag. Just as if any bugger were to mess with you now, sweet lips. I'll send them to the devil in no time."

She burst out laughing. "Oh, Fergus, for a modern man, you are quite traditional. But why do you hold her as a secret?

She is such a darling," she asked with a disappointed frown and a sway of her head.

"I don't keep her a secret. She spends most of her time here. So, not many people know about her. She doesn't bear my name."

"What? Oh, Fergus, how could you?" She sprang to a sitting position on the bed. "That won't do," she said indignantly. "You are her father!"

"I know! At the time, Natasha rushed to the town hall to declare the childbirth and put 'father unknown' on the birth certificate without telling anyone. I only found out about this a couple of years ago when Lucy started play school and we had to provide documents. But Natasha had gone by then. She had done it so I would not take the girl away from her. She had always feared this, though I reassured her constantly." He paused, pensive for a second. "But what's done is done, and I am working with my lawyers now to change that, to give her my name."

"Good! She is of school age now; it would be good to put things right," Marguerite agreed. "And another thing, if we are to be a family, both Lucy and I must be with you. She is not staying here if you are in Oxford, and neither am I," she declared, raising her chin. She moved close to him, staring him down with a scowl.

He laughed and pulled her to him for a kiss, but her furrowing brow told him she wouldn't budge, no matter how sweet he was to her. "You'll get bored when I am working long hours in town and—"

"Fergus Waltham, if you think you'll hide your daughter and me here, in the countryside, as much as I love the place, you have another think coming. Understood? I won't have it." She was about to leave the bed, but he got hold of her wrist and stopped her. He drew her to him with a forceful tug. She yelped, and he kissed her ravenously, devouring her.

She soon mellowed again.

"I couldn't, even if I wanted to, sweet lips. I can't stay away from you. It would kill me," he said in all seriousness, with tenderness in his eyes.

"Good, I am glad to hear it." She caressed his face and kissed his brow.

He scoffed. "I can't believe it how easily Lucy has taken with you, Marguerite. She already adores you. She told me you are lovely."

"Aww, did she?"

"And I happen to agree with her." He moved closer to caress her, giving her a lick on her neck.

She giggled and playfully shoved him away, but he grabbed her, stealing a kiss. "Well, go on, what happened next?" she asked again when the kissing stopped, her fingers caressing his chest in tiny circles as she spoke.

"Anyway, birth certificate aside, when Lucy was born, we decided she should live with Natasha. I saw her often. I mean, she is so adorable. I couldn't keep away from my daughter. Another reason I quit searching for you. I didn't want to leave Lucy for long. But you were in my mind. I swear, you have been all these years," he said, caressing her face, giving her small kisses over her eyes and nose.

"Yes, handsome, you were, too, always," she replied, and her pink tongue flicked on his neck.

He groaned. "Funny how we both felt the same, though circumstances got in the way. Believe me when I say Chloe or any other woman before you meant nothing to me. Only you, my love, then and now. Only you," he said, lamenting the wasted years.

"I know," she said with a coy, satisfied smile.

"Are you happy we got a second chance, darling?" His hand stroked her tummy.

"More than anything!"

"For the first few days, I cursed my father. I must admit, now, I send him a *thank you* prayer every night. Well, not in the orthodox sense of the word, but a prayer all the same." He laughed.

She caressed his chest, placing more random kisses on him. "Tell me, how did she die? Natasha, I mean, was it an accident?" She was curious about the mother of his child.

"No. She got sick; an aggressive form of cancer took her in six months. It devastated us; my daughter was only three. So Lucy came to live with me. It was difficult at first. She missed her mother, but we managed. Her granny, Ruby, Natasha's mum, lives on the estate too. She is out visiting a relative this week. You'll like her. She is a no-nonsense lady, a wonderful grandmother."

"What sort of woman was Natasha?"

"Attractive. Sweet. But I didn't get to know her when we had our affair. We were not in love. It was just sex. Then we became friends when the child was born. We got on well. She had a restlessness about her. Sometimes we argued about Lucy. But we always reached a compromise."

"I see."

They kissed for a while until he was on top of her, brushing her forehead, her eyes, her nose with his lips.

"Fergus?" she called out to him.

"Yes, sweet lips?"

"If we hurry, and go to yours, to the earl's bedroom, I mean, we will not break with tradition. We would have just enhanced it with making love in the countess' bedroom, too," she said with a light laugh. "Besides, I have not seen your bedroom yet."

"So, be it, my countess!"

He rose and pulled her up in his arms while she shrieked with joy. "Shush!"

"Darling, wait, we cannot go in the hallway like this,

naked, even if it is down the hallway. What if someone sees us? Besides, what about Crispin, tomorrow morning? Won't he come into your room?"

"He won't dare come in. The moment I knew you were coming to the estate this afternoon, I gave him two days off."

"I see, but you cannot carry me naked in the hallway. It won't do!"

"Fine." He deposited her back onto the bed. He took her gown and wrapped it around her, as if he was wrapping a parcel. She giggled all the way. He lifted her in his arms again, and another high-pitched squeal left her lungs.

"Shush, what a noisy wife I've got! Um…"

She laughed as he jostled her, trying to open the door. "Fergus, but you are still stark naked."

"Oh, bloody hell, it doesn't matter, now. It's late, everyone has gone to bed," he said, as she reached for the handle and opened the door, still scooped up in his arms. He made a run for it.

When Briggs suddenly appeared on the landing from the floor above, the housekeeper halted and gasped, astonished at the naked lord.

"Sorry, Briggs, on wife's duties!" He chuckled, nonplussed in his nakedness, while Marguerite blushed furiously.

Mrs. Briggs flushed too, as he made a beeline for his bedroom and disappeared down the hall, exposing his well-toned, muscled derrière to the unsuspecting woman.

Chapter 19

They remained on the estate for the entire week. He postponed his appointments, and they spent a marvelous time as a close-knit family. On the day after her arrival, Fergus took it upon himself to introduce Marguerite, formally, to his staff, as his countess.

It secretly delighted his team; at last, the earl had settled down. The reason for their joy, he would be more obliging for all matters associated to his obligations as an earl and the estate now he had a wife.

Not to mention, his sweet new bride enchanted them when the cook made the newlyweds a splendid welcome cake, and the lady asked them all to share it with them, while Fergus opened a few bottles of champagne from his reserve to toast the auspicious moment. The impromptu household party was a great success. They had never seen him so relaxed and contented.

Fergus gave her a tour of Penningbrooke Hall. He revealed the splendours of his stately home, one-by-one. He roamed around the residence with his wife, Lucy trotting ecstatic with them, too. His three dogs followed them everywhere at the rear, sometimes overexcited, they got in their way at the front.

She loved the huge central hall entrance. It never failed to mesmerise Marguerite as she wandered through it. The enormous proportions of it, with its marble floor and the crystal chandelier, coming down from the soaring ceiling like a haughty gleaming star in the firmament, impressed her anew on her way in and out of the house every time.

He showed her the staterooms on the first floor, where it was said, in times bygone, kings and queens had honoured the family with a visit. They inspected several of the morning rooms and the drawing rooms of varied sizes and colours on the same floor.

The famous Penningbrooke's ballroom was renowned for miles around the county. It was massive, light, with huge arched windows and high ceilings, several hanging crystal chandeliers, and intricate parquet wood flooring. It shimmered all around, with the light of the crystals reflecting on the walls. It seemed to her she could hear the music reverberating in the room. In the past, glittering balls had come to pass when his mother was alive, but very few since.

Two still influenced the social calendar, though, the Harvest Ball in September and the Christmas Ball. These had long traditions. The family held them on alternate years now, rather than both every year as it was once. Close friends, tenants and neighbours attended in great finery.

"As my wife, the Harvest and the Christmas Balls will fall on you to organise and deliver," he said in all seriousness.

Marguerite gulped, and she blinked fast, gazing at him.

"Don't worry, darling. We'll help, won't we, Lucy?" he added with a wink to his daughter, seeing his wife's anxious face. He ruffled the child's hair, who nodded eagerly, and he placed a kiss on Marguerite's cheek.

They stopped at the small chapel with its cavernous vaulting roof and tall alabaster pillars. Its tinted glass windows had enchanting celestial paintings on them.

"I wish we had married here, it is so lovely," Marguerite replied, then she blushed at her unwitting remark.

A regretful smile formed on his lips as the memory of having ruined her wedding day flashed back to him. A pang of remorse ate at him.

"I guess you must make it up to me for not marrying me in this beautiful chapel, don't you?" She giggled, almost as if she read his mind. He leaned over and kissed the top of her head.

"You mean instead of the mausoleum in Oxford?" Fergus scoffed, "I will, my love. I promise."

They strolled through the portraits and landscapes gallery, where prestigious mesmerising watercolours and oils reigned supreme. His impressive collection of paintings, with many originals from famous masters, was priceless. He told her old folk tales as they looked at some of his ancestors' portraits, those with a more colourful past.

She threw her head back. A silly snort escaped her. "Well, I never," she repeated through some of the more spicy stories.

"Darling, stop saying that," he uttered. "What should she say, Lucy?" he asked in humour, turning to his daughter.

"Your ancestors are splendid, my lord," the child replied, full of pomp, solemnly. They both laughed, while the little girl looked at them with a crease on her forehead, but he scooped Lucy up in his arms and twirled around, to his daughter's delight.

"Your forebearers seem a bit shameful to me. I understand now why you are the Dark Lord, with such pedigree," she whispered in his ear in amusement when he stopped twirling.

He put Lucy back on her feet, and then he swatted his wife's ass.

She yelped, holding her butt, and raised her eyebrows, shaking her head, warning him to be wary of the girl. A playful, intimate smile spread on his face that said, *'I'll remind you later!'*

Marguerite had never seen a stately home so grand, aside from Versailles. Jones had told her on that first afternoon on the hill, *'it is a lavish house.'* Though nothing had prepared her for the extensive luxury, art collection, and grandeur of it.

"Don't forget, darling, as my countess, you are now the mistress of this house. Of all of my houses, as a matter of fact."

"How many houses d-do y-you have?" she asked him with a trembling voice, in wonderment, dreading the answer.

"Um... I'll ask Perkins for the exact number. Perhaps twelve in Britain, I'm not sure. They are all large residences, but this is the largest. There are others overseas. You must also dart an eye on my brothers' estates, as they are working abroad this year. These should have been part of my holdings as firstborn, too, from my mother's family. But at a young age, I concluded my father's patrimony was big enough for me to handle. So Sebastian and Frederick will take over the estates inherited from mother's side of the family at some point. Assuming the blackguards will stop messing around and settle down. Oh, and as for Belinda, she'll be a wealthy woman on her 25th birthday, God help us all!" He raised his eyebrows with an ominous smile.

She returned a small tentative one, gawping at him, and blushed to the roots of her hair. She shivered. Would she be up to the challenge? She wasn't sure.

"Don't be anxious, sweet lips. Briggs and Bancroft are here to help you." This time he gazed into her eyes and his grin was tender and amorous.

She nodded solemnly, indicating she understood her role. His father had explained it extensively to her when he came looking for her, but she had never imagined the extent of it, the extent of his wealth.

Then it was time for Fergus to show her the luscious gardens, exuberant and so pretty.

The sun was bright and high in the blue sky, a few wispy clouds meandering the celestial mantle. The breeze was crisp, bringing with it a myriad of sweet fragrances from the flowers in bloom around the grounds. It was an enchanting spring day. In that beautiful setting, with her loving new family around her, Marguerite believed she had entered a magic fairytale, as if she were in a dream. *Perhaps my troublesome past is truly over, and my future will be a joy. Please, God, don't make me wake up if I am dreaming.*

His voice took her out of her reverie. "There are two hundred acres of formal gardens, lawns, pleasure grounds, and lakes, many places for us to wander. You'll enjoy them, darling."

"They are gorgeous!"

"On the left of the estate, there are 1200 acres of woodlands, where deer roam free," he said as he came closer to her. He put his hand on her shoulders, turned her body to look toward the woods, and pointed with his finger in the general direction.

She raised a hand over her eyes to gaze in the distance at the deer park.

"Of course, farmlands surround it all, acres and acres of rich land, all tenanted. I must introduce you to the farmers and their families. And don't worry, Chloe has promised to behave," he whispered this last sentence in her ear nonchalantly while she flushed. But he rushed on before she could make any comment to his last statement, "It's customary for the farmers to meet the new lady of the house. We'll visit them in the next few days on horseback if the weather holds."

"Horseback? I've never ridden a horse in my life."

"Don't worry, my love, you'll learn. Nothing to it, is there, Lucy?"

"It's easy, Marguerite. I can teach you," the child said, eager to please, holding her hand.

"Oh, that would be wonderful, sweetie, but you must be patient with me." She kissed the top of the girl's head.

They were approaching the lake. They strolled down to it, where bluebells and marigolds were in bloom.

"As if I had a premonition, the marigolds are in your honour, my lovely Marguerite," he said, with an enamoured smile that took her breath away.

Sweet Jesus, he is so handsome, she thought as they wandered on. He must have picked up something in her face as he caressed her arm with his fingers with a knowing look and winked at her.

The path was stunning, with the grounds carpeted in blue and orange. They passed the marble statue walk, astonishing with its carved, beautiful sculptures.

On their return to the house, Lucy took her hand and pulled her into the maze. They played with the child and the dogs for a while as he explained how, as children, he and his siblings used to love getting lost in there, playing hide and seek.

The next day, they had a picnic on the lawn, enjoying the day outside, to Lucy's delight.

Fergus gave them time alone, too, so his wife could get to know his daughter while he caught up with urgent businesses commitments in his study.

He couldn't believe how everything had changed for him, now she was in his life again. It was as if a dark cloud had lifted from the sky, and from his soul, and in its wake, joy and love were pouring light into his world.

━━━━━

On the next two days, they roamed the woodlands and the farms on horseback. Sometimes, she sat behind Fergus' stallion on short horse double rides. Lucy was already an excellent rider on her pony.

"I have a surprise for you," he said on the third morning.

"What?"

"Come with me."

"What is it?" Marguerite asked with a childish grin. Her eyes sparkled, eager to know what he had in store for her.

"Well, you must wait and see."

They left the house and walked toward the stables, Lucy trotting behind them as well as the dogs.

"Come on, Lucy, keep up," Fergus said and winked at the child as she caught up with them.

"You'll like your surprise, Marguerite," the girl said in a high-pitched voice. Her excitement was bursting as they reached the stable and she got a fit of giggles.

"Morning, my lord," the stable master said, "shall I bring it out?"

"Good morning, Rory. Yes, please," he said, as they exchanged a few words of pleasantries.

A few minutes later, Rory came out with a fine, tall, elegant horse. The coat was a vibrant, light chestnut, with a whitish, long mane and tail.

"Your wedding present, darling, a lovely Haflinger mare, with a beautiful temperament and a quiet nature. She will be ideal for you to learn to ride," he said with a proud smile.

Everyone in the family had their own horse, including a few thoroughbreds for racing. Fergus had spent two hours each day teaching her how to ride. But his bride didn't have a horse of her own until then.

"Oh, my God, Fergus, she's beautiful!" Marguerite's eyes glittered, and she gave him a little bump with her shoulder, then rubbed the horse's nose. She accepted an apple from the stable master to give to the mare. The horse devoured it and nuzzled her new owner.

"It's a great breed for beginners. Her name is Pretty, she is so gentle. You'll enjoy learning to ride her."

"Oh, the name suits her so well. Hello, Pretty!" She patted the horse's neck and nose lovingly. Lucy held her hand up with another apple.

"You can ride with me and Lucy to the farmlands this afternoon. I'll introduce you to a new tenant. It'll give you confidence. Learning to ride will be fun, darling, but Pretty won't spook easily. She is safe."

So they did. She was bursting with pride, sitting on her new horse. To Marguerite, the magic dream got better every day.

The week was at an end. They would move back to Oxford the next day, with Olivia, Lucy, and her grandmother joining them in a day or two.

Marguerite made a point. If they were to be a family, they'd need to be close. She was firm on that. If Fergus must stay in Oxford, so would his wife, daughter, and her grand-mother. They would be where he was.

Though Lucy's grandmother, Ruby, would be coming and going as she pleased, now taking a back seat, and enchanted, the child cherished her new mother. They would embark on a new life together.

That night, in their bed, in the earl's room, Marguerite

kissed him tenderly. "I am so glad I took your father's challenge and married you. I was dubious and didn't know what to expect. I adore your child. I am devoted to your family," she said as a tear came down on her cheek. "There were times in my life I thought happiness did not exist. That life was only sorrow and fear, but now... Oh, Fergus, I am so happy. I love you!"

He caressed her hair with an intimate, adoring gaze and brushed the tear off her face with his thumb. Then he kissed her, satisfied and proud of her love.

"I am so glad that you took the challenge, my darling. I thank you for being so brave and taking me, my daughter, and my family on. And I worship you! I'll never let you go again. Never!" he said, and to the ravenous kiss, followed more.

Chapter 20

He was pacing the hallway as if he were a caged animal. Seemingly, to relax for a few minutes, but he was far from composed. She'd ordered him to take a break, even if he didn't wish to.

"Would you like a cup of tea, my lord? I can serve it in your study if you prefer, with a dash of brandy perhaps?" Mrs. Briggs asked him, seeing him agitated as he walked up and down the hallway with a frown on his face.

"She virtually threw me out. She lied, of course, suggesting sweetly I need a break instead, but I don't want to leave her, Briggs," Fergus blurted out, dragging a hand through his tousled hair. His locks, dishevelled, were going all over the place. He was flustered, and his restless energy continued as he paced the hallway anew, flexing his fingers repeatedly.

"I understand, my lord. It's natural you should worry. But perhaps a brief rest would do you good," the woman tried soothingly, but he rubbed his temples, puffing out a breath.

"No, I'm going back in," he replied with no qualms. His mouth was dry. He could have done with a brandy, but he could not bear staying away from her for a minute longer, whether or not she liked it. So five minutes later, he opened the door to the room and stepped inside.

"Fergus! I thought I told you to go for a walk," Marguerite said with a heavy sigh. A flush appeared on her face, and she rubbed her tummy.

"A walk? When you are in here like this? I am not going anywhere, love. No!" he stated with finality, shaking his head. He gazed at her without blinking. When her eyes narrowed on him at his stubbornness, she muttered an oath under her breath.

He lowered his gaze and rubbed the back of his neck.

"Oh, darling, please…" she implored him, inclining her head on one side, pouting.

Nine months thereafter, from the evening when they first made love in the earl's bedroom, almost precisely to the day, his wife was ready. The baby was coming!

The end of January, and what better way to start a new year, he thought. His palms were still sweaty. Thank God, at least his heart rate was slowing down since he had seen the puddle on the floor at dinner, under her chair, when her waters had broken.

He had known this moment would come. He had been preparing for it. Now that it was upon them, despite his usual self-control, he panicked, while Marguerite had looked on at him coolly and calmly, with amusement in her eyes. She reminded him to call the midwife and the nurse, as they agreed. But it took him a little while to get himself under control.

During the previous months, he had insisted on a hospital birth, but Marguerite had refused. She had stood her ground. She wanted the baby born at Penningbrooke Hall, in the earl's room, no less. And that was exactly where they were that evening.

She had stubbornly said that all his predecessors, all those earls who had held the room before him through the centuries, were going to look benignly upon the newcomer. They would wish her well on the birth of the new heir, and she would auspiciously bring her son into the world.

They had known the sex of the baby in advance, and Marguerite had built herself that mystical notion, with a pigheaded conviction about her. Nothing he said or did through the months would persuade her out of it. He could not change her mind.

He tried to dissuade her, time and time again. But she would not hear of it. So, reluctantly, and against his better judgement, he had agreed to it.

She wanted a natural birth, in a peaceful and familiar environment. So, the earl's bedroom, where she had spent many happy hours with her husband, was that place for her.

Fergus was not taking any chances, though.

Three doors down the hallway, there was a room ready for an emergency. He had hired all the medical equipment necessary for an operation if she should need a cesarean section. An obstetrician strolled on the grounds, not straying far from the house, in the event they should need her to perform the procedure.

Marguerite was annoyed at this, but she allowed him that eccentricity as long as it didn't interfere with her or the birth. But she wished to see none of it.

"What the hell are you doing up? Are you mad?" he said frantically, seeing her walking around the room.

"Fergus, my contractions only began less than two hours ago, and they are so random and way apart for now. Not that I am complaining, but they are rather mild. They feel more like cramps. I promise you, they are not uncomfortable. I can walk well enough," Marguerite tried to reassure him with a mellow voice, as if he were a petulant child.

She had a nurse and the midwife in attendance for the birth. And of course, her husband was there, too. But if she had to confess, from the instant Marguerite's waters broke, Fergus had been more of a hindrance than a help.

"All the same, I don't think—" he ventured, but the midwife stopped him.

"My lord, it's beneficial for your wife to walk around the room for a few minutes. She is at the early stages of labour. You are in for a long night, no reason for alarm. Give her your arm so she can lean on you while she does it," the experienced woman said, trying to sound not too condescending to a worried, expectant father.

"If you say so," he said with a sigh and gave Marguerite his arm. She leaned on him and gave him a sweet smile, holding her enormous belly, caressing it.

Fergus wasn't a first-time father. He already had Lucy. But Natasha did not disclose to him she was expecting his child until she was well into her eighth month. So he didn't support her on specific experiences, such as prenatal or childbirth classes or clinic visits. When he got his head around the fact, it was time for her to give birth. Natasha had a quick delivery, too, and by the time Fergus went to the emergency room, he was too late. Lucy was in the world and waiting to meet her new dad. So, his experience was limited on these matters, almost nonexistent. Hence, he had been determined he would not miss a thing with Marguerite.

This time, he stayed closed to his wife during the experience. As Marguerite's pregnancy progressed, his interest in it increased. He chose an active participation in every minor aspect of it. So far, he had enjoyed the experience. He learned more than his wife on every detail, while she focused on the practical things instead.

Fergus read countless books on pregnancy and childbirth. He was nervous about it, rather more than his wife.

Marguerite had chosen this period to be calm instead. Besides, he wasn't sure what to make of it all. He trained his mind to expect the unexpected.

That night, Marguerite felt peaceful, the most tranquil she had been throughout the pregnancy. She would say throughout her life. Nothing seemed to disturb her from her peace of mind and from her focus. When her waters broke, a joy and a composure had taken possession of her. She was determined to deliver her son into the world in a harmonious and serene atmosphere. That was, Fergus permitting, who had chosen that evening to turn his natural self-control and self-restraint into a nutcase.

She kept herself calm through the early stages of labour. She remembered to perform her breathing exercises. She was strong and dignified in the face of pain during her contractions. She walked around the room. She leaned on him. When he got agitated, again, and insisted she was tiring herself and she should go back to bed, she scowled at him, her lips in a thin line.

"Darling, breath, relax. I am fine," she said to him. There was a hint of amusement in her eyes. Seeing her normally calm husband so put out and anxious, was hilarious for her. That was until he got on her nerves and he became too irritating. So, she sent him off, out of the room, for another break.

"Take a stroll, Fergus. And this time do it. Don't dare come back for an hour. Do you understand? You are panicking!"

"An hour! Panicking? Me? I am just—" he echoed, incredulous, but she didn't let him finish.

"Out, or I won't let you in again! There is plenty of time. Go for a walk. Relax. And when you return, you'd better be calm." Her temporary distress brought on another contraction, which took her by surprise. He tried to grab her and put her to bed.

"Out, you are making me nervous. Don't show your face until you can control yourself. Do you hear me?" she screamed at him, "Nurse, take this man out of the room."

Fergus decided a little fresh air would do him good to clear his head. He didn't want to upset Marguerite again, given the circumstances. She was too damn right; he had to compose himself. *What's wrong with you, man?* he rebuked himself. *Take a grip on yourself!*

He walked around the grounds with his three dogs, Dolly, Vronsky, and Levin. He was reading Tolstoy's books, when the dogs had first arrived at the house years ago, hence he had chosen the dogs' names out of characters in one of his book. That night, he was glad to spend time with them. Fergus played with them. Dolly, his large, black shorthaired Labrador, rubbed her fur on his leg twice, always in-sync with her master. The intuitive dog recognised he had something on his mind.

Fergus stroked her. "You silly girl!" He scratched Dolly's nose, relaxing somewhat. Soon, impatience got the better of him again. He went back to the house and moved to his study for a brandy. As he was sipping his drink at his desk, he saw the envelope on the counter.

The one Perkins, his secretary, had sent to the estate that afternoon. He had forgotten all about it with the chaos of his wife in childbirth. The man had marked it *urgent*. He recognised his secretary's handwriting.

Fergus glanced at his wristwatch. It was nowhere near the hour yet that Marguerite had ordered him to stay out. So he opened the pouch. There was a note from Perkins, with a second envelope inside. He darted at the postmark. It came from France. His secretary's note asked him for instructions on the matter. Then, he read the letter from an acquaintance at the French Prisons Bureau. His eyes almost bulged out of their sockets. His face blanched, and his jaw tightened. Alain Basset's case was going to the Parole Board in three months!

Curses as black as the night tumbled out of Fergus' mouth. He would have to send Perkins instructions on this. How strong was the bastard's case? Could the brute win it? Alain could be out soon! Fergus would not let that man near his wife again. He would kill the bastard if he did. He replaced the letter in the envelope and locked it in his drawer. Then he replied to Perkins with instructions.

Was this an omen? To read this letter the day his wife was about to give birth to his son? He must not tell Marguerite. She believed in these things. It would freak her out. *She will not know,* he vowed.

Strangely, the letter sobered him up in an instant from the giddiness of having a child, of becoming a father. His calmness descended over him like a mantle. His head cleared. The warrior instinct took over him instead. He would protect his wife and children with his life.

The obstetrician had a cup of tea and was reading a book when Fergus entered the library. He shared a cup of tea with the woman, who reassured him all was fine.

Soon his feet drew him back to the room. He listened from the outside; there was no sound coming from it, and everything seemed well. Still, ten minutes before the hour was up for him. He felt restless, thinking about the letter. *Marguerite and the baby are my priority right now. Focus on her, on my son's birth.*

He sighed, discontented. He went up to the nursery to see

Lucy. The child was asleep. So he sat in the armchair next to her bed, looking at his sweet girl, and a tenderness filled his heart. Watching her sleep calmed him even more. It worked its magic. His self-control had flooded back. The usual Fergus was in place.

He returned to the room with a renewed energy, focused and chilled. He would not say a word to Marguerite about Alain. *She must not know*, he resolved.

There was no point in worrying her. She had a baby and Lucy to think about. Nothing should distract her from her rediscovered joy. She was happy with her new life, an existence that included Fergus and children. He would not allow that man to ruin her happiness again. Ever! He would kill the bugger if he came anywhere near his wife again.

Marguerite's contractions increased in number and length. They became sharper and more severe. When dawn came, they were five minutes apart. *Things are heating up*, he thought. She was almost ready for birth.

Fergus peeked. He spotted a crown of dark russet hair ready to pop out of her. He felt a pang in his heart for mother and baby. It reminded him of the beautiful painting he had once seen in the Pezzoli Museum in Milan, the Madonna of the Book by Botticelli. Visions of his wife and infant in months to come, in a similar stance as that in the painting, assailed him. An outpouring of love so intense rushed out of him and would soon unleash on them. *I must concentrate on encouraging Marguerite*, he told himself. *Don't lose focus now.*

But his boy was in no hurry to meet the world. The contractions didn't let up for her. They had become fervent. She tried to change positions on the bed, side-to-side, squatting. She couldn't find one that suited her or eased her suffering. The firm pressure on her pelvis was forceful. She was bracing to push. The contractions had altogether ballooned, with brief intervals between them. Marguerite's urge to push was strong.

Throughout the last hours of her ordeal, Fergus sat on a chair next to the head of her bed, holding her hand. He was cool and collected, composed, assisting her while the nurse and the midwife did their jobs at the other end.

Every time the pain came, she squeezed his hand hard. He thought she must have crushed several bones in his hand. But he smiled at her serenely, with no complaints or a hint at his discomfort.

"Breathe, darling," he would say. He would breathe in sync with her. Though it was also a comfort for his battered hand and the depressing thoughts about Alain.

But she had courage! How on earth was Marguerite enduring such an agony so bravely? It was beyond him.

The baby's crown on show, the last stage was upon them now.

"Push, darling, push," he said between sharp breaths, as they taught him at prenatal classes.

"Stop telling me what to do!" she wailed at him, while another severe contraction took her breath away. Fergus winced in anguish when she squeezed his hand so hard, he thought his wife had developed nutcrackers instead of hands. He didn't let on, though. He carried on caring for her with an impassive face, and within minutes, the baby was born.

Marguerite wept when she heard her child cry for the first time. The lad had a good pair of lungs on him. While Fergus was dumfounded, he had no words. He just grinned at her, from ear to ear, at the most wonderful mystery of nature.

"Your son, my lord, handsome and healthy," the midwife said, businesslike. The nurse flashed the bundle of joy in front of him for a second as she placed the baby on Marguerite's chest.

His wife caressed her boy and sobbed, kissing him. Then she put an arm around her husband's neck and kissed him too. He patted the boy in her arms with his huge fingers, contrasting with the boy's tiny face. They were too busy getting to know their new son to even notice Marguerite had delivered the placenta, too.

The nurse picked up the baby to dress him, while Fergus caressed his wife's cheeks, awestruck. When ready, the midwife gave the child to Fergus. Then she helped Marguerite to freshen up, to make her comfortable again.

He strolled the room and noticed no one and none of the surrounding activities. He launched proud smiles at his wife while she watched them with tenderness.

Her heart ballooned with emotion for the two men in her life, and with Lucy, her family was now complete. Though her husband had told her several times he wanted an army of children, she shivered at the thought of it right now.

The maid and the nurse transferred Marguerite to her own bedroom, clean, fresh and ready for her where she had a well-deserved cup of tea and biscuits.

He followed and paced around the room with his boy in his arms.

Her heart thumped so hard in her chest. She couldn't contain her joy, just looking at the love of her life, happy with his son, the new heir.

He sat next to her on the bed, still holding the baby. "I can't believe I have a boy, too. Thank you, sweetheart," he said with a crack in his voice. He kissed her, while a tear of joy ran down her cheek.

"Daddy! Marguerite!" Lucy squealed as she burst into the room. "I want to see my brother," the girl cried out, full of excitement when they had allowed her in. She ran to them. "He is small, isn't he?"

"Yes, pumpkin, he is," Marguerite said with a smile.

The girl kissed the baby's cheek. "Can I hold him?"

"Sit here, and hold him carefully," he replied, pointing at the armchair

The girl delighted in holding her little brother, with lots of cooing noises. "He doesn't do much, does he?" Lucy blurted out, rather disappointed, her lips curled down.

"Not yet; you must wait a while before he does." Fergus chuckled, and she returned the baby to her father. He sat in the armchair by the bed, while the girl lay next to Marguerite.

"Darling, Marguerite is exhausted, you shouldn't—"

"That's okay, Fergus. Here, Lucy, get comfy in the bed with me." So the child cuddled up to her. She had taken up the habit to do this in the mornings.

He looked at his baby boy in his arms, then at his wife and his daughter snuggled up together, while his woman caressed the girl's hair tenderly.

"I love you, girls," he whispered to them. He would protect his family for as long as he lived.

Marguerite mouthed his words back to him.

They realised this moment would be in their hearts forever as the happiest of their life.

The End

Raffaella Rowell

Raffaella was born in Italy and grew up in South America. She moved to England in her mid-twenties, where she currently resides. She is married and has two sons.

She has a university degree in Modern Languages and Literature. She loves a book in any genre, reads anything and every day, with a weakness for crime/thrillers, romance novels, classics and historical figures.

Raffaella writes romance novels with a twist of suspense, spicy and sexy in the midst. She also enjoys gardening, baking (legendary for her delicious baked cheesecake), and playing the piano.

Email: raffabellano@gmail.com
Instagram account: @raffaellarowell
Twitter account: @Raffaella Rowell - Author
facebook: www.facebook.com/raffaellarowell
Visit her website here:
www.raffaellarowell.com

Don't miss these exciting titles by Raffaella Rowell and Blushing Books!

The Siblings Series
A Matter of Wife & Wealth

The Trouble with Molly series
The Perfect Pairing
The Trouble with Mollie

Single Titles
Ice, Spice and Red Lace

Blushing Books

Blushing Books is the oldest eBook publisher on the web. We've been running websites that publish steamy romance and erotica since 1999, and we have been selling eBooks since 2003. We have free and promotional offerings that change weekly, so please do visit us at http://www.blushingbooks.com/free.

Blushing Books Newsletter

Please join the Blushing Books newsletter
to receive updates & special promotional offers.
You can also join by using your mobile phone:
Just text BLUSHING to 22828.

Every month, one new sign up via text messaging will receive
a $25.00 Amazon gift card, so sign up today!